Leah Lake is a working mother of two and wife settled in the British county of Cambridgeshire. She enjoys spending time with her family and relaxing at home where she tries to write fiction in her spare time. Her inspiration comes from reading romantic thrillers and indulging in far too many box sets that help to cast her mind into other worlds to create the escapism and fantasy that comes from losing yourself in others stories. Her love for this encouraged her to begin to pen down her own ideas and before she knew it, her book and characters unravelled and she lost herself in her own story that she now hopes to share with you.

To my husband Pat, for encouraging me to keep on writing even when I had other things I should be doing. For taking over the everyday jobs to allow me to do it. To my boys, Oscar and Archie, for asking me what felt like a million times if I had finished my book yet. Yes boys, Mummy finally has. I love you all, to the moon and back.

Leah Lake

Stars Aligned

Austin Macauley Publishers

LONDON * CAMBRIDGE * NEW YORK * SHARJAH

A CIP catalogue record for this title is available from the British Library.

ISBN 9781398414525 (Paperback)
ISBN 9781786934109 (ePub e-book)

www.austinmacauley.com

First Published 2022
Austin Macauley Publishers Ltd®
1 Canada Square
Canary Wharf
London
E14 5AA

There is one person who without her encouragement, this book wouldn't be real. For reading the first few chapters of my book and telling me to write more and more. For practically begging me to send it to publishers and being my number one fan from day one. Natalie, I can't thank you enough. This acknowledgement is for you.

Chapter 1

It started with a touch, an electrifying connection I felt immediately the moment our hands brushed. It was an innocent moment, handing over cash to pay for the items I had just delicately packed into a brown paper bag. I felt sure you felt it too, your eyes and the way your breathing changed as I snatched my hand away; you felt burned, not only physically but mentally too. It was obvious you had never felt rejection, you could click your fingers and women would flock to you, too much choice to ever worry about the chase. It wasn't that I was denying you, or I didn't wonder in that moment exactly how your hands would feel running slowly down my body, it was the pure fear of allowing myself to be in wanting, to need and desire someone who I knew would never take a second look at me. The disconnection between us as I broke your touch brought me back into the room, the small card and gift store I worked in to make ends meet. I braved my retail face and smiled politely, handing over the bag I had just packed, the anniversary card that had the words 'Wife' stretched big and bold across the front in a delicate pink shade along with a singular red rose. Married, inside I feigned disappointment. He smiled back, a genuine and delicate smile, his eyes lingering on me longer than was polite. He turned graciously, heading towards the door, me admiring his broad shoulders and perfectly fitted suit when he suddenly stopped in his tracks, without turning fully to face me, over his shoulder, he breathed the words that floored me, "So, Emily, Jason Elliot was right, you ARE a force to be reckoned with." I felt the blood drain from my face and the floor wave beneath me as I watched him move in slow-motion across the shop and out into the rush of the shoppers passing by. How did he know Jason? And more importantly, where was Jason now?

I had felt you before I had even seen you enter the shop, a familiar presence that made the hair on my arms stand up. Like my body remembered the aura that surrounded you from that very first time I had seen you, kick starting my senses

9

into hyperdrive. You were the type of man that people subconsciously looked up from their papers and lattes as you drifted by, women would look you up and down admiring your physique, but you would always be none the wiser, completely oblivious to the effects that you had on others. It was the first thing that I noticed when I, along with many others in the lobby of OSAR Books laid eyes on you, your dark eyes and rushed strides, as if you were trying to block out everyone around you, set intent on avoiding all interactions even though you could easily captivate anyone in the room. Was it ignorance, lack of confidence, who knew? The only information I drew from that first moment was that you were seemingly a very private man, allowing perhaps only a small handful of people close and everyone else outside of that circle would remain there. I estimated you to be around 6'3", an avid gym goer, although not in the muscular over the top sense, just fit, and well-toned with short dark hair and equally as dark facial stubble. The tailored navy-blue suit you wore conformed and flattered in all the right places and really set the precedence of "Important person." I felt my heart race and my skin flush as my eyes followed you possessively across the foyer, I wondered who you were, what kind of man could have such presence and dominance over a room without even uttering a word, but before I could ponder anymore, you passed through the escalating doors and into the back seat of a black tinted Bentley before the car eased into the flow of traffic and off towards the city. I leaned back into my chair and let go of the breath I hadn't realised I was holding. Who was this beautiful, dark man?

That first encounter had been a week ago, I had been there for an interview, hoping to earn a position as personal assistant to Alicia Clines, the company administrator. The interview had passed by in a confusing blur, my mind tainted with vivid thoughts of Mr Mysterious, too flushed and encapsulated to concentrate on the task in hand. I wasn't too surprised when I received the email two days later advising me that the position had been filled but they would keep my resume on file. It was intended to be a steppingstone for a fruitful career in something I was passionate about – books. With no qualifications, and no real job skills, I already knew it was wishful thinking, but it was still a dream, nonetheless. I felt defeated and hopeless with nothing left to live for, my existence merely dragging from one day to the next, numb inside yet always portraying a different image on the outside for others to see. I had moved to Miami from Michigan in the hope to start afresh, and make a life for myself, and so far, a year in, life was going well. I had a couple of close-knit friends I had met through various avenues of the city and my job at M's Cards & Gifts was keeping me afloat financially until something better, more permanent came along, but the desire and drive in me to press forward had become more nagging and I knew I needed a change before I slipped back down a road I didn't want to go. I had headed home that day with a mission to unfold. I had managed to discover, after a serious case of social media stalking and google guessing, that Mr Mysterious had a name. Alex Hutchinson, 30, owner and co-founder of OSAR Books. I can't say I was shocked; it explained his presence and matter-of-fact attitude to those around him, but it also slammed down any very-farfetched ideas that may have crossed my mind that perhaps he could have noticed me. What would such a powerful, successful man ever want with a 26-year-old, broke card store worker, living in a drab apartment, with no real future plans and a ton of baggage want? Nothing. I had simply drawn a line under the experience, thought myself grateful for catching a glimpse of such an easy-on-the-eye-guy and carried on as usual. Yet here you were, a week later, the other side of the city in a small quaint family-owned shop buying items that I know you could get closer to OSAR, seemingly knowing more of my business than I care for you to know and creating a sexual tension I hadn't realised had been lingering for the seven days since I first saw you…or did you first see me? I had to figure out what this meant and what his intentions for me were, especially now Jason was in the picture – a dangerous and vindictive man I thought I'd left behind in Michigan.

I had been in a relationship with Jason, up until around a year ago, shortly before I made the decision to leave him. We had grown up together in Wisconsin, having been high school sweethearts, my first love, or so I thought. I had all my firsts with him, first kiss, first date, along with my first torrent of emotional abuse that would follow in the years to come. We had gone our separate ways for a few years after school, doing our own thing, living life before a chance meeting found us rekindling our romance after bumping into each other one evening while having a drink in a local bar. We had spent hours talking, falling in love all over and agreeing over to many double Malibu orange juices, that we would try to make things work. It was crazy, spontaneous, and almost desperate, but I was broken, in need of someone familiar and he was the only person who knew me, the only one who could read my mind by looking at my face, the only one I trusted. We were inseparable from that very night, gathering up what little possessions we had and driving hours away from where we grew up together, leaving our old lives and memories behind before eventually settling down and finding our feet after living out of his for what felt like forever. We were together and had each other, that's all that mattered. That trust and contentment over time soon turned to possession, ownership, and misery. A man who promised me the world and then snatched it all away while just to see me crumble. He was my escape, the one who was supposed to save me from the life I had, to start fresh with, take walks on the beach while our grandchildren played in the sand. We had spoken of it all, big plans, and life ambitions. For a couple of years, we had a "normal" relationship, loving, trusting, a happy partnership. It took me two long years of "new Jason" to realise the truth, I was there for his amusement. To wind me into a ball so tight and fragile I was too scared to leave, to make me feel worthless, unwanted, and ugly. New Jason had appeared the summer before last. It was a cold, fresh, early morning, and darkness still lingered outside. I had rolled over pulling the covers with me to find the bed empty. We had gone to bed together around 10 pm, said goodnight, had a cuddle and drifted off to sleep. Nothing out of the ordinary, yet my senses were telling me this was anything but ordinary. My head felt heavy, foggy, a queasiness in my tummy. A faint smell of fuel hung in the air, and I could hear the shower running in our En-suite. I swung my legs over the side of the bed knocking my bedside table, the lamp clattering over. Immediately the water stopped in the shower.

"You up?" Jason whispered. My breathing quickened and everything felt wrong. It wasn't a question, it was a panicked plea, him secretly hoping for no response. I stayed still, my eyes focused on the unfamiliar clothes piled by the door, blood stained with a silver locket, a distinctive teal stone in its centre which was placed delicately on top of a pair of lacy black knickers. The door creaked slowly open, my eyes snapped to meet his, dark pupils dilated – fear. He immediately broke my gaze and glanced at the pile of clothes, then back to me. He knew I had seen, knew that I had seen into his soul, the real him. That was something he couldn't hide or change, it was too late. I needed to be silenced, stopped. He lunged forward, his hands wrapping tight around my neck forcing my body hard into the mattress. His face tensed and his grip tightened harder. I fought back, kicking, his grip was too strong, his body too heavy. The room waved around him as a single tear fell from the corner of his eye then the blackness took over me.

My eyes snapped open as I took a deep breath sitting bolt upright. Beside me Jason lay sleeping, breathing softly, content, the clock blinking 07:42 am. Confusion flooded me. I clutched at my neck, swollen sore, the fuel smell, fainter than before but still there. I had woken a few hours earlier. I remembered Jason had strangled me, I could still see the sickening look in his eyes, the anger and malice. I jumped backwards off the bed, landing in a panicked heap on the floor. Did he try to kill me? No, he wouldn't, he had never laid a hand on me, never uttered a bad word. Surely, I had been dreaming. The fuel smell and raw skin around my neck confirmed I wasn't crazy. Jason woke with a startle as I hit the floor noisily, jumping up out of bed, his hands reaching out to me in a tender way.

"Emily, are you OK?" He breathed gently. I subconsciously reached up for him, my mind not believing what I thought I had seen. Pulling me into his lap he nuzzled my neck, kissing the tender soreness. "You had a bad dream last night," he whispered. "You really scared me, started clawing at your neck, saying you couldn't breathe." I stayed silent, waiting for his explanation. "Yeah, it wasn't nice to see, I had to hold you down, you scratched me, look." He cocked his head to one side, raw nail marks trailed down the side of his neck, dried blood covering them over. I glanced down at my nails, short, too short to draw blood, and clean. Not one trace of blood. He was lying. Trying to cover his tracks and make me believe what he wanted me to believe. My body clocked into survival mode, knowing he wouldn't allow me to leave this house alive if I questioned him, I squeezed my eyes tight and placed a delicate kiss across the marks on his neck.

"Sorry baby." I faked. "I think I must have had more wine than I thought last night." I rubbed my head feigning a headache and stretching gently as I snaked out of his grip, the room still waving as I stood. The room was clean, no blood-stained clothes, no necklace. I faked a yawn and huffed my disappointment at having to run to the store for milk, his eyes not leaving my face the entire time. I had remembered there only being a tiny bit left, trying to find any excuse to leave.

"OK, babe," he chimed. "You sure you're OK to go?"

"Yes of course, I'm fine, I promise." I smiled my most convincing smile while throwing some clothes on and making my way down the stairs and out the door leaving Jason in bed. A million thoughts were going through my mind. Had Jason killed someone? Whose clothes, were they? I didn't recognise them. Why was he acting like this morning hadn't happened? He had strangled me until I passed out. If I was to get to the bottom of this, I would have to play it cool, or I could end up his next victim.

I returned from the store 25 minutes later. I pulled into the driveway slowly and sat with my hands on the wheel, contemplating reversing back out. It only took me the time I had been gone to start doubting myself again, starting to believe what I desperately wanted to. I had previously had erratic dreams; we had always joked about my sleep talking and how he could get anything out of me if he questioned me while I was asleep. Maybe he could be telling the truth, and this was all just quite literally, a bad dream. I took a deep breath and sauntered up the driveway back into the house. Jason was in the kitchen leaning up against the worktop, two clear mugs, tea bags brewing, steam rising out the tops, stood nearby.

He smiled and took the milk from my hands. "I was worried you wasn't coming back," he joked lightly. "Why did you drive, the store is only a minute walk away?"

I looked away, not able to lie to his face, of course I couldn't tell him I thought he had murdered someone, drugged, and strangled me then was trying to convince me it was a dream and that I had been planning on driving and driving until I was far away from him. "Cold." I snapped, more impolite and curter than I had intended it to sound. Silence filled the room, eventually broken by the sound of him pouring milk into my tea. Desperate to convince him things were OK, I sided over, brushing my hands down his arm as I reached down for my tea. Before my hand reached the mug, his hand snapped tightly around my wrist, pulling it towards him and twisting hard. Panic and fear rose in my chest, my acting skills hadn't fooled him. I hadn't been fooled either, we both knew it. His face lowered to mine, and between gritted teeth he spat out words so venomous, so full of hatred, I knew he had got me, I was his, fully suffocated by his evil, encapsulated, a prisoner bound by unconditional love to keep his secret.

"You breathe a word, one word and I will visit that pretty little daughter of yours and ensure she takes her last breath at my hands." It was an instinct that naturally prevailed, maternal. Sickness waved over me, like all my worst nightmares had risen. I couldn't let him get to my baby girl, my perfect beautiful Ivy, so innocent and loving. I was trapped, I stared back, anger coursing through my veins and nodded. I knew in that moment, his secret would have to die with me, in order to protect my baby.

Chapter 2

How long had I been standing here since he left? The shop was empty, and darkness had begun to fall outside. Alex had clearly come here for a reason, a reason that was completely eluding me. I glanced down ay my hands, cold, shaking to see a small white card left on the counter. I picked it up and immediately felt sick. Alex had left his business card for OSAR Books, specifically for his PA. The name blazoned across the middle was his, Jason. He was Alex's personal assistant, how on earth could this be? I had left Jason over a year ago in the middle of the night, leaving only a note saying "Don't try to find me, your secret is safe."

Why was he now in Miami? Fear coursed through me, Ivy. My daughter had been placed for closed adoption here five years ago. I was young, too young to become a mother and with nothing to offer, it was the hardest decision I had ever made but not one I had forgotten about. I thought of my daughter every day, wondered what type of life she was living and if she remembered my face. I remembered hers, that perfect round face, brown eyes staring up at me as I held her for the first time. It was an unconditional and powerful love I had never felt before. Handing her over to the social services hours after she was born broke me. Even though I knew it was for best, and I knew she was going to a family who could offer her far more than I could, it didn't make it hurt any less. Choosing a closed adoption, the only information I knew was that her new home would be Miami, the sole reason for me heading here, to be closer to her if she needed me, even though I had no idea exactly where she was, and she had no idea I existed. It brought me peace knowing that Ivy was close by. It was about a year later that I had bumped into Jason in that bar, feeling brave and honest after one too many Malibu's, I had told him all about Ivy, where she and her new family lived, and how much I loved her. He comforted me and told me all the things I wanted to hear, taking away some of the guilt and pain I had been harbouring. Little did I know that that conversation had caused the opposite of what I wanted; she was now in grave danger. Anger and fear flooded my senses, he couldn't have found her, it was a closed adoption, he would have no idea where to start. Then the memories of the last two years of our relationship, if you could call it that, came flooding back, the knowledge of what a monster Jason could be. The emotional abuse far outweighed the physical, being reminded every day of what a terrible mother I was to give up my child, not being allowed to wear makeup or own a phone, moving me to another state entirely, leaving everything I knew at home in Wisconsin before trying to create a new life for us in Michigan. I was secluded, alone and scared. He ground me down into a shadow of my former self, no friends or family to notice a change in me. I feared this man, feared him that much that I couldn't go to the police, what could they do two years later when my memories of what I thought I saw that night were hazy and uncertain, all evidence long gone. The threats he made to my daughter were the only thing that kept me there, believing every word he spat when he would threaten to end her life, preaching about how it was what I deserved. I have no idea where I found the courage to leave that night while Jason slept, but I did exactly what I had wanted to do that morning I went to get milk, I snuck out leaving my handwritten note by the bed and I drove. I didn't know where I was heading but I found myself heading towards where I knew my baby was. I had to protect her. I had managed to keep some money aside, 2000 dollars that I had in cash under the floorboards from previous birthdays and odd jobs. That and the clothes on my back where all I left with, lesser the emotional torture of Jason, but replaced with a heart full of love knowing that every mile I drove, I was closer to her.

I hurried over and locked the shop door, doing a quick visual sweep of the street, I couldn't see Jason. Still shaking I picked up my mobile and dialled the number on the card. Not knowing what I was going to say, or how I was going to feel hearing his voice, it had already started ringing. After a few short rings, he answered.

"Hello, Jason speaking, PA to Alex Hutchinson, how can I help?" his voice was animated and fake, an over-the-top effort to conceal his real persona. I stood frozen, words refusing to pass my lips, a sickening feeling washing over me. A few moments' silence passed before I heard the real Jason. "Ahh Emily, I wondered when I'd be hearing from you."

"What do you want, Jason?" I hissed back furiously. "Why are you in Miami?"

"Woah woah, there, missy, so many questions. I thought you would be glad to hear from me, I mean it's been a year since you left me in the middle of the night, what the fuck was that about?" he shouted furiously.

"How did you find me, Jason?"

"Well, Emily, it wasn't hard to work out that you would want to be near your daughter, what with you believing her life was in jeopardy, so I headed this way around a month after you left, I tried tracking you down on social media, online – nothing. I had almost given up when would you believe it, there you were sitting in the lobby of OSAR Books. I could hardly believe my luck, like we were destined to be together, a third chance for us to be in love. You of course didn't see me, your eyes too fixated on *him.*" He spat the last word with so much hatred, so much malice that for a moment I could see his face, tensed, full of anger, mirroring that morning he strangled me. He continued, his voice softening as he spoke.

"So, I thought I would do you a favour, I saw that you had applied for the PA job for Alicia but didn't get it, so I put in a good word with the boss, told him what a good person you were, a kind-heart blah blah blah and got you a second gig. See I'm not that bad right?" My initial reaction was to tell him to shove it, why would I want a job anywhere near that psychopath was beyond me, but my inner strength told me I had to be smarter than him, not allow him to pull me back into that person I had worked so hard in the last year to get rid of, to play him at his own game.

"Oh, Jason," I chimed sweetly. "That is so kind of you, thank you, when do I need to be there?" I could almost sense the confusion coming through the phone.

"Umm, oh, err…well tomorrow at 8 am, OSAR suite, top floor," he blurted out quickly.

"Thanks, goodbye, Jason." I hung up before he had chance to respond. So, Jason had a dirty game to play, I was pretty confident he had no idea of Ivy's whereabouts, he would have most definitely used that as leverage and had he have harmed her, there would have been a media frenzy in such a tourist ridden area. I just had no idea why he would want me working with him, what his motive was but I imagined it was to hold me at arm's length, torture me some more, but I was stronger now, I just had to be two steps ahead of him at all times, get him to slip up about that morning things changed and what he had been doing that night with the blood-stained clothes. When I had all the information and his confession, I could hand him over to the police. I could do this, working closely with him would be an advantage, I could worm my way in, break him, and expose him for what he truly is. I just had to be strong and keep my cool. I could do this, I needed to do this for Ivy. I took in a deep breath and headed home. Tomorrow was the start of the end of Jason.

I didn't sleep well that night, I spent most of it tossing and turning, my mind running over various different ideas of revenge, potential scenarios, and trying to work out how I would keep this on the downlow in front of offices full of employees. I lived in a small, one-bedroom apartment on the second floor of a dingy corner set apartment block, not being able to afford anything better, what with arriving here with hardly anything and having a minimum wage job. The area was not in any way desirable, so I should have been used to all the noises, people mulling around during the early hours seeing to their business deals, but still, the occasional odd noise from the street below sent chills up my spine, me wondering if it was Jason finally coming for me. At one point I had laid there frozen still, too scared to move as I heard the metal trash cans just below my window topple over, before wiggling the window latch to make sure it was secure, then dashing to my front door to make sure it was locked too, despite checking it multiple times throughout the night. After a pretty much non-existent night of sleep I made a pact with myself, I couldn't, and wouldn't let him win, I couldn't live like this. I was already awake when my alarm went off at 6:30 am. OSAR was around a 20-minute bus ride from me, so I knew I had less than an hour to sort myself out. I clambered out of bed and headed to the bathroom, glancing in the mirror, my night of turmoil was obvious, wild hair, dark bags, the only positive was the sun kissed glow I had acquired since moving to the sunshine state. I sighed and jumped straight into the shower which I always had far too hot and quickly attended to all my needs. I immediately felt better. I wrapped myself in a towel and started sliding clothes across the wardrobe, no, no, too sexy no, before sliding the previous one back into view, too sexy? It's not every day a girl gets a forewarning that she's about to bump into her ex. Part of me said I didn't care what I looked like, not to him anyway but I wanted him to see I was doing OK, more than OK, and that I wasn't to be messed with. Yes, I'd go with that. I spent more time than I usually would, waving my short dark hair into a messy but chic do and slicked on some makeup, still natural looking but again more effort than I would usually make. I had attended the interview last week in black ill-fitting trousers and a lilac blouse that buttoned up to my chin, yet here I was slinking my way into a dark navy-blue dress that hugged my curves and skimmed off my behind in a sexy, but not too sexy way. Teamed with a pair of nude heels and a matching bag, I was ready to go. I glanced in the mirror and hardly recognised myself, I looked…wow different. Confident, sexy, curvy, a completely different woman to the day before, like Jason had given me that final push to rid the old me and take up permanently the new one. I'd got this. Before I knew it, I was crossing the OSAR foyer heading for the desk at the back of the space. It was a vast area, mostly finished in marble, with sleek cream leather loungers placed in little huddles around the edge where people sat drinking coffee, waiting for meetings or waiting for job interviews which was my case last week. A young man with a kind face sat at the main desk tapping away at a computer, a small silver badge on his shirt told me his name was Tom. He was talking occasionally into his headset, clearly taking phone calls, a multi-tasking pro. I smiled as I reached the desk and his head whipped up to greet me politely. "Ahh Miss Moore, Mr Hutchinson will see you right away, take the elevator to the top floor, his office is to the far right as you exit." I felt sure the shock on my face was obvious as he almost immediately whispered, "Is there a problem, Miss Moore?"

"I…err, no, um…I just was under the impression that Miss Clines was interviewing me seeing as that is the position I was applying for," I replied, smiling sweetly so as to not seem like I was being awkward.

"Miss Clines isn't here today; she is on leave. Mr Hutchinson will take your interview today, Miss." He gave a side smile seemingly understanding my apprehension, covering his mic with his hand he leaned into me and whispered, "I'm almost *certain,* you will make his day," giving me a cheeky wink and looking me up and down. Shocked, I almost had something to say until he held his hands up in a defensive stance. "Don't worry, honey, I'd absolutely prefer the company of *him*, not that you don't look absolutely fire!"

"Go get him, girl," I suddenly felt stupid and laughed, not every man had to be bad.

"Thank you, Tom, I'll let you know how it goes," I chirped back, as I headed confidently towards the elevator.

I could feel my heartbeat in my ears, seemingly strumming in time with each floor that passed, 125, 126, 127, I was there, the top floor. I was giving myself a bit of a pep talk, re straightening my dress and smoothing down my hair when the doors pinged open, and there he stood. Mr mysterious who I now knew to be

Alex Hutchinson, CEO and owner of OSAR Books. He smiled, reached out his hand for me. "Emily."

My breathing caught in my chest and all I could manage was a deep sigh. Realising I was being rude I stepped forward and took his hand, his touch was warm, strong. He gave it a firm shake and introduced himself. "Emily, nice to meet you properly, I'm Alex, I apologise our meeting the other day in the card shop was so brief, I happened to be passing by and remembered Jason mentioning what a good worker you were and how you would be an asset to the company. I couldn't resist popping in just to see what all the fuss was about." He held his arm out gesturing towards his office.

"No problem, nice to meet you too," I replied bluntly. What was the matter with me, how had I all of a sudden forgotten how to walk and talk? Shake it off, I thought to myself, as he led me down the corridor. It was only ten metres or so, but we walked in silence, for what felt like eternity. Say something, sell yourself, I scolded in my head. As we reached the door, he held it wide open for me, leaning slightly into the doorway in order to hold it fully open. I brushed past him as I went through, hearing him audibly exhale and seeing him tense at the same time. His office was a corner space, glass floor to ceiling windows wrapped around the entire office giving us a primal view of the beach, white sands, and turquoise waters. It was truly stunning, nothing like I had ever seen. The furniture was sleek glass, with white marble floors and cream leather sofas following the décor of the foyer. Any other day I would have felt out of place, too frumpy, but today, I know I looked the part. I realised I had been standing admiring the view for perhaps too long when Alex's voice broke my attention.

"See something you like, Emily," he purred. I shot a glance in his direction, our eyes meeting, his full of lust, a cheeky smile on the corner of his mouth. Of course, I knew he was being suggestive, but I wasn't biting, I was here for a job interview.

"Yes, the beach is beautiful from up here," I replied plainly. His eyes cleared and the cheeky smile disappeared. He gestured for me to sit down on the chair in front of his glass desk while he made his way round to a huge black leather seat, seemingly back in CEO mode. He took a seat, his eyes never leaving mine.

"So, when do you want to start?" he quipped out of the blue.

"Umm excuse me, I thought you were interviewing me, I haven't said much to sell myself." I looked down at the floor embarrassed. Clearly not liking the broken eye contact he stood up abruptly, drawing my attention back to him.

Leaning forward onto his desk and lowering his head in line with mine. I trust the opinion of my employees, if Jason says you're the real deal, I'll take his word on it, remind me how you pair know each other again?"

Oh no, I hadn't pre-empted this, what had Jason told him, did he know we were ex-lovers, that I had left him in the middle of the night? I couldn't get caught up in a lie before I had even started.

"We went to school together," I said smiling, "back in Wisconsin." I wasn't lying but I also wasn't giving too much away.

"Ah I see, I think Jason may have mentioned something along those lines. So, I know you were applying for the position working with Alicia, but that position has now been filled, I am looking for a new assistant, to work alongside Jason, I have lots that needs attending to so I thought two assistants may lighten the workload, what do you think?"

Shock and panic shot through me, work alongside him I thought, urgh this wasn't something I was anticipating, we would have to compare schedules and have more to do with each other than if I had of been on the 125th floor with Alicia. Then the reason I was here in the first place resurfaced, to out Jason. "Yes of course, I'd love to take up your offer. I don't need to give notice for the shop so I could start Monday."

"Monday it is," he replied cheerfully, "but before then, I'd like to take you over to my place, I often work from home and have an office set up there, I need you to familiarise yourself with the workspace and what is expected of you, as you will be working at my home as well as here." Before I could answer or make sense of what he was saying he chimed, "Saturday at 7 pm, I will have my driver pick you up."

"Saturday at 7 it is." I grinned like a cat who'd got the cream. Phase one – take down Jason complete.

Chapter 3

The next few days dragged by, I laid up on my bed working through my head my plan. I had got through the so-called interview, and bagged myself a decent job, all be it with some baggage in the form of Jason but fortunately I had managed not to bump into him on my way in or out of OSAR. Alex had ridden all the way down to the foyer with me, his hand placed in the small of my back guiding me though the building. His touch had sent shivers, I remembered fantasising about him pulling down the zip on the back of my dress, sliding his hands gently around and caressing my breasts while kissing my neck. Tom on the front desk had given me a cheeky thumbs up as we walked to the entrance. I giggled inside and shot him the biggest smile that told him it went well. "My driver will take you home, wherever you need," he said while holding the door open to the black Bentley, I had seen him get in the other week. I wondered if he was so attentive to all his staff.

"Thank you, Alex!" I gushed perhaps a bit too enthusiastically.

"No thank you, Emily." He breathed as I sided onto the back seat. "Oh, and by the way, you look absolutely, breath-takingly beautiful today, Emily" He smirked as he closed the door. Laying here now, alone on my bed, I pushed my thighs together at the memory, remembering Alex watching me leave that day, my skin felt flushed, my body wanting his touch again. Oh shit! I sat bolt upright; my breathing heavy. Wife, he had bought a card for his wife that day in the card shop, what was I thinking? Oh goodness, I had been reading him completely wrong, reading his signals as flirting, the look in his eyes as lust. I had been drawn into that entity that he oozed without even trying, the one I imagined many women had fallen into. I threw my head back and covered my eyes, completely embarrassed, but also, secretly gutted too.

Before I knew it, Saturday was here and I heard a car beep outside my apartment, Alex's driver was here to take me to his. A professional meeting, part of my job. Nothing more. I knew this yet I had found myself again picking out a sexy black dress, fitted, perhaps too fitted on my large breasts but covered up, heels, sultry hair, and makeup. I wonder if his wife would be there, oh god it was too late to change now, the driver was here. I rushed down the stairs and out across the foyer, hopped into the back seat of the tinted Bentley before hearing the voice that froze me, "Hello, Emily."

Jason. Fear engulfed me, I felt sick, confused, but I wouldn't let him know it. I was safe, a driver overhearing our first meeting after all this time, ignoring our chatter as he drove. I turned to face him, planting on my fakest smile. He grinned, looking me up and down wetting his lips with his tongue. Instantly regretting my dress choice, I felt sick, repulsed but had to put on a show. "Jason, how are you, nice to see you." I could instantly see the change in his face, he was annoyed, annoyed at my non-melancholy, annoyed that he didn't affect me.

"So, you're this neck of the woods, are you? I wondered where you were hiding out," he said the words so innocently that the driver would suspect nothing but to me, it meant everything. He now knew where I lived.

"Yeah." I fake smiled back. "What are you doing here anyway, Jason? I wasn't expecting you."

"Oh, I just got done at the office, Theo is taking me home, I guess he thought he would pick you up on the way through to take you…?" he shook his head questioningly whilst admiring my tight dress yet again.

"To Alex's," I shot back confidently. I remembered his tone when he had commented on me looking at him in the foyer, bitter, jealous. *Come on, Jason, show your true colours.* True to form, I saw the rage sweep over him, his fists clenched, and his jaw tightened.

"I see," he spat.

"Yeah, he felt it appropriate for us to familiarise with each other and his place seeing as I will be working closely with him now." I saw the confusion hit him.

"I thought you were going to be Alicia's PA," he questioned, anger still brewing. We pulled up outside a huge apartment block reaching right up into the sky, *It was undoubtedly Alex's place,* I thought. Stepping out of the car I turned to look at Jason.

"No, as of Monday, I'm Alex's PA." I smirked and closed the door on him, watching his face process the information I had just given him, followed by a sarcastic wave as the driver pulled off into the traffic. I thought our first meeting was going to be traumatic, affect me more but as far as I was concerned, it was one nil to me. I had a spring to my step as I began heading towards the building.

23

It must have been the tallest apartment block I had ever seen, lush trees lined the entrance, and the people who milled about wreaked of money. Expensive watches, designer dogs, I even spotted a lady being escorted to her chauffeur driven car by a man holding an umbrella over her head, it was neither raining nor sunny, so I took that gesture as a statement and giggled. "Something funny, Miss Moore?" Alex. His voice eased me, made me feel like the only person around, how did he do that? I spun around to meet his dark gaze, suited up, leaning casually up against a pillar, his eyes admiring my figure.

"I'm just laughing at that lady with the pointless umbrella." I glanced over and pointed my nose in her direction.

His face hardened, "That's my mother." He waved in her direction and she waved back.

Shit. "I'm so sorry, I err…"

"Oh Jesus, lighten up you, I was joking." He laughed loudly whilst gesturing me inside with an outstretched hand. "That's crazy Ann from apartment 603." He whispered whilst leaning into me as we walked, like a giddy boy sharing a top secret, smile a mile wide.

"A million cats divorced five times, filthy rich, you get the picture." He laughed again. "That will be me one day I tell you," he joked.

"Divorced five times?" I jibed, remembering the wife.

He looked at me with a cocked head and winked. "Just the cats."

We walked through into the lobby and around to a key coded door. He swiped his palm over the panel and the door clicked open, an elevator door concealed behind it. I revelled in the high-tech aspects of the place, wondering why he would need such high security. "We don't want any old riff raff getting in, do we?" He poked, answering my unsaid question. I smiled playfully and looked myself up and down, "Riff raff, are you huh?" he winked. "We may have to do something about that," he whispered suggestively.

Wife, wife, wife, I kept saying over and over in my head as we took the elevator to the top floor. When we reached his apartment, I was astounded by the vastness of it, huge open plan rooms leading on to each other. Exquisitely decorated to a high standard with small intricate touches, paintings, and vases I could only imagine the cost of.

"Wow," I gasped.

"You like?" He questioned, watching my face as I scouted the room admiring its beauty. I spun round to face him, not realising how close behind he had been following and bumped straight into his chest. He caught me by the arms and stared down at me.

"So beautiful." He breathed slowly. His body was hard and rigid, warm, and smelled like musk. He towered over me in size, could easily overpower me, yet his demeanour and chivalry shouted gentleman. His hands moved slowly down my arms until they found my hips, his eyes not leaving mine, he leaned in slowly and kissed my neck gently.

"Shall we get a drink," he whispered into my ear. I inhaled deeply, realising I had forgotten to breathe, my heart racing, skin flushed, butterflies. A nod was all I could manage, he released me moving his hands back to my arms.

"OK?" He questioned. I simply nodded again and watched him head towards the kitchen. Fuck, wife! *What is wrong with me, no what is wrong with him.* That is not how you act when you are married. Furious that he could make me forget the important details when he touched me, I gathered myself and stomped after him.

"Actually no!" I shouted, his head whipped round, and his confused gaze met mine, speaking a silent question. "Why on earth do you think it's OK to act like that when you have a wife, it's appalling, embarrassing, you're a pig!" Tears filled my eyes in anger. "I forget every single time you touch me, then remember straight after and it makes me feel awful, I'm not that kind of girl!"

"Wait, what do you mean married?" He looked at me questioningly, moving closer.

"The card shop, you bought an anniversary card with wife on it!" I spat back shaking my head.

"Emily." He laughed. "Calm down, I'm not married, that was for my dad, well for my mom from my dad. He is wheelchair-bound and I was picking it up for him, it's their 30th wedding anniversary coming up and he struggles getting out and about, it's become somewhat of a tradition me collecting it for him." His words genuine and honest, he had me in his grip at this point, holding me tightly by the shoulders, I just stared at him. "I promise, single, nada, nothing." A moment of silence passed. "Only you," he added quietly.

My breathing quickened and my heart raced as I stretched upwards, my hands in his hair, my lips on his; he immediately took control, picking me up in one swift move and setting me on the countertop, kissing my neck in a desperate and feral way down to my chest, his hands explored my body, cupping my breasts, his thumb tracing over my nipples, now hard and wanting. My whole body was wild with lust, unable to control myself, my hands lowered to his waistband. I could feel the straining of the fabric as I was undoing his belt, his hands finding the zip at the back of my dress and undoing it in one swift pull. The fabric pooled around my waist, exposing my breasts, covered by my lacy black bra; he hummed in appreciation as he leant back to get a better look. I pulled him back roughly, not wanting to stop. I lifted up and pushed my dress under me, it falling to the floor. I was now sat on his kitchen counter in nothing but my underwear, it seemed to do the trick though, the fire in his eyes and the desperation in his breathing spoke a thousand words. His head lowered to my stomach, him trailing kisses all the way to my thigh, missing out where I wanted it the most. I moaned and writhed around, throwing my head back trying to force my body closer to him. He kissed his way slowly back up my thigh until he found my sweet spot, pushing my underwear to the side he kissed and teased me with his tongue, back and forth, getting stronger and stronger until I found myself building, my hands gripped his hair hard, noises coming from me that I didn't recognise as myself. He laid me gently onto my back, my body greedy wanting more. He lowered his trousers and took himself in his hand, stroking up and down not breaking my gaze while I watched his breathing change, his pace quickened. Wow, I had never seen anything more erotic in my life. My hands traced down my body desperate for some friction.

"Ah ah ah," he teased pushing my hands away. "I'll see to that don't you worry." He smiled while pushing a condom down over his impressive length. He slowly moved over me, kissing every inch of my body until he reached my lips, he kissed me softly at first, pushing himself into me, filling me until I could take no more. The feeling was exquisite, satisfying, full. He started to move slowly, teasing me into wanting more before upping the pace, faster and harder until he was fucking me so furiously, he was hitting my sweet spot, thrust after thrust, his fingers digging into my hips as he pulled me in tightly with every move.

I could feel myself quickening, reaching that point where I knew I was going to explode, "I'm almost there," I murmured through quick breaths. I felt him smile as he was kissing me, like he was in on a secret I didn't know about, and boy did I have no idea. He pushed his hands round to the small of my back, raising me to him allowing him that little bit deeper and fucked me like I'd never been fucked in my life, relentless, quick, deep, hard thrusts slamming into me and hitting me right there until I came apart around him. I scratched my nails down his back, breathing his name in pure ecstasy as he came too, ragged breathing, his fingers digging harder into me slamming my hips against him until he was fully empty.

I lay there, fully sated, exhausted, Alex leaning over me nuzzling my neck. We laid there for what felt like forever, when without saying a word, he picked me up and carried me down the hallway to his bedroom, before lowering me gently down onto the bed, and climbing in beside me. He pulled me close to him, his arms completely wrapped around me. I felt amazing, safe, satisfied. He kissed the back of my head and murmured my name. I was unsure of what was going on, how on earth that had just happened but for some reason I couldn't explain, it felt incredibly right and like everything that had happened had led me to him, and him to me. We lay there entwined in each other before we both drifted off into a deep sleep.

Chapter 4

My eyes opened slowly; the room dark. I stretched out, my body feeling achy but sated, when I suddenly remembered where I was. I sat up quickly throwing my hand over my mouth in shock, I had slept with my boss, what on earth was I thinking. I felt embarrassed, confused, and wondered if this whole visit was exactly how he had it planned out. A million questions coursed through me as I looked over at the man next sleeping softly next to me. I pulled the covers up around myself realising I was still naked, in doing so, accidently pulling them off Alex, equally as naked, the cover now only barley hiding his modesty. A small slither of light was shining through the gap in the blinds, lighting up a strip across his now exposed muscular upper thigh, trailing up over his stomach and through the dark hair and ending under his stubbly chin. This man was perfect, chiselled, and strong, I licked my lips before reaching out, my fingertips gently making contact with the start of the light, drawing me in. I knew I shouldn't be touching him, that last night shouldn't have happened, the guilt still eating away at me, but my body was disobeying me anyway like it craved that physical connection with him. I began slowly tracing upwards, his body warm and hard, as I reached his groin I stopped, my mind wanting me to reach down and explore, I circled my fingers around in his hair before his breathing changed and his hips began circling, matching my fingers, I looked up at his face, still deep in sleep. His body began to tense as his hand moved from the back of his head slowly down his chest meeting mine, I kept completely still allowing his hand to pass mine as it disappeared under the covers, the covers began to move slowly, his back arching off the bed slightly, yet his eyes still shut, still sleeping. I watched in shock, as his movement got more vigorous, he was now completely uncovered as the covers fell away from him. He was busy smoothing his hand up and down his impressive length, now rock hard. I couldn't stop watching, this beautiful, dark man laying right next to me, pleasuring himself, his breathing was becoming faster and faster as he upped the pace, his mouth in an o shape. My hand was still paused on his groin, my mind and body betraying me further it began moving towards his subconsciously, I reached his elbow and he paused, my hand slowly trailing towards his, as I reached him, he slowly released himself, before taking my hand and placing it where his had been, covering mine entirely with his. His hand squeezed mine and he began to move us both up and down, harder and faster, I could feel him pulsing beneath my hand, his hips moving upwards with our strides. I couldn't remember ever seeing anything more erotic in my life, and now I was becoming very aware of the ache between my thighs. Suddenly my mind came back to me, no longer betraying me, as I whipped my hand away furiously, his hand not hesitating to replace where mine had been and continuing as he was. I jumped up off the bed and gathered up my belongings quickly, sensible me now back in full swing, guilt filling my mind and telling me to keep my main objective at the forefront. I had to work with, no work for this man and having a sexual relationship with my boss was not a distraction I needed right now, I took once last glance back at Alex, now undeniably close to finishing and closed the door quietly behind me.

It was just turning 6:30 am as I arrived back at my apartment, getting a cab home wasn't difficult in the city and the look on my door man's face as I proceeded with the walk of shame from the curb to the main doors told me he knew the story and had probably seen it a hundred times before. Make up smudged, hair a mess, last night's dress and shoes in hand, I forced an awkward smile and whispered thanks as he opened the door for me as I passed through, eyes fixed on the ground in shame. I instantly felt better as I closed my apartment door behind me, my safe haven and private space, leaning back on it and closing my eyes I sunk to the floor. Last night had been amazing, more than anything I could ever imagine, but I shouldn't have allowed it to happen. It was unprofessional and complicated, I was now going to be working with my ex who I was trying to out, as well as my smoking-hot boss who I had just had mind blowing sex with and watched as he got himself off in his sleep, and I would be lying if I said I wasn't completely and utterly drawn to him at every moment, then, to make things worse, neither man knew of my relationship with the other. This was such a mess, I weighed up the options of not turning up on Monday and just going back to the card shop, but Ivy came to my mind every single time. I couldn't walk away knowing that at any moment Jason could find her and make true of his threats. I had to see this through, I stood up confidently and headed to the shower while talking myself into my plan. As the hot water cascaded over me, I felt the previous night wash away, technically I wasn't working for Alex yet, my job didn't start until Monday so I told myself that yes it was a crazy night, the most amazing night but that as I hadn't actually started yet, I hadn't actually slept with my boss and that Monday I would start afresh, remain professional, and try to find out all I could about Jason by continuing to work with him.

By Sunday, I was feeling more optimistic, I had not heard from Alex or Jason since Saturday and even though less than 24 hours ago I had been in bed with Mr Dark it felt like a lifetime ago. I was meeting one of my best friends – Molly – for lunch and although she didn't know the full details surrounding Jason, she knew he was my ex and I had given her a brief panic phone call earlier in the week to tell her he was now here in Miami. In typical Molly-form, she wanted to know all the details right now but I told her it was too complicated and I would meet up with her and fill her in on Sunday. Feigning disappointment, she had reluctantly agreed and had been texting me all week counting down the days telling me how much she couldn't wait to catch up, little did she know I had a whole other array of gossip in the form of "A night with Alex" to fill her in on also.

As I walked into the foyer of my favourite Italian restaurant, I saw Molly sitting towards the back of the restaurant, her smile beamed as she met my gaze and she waved enthusiastically, I noticed her sister Ali sitting next to her, a welcome addition as I was more than good friends with both girls. I had met Molly when I first started at the card shop, she had been there for a few years and I knew instantly that we were going to be good friends, she had lived in Miami all her life and really took me under her wing when I needed a friend and introduced me the city. I was devastated when she left a few months later to work for a local chain waitressing as the hours worked better around her two young boys but we remained really good friends. Her sister Ali I had liked straight away, she was a wild case, always saying the funniest and most inappropriate things that had me laughing with tears on more than one occasion and we had some of the best times since. I classed both as really good friends and I was so glad to be here with them to gossip with and explain my hugely awkward situation I had got myself into.

As I approached the table, Molly jumped up and gave me the biggest hug, "Aww, are you OK, Em?" she whispered as she pulled me tighter. I felt myself well up, all the drama over the last week had really taken its toll on me and I hadn't fully realised until I had got here, with people I trusted, and I was ready to finally let my walls down, let it all out. I simply nodded in response, typical me, not wanting to burden people with my dramas. I pulled myself together and sat across the table from the girls, and they both stared, not saying a word, waiting for me to spill the beans on everything that had been going on.

"Well, come on then, what the hell happened?" Ali chirped up bluntly.

"You want the long version or the quick one?" I smiled, already knowing they would want to know every little detail.

"I think we should order some drinks first." Molly laughed beckoning over the server.

An hour and a half later, far too much alcohol and plenty of good food done, I had filled them in on everything, starting from the strange night in Michigan that Jason had strangled me and potentially murdered someone, Ivy's adoption, all the way through to my night of passion the day before.

"Wow, what a dick," Ali moaned, "I can't believe that creep would follow you all the way to Miami to try ruin your life! You need to report him to the police."

I placed my head in my hands shaking it. "What have I done!" I whispered to myself.

"She can't," Molly chimed in, "she's got no proof of that night, and she isn't a hundred percent sure what she even saw. Plus, he hasn't actually done anything bad to her since being here, in fact, he led her to Mr Hot!"

She lowered her voice and leaned in close to me, "Just describe to me again how he placed his hand over yours while he, you know, ahem," she whispered, laughing followed by a suggestive wink.

"Molly!" I cringed, embarrassed that I had gone into so much detail explaining how I had groped him while he slept, the girls hanging on to my every word wanting more.

"I need to see this man for myself, see what all the fuss is about," Ali muttered. "It's been far too long. I could do with some juicy sex stories seeing as I'm not getting any myself." She folded her arms across her chest in a huff. I laughed and told her we would have a girls' night out soon and find her someone hot to take home. That was something I loved about Ali, she was a free spirit, young and mischievous, living her life to the full. I envied her.

In typical big sister fashion Molly had her say, "Ali, you do not need to go home with some random guy just to have fun; you need to find someone long term, it's so much more meaningful," she said softly.

"Urgh, boring!" Ali wafted her hand over her mouth fake yawning. We all laughed together, I had really needed this, felt better for getting it off my chest and having the girls give their opinions. We had concluded that I would remain professional, they agreed with my theory that as I had not actually been working for Alex on Saturday, that I could take the free pass and start afresh on Monday. They were also going to do some social media stalking to find all they could out about Jason, helping me to take him down. These girls had my back fully and I felt so much better knowing I was not doing this on my own, I felt stronger, and more determined than ever to rid Jason out of my life for good. I suddenly willed Monday morning to come quickly.

Chapter 5

I rolled over and looked at the clock, 6:05 am. My alarm didn't go off for another 55 minutes, but my body had other ideas. I hadn't slept well that night, nerves and excitement about my new job kept me tossing and turning most of the night and I finally decided to give up. Wrapping myself in my oversized dressing gown I headed to the kitchen and put the kettle on, my morning cup of tea was something I needed to get me moving in the morning, followed by far too many during the day to see me through to the end. I sat at the kitchen breakfast bar with my eyes closed, hands wrapped around my cup imagining all the possible scenarios that today could present. How would Alex be with me? He hadn't tried to contact me since Saturday which if I was being honest, slightly annoyed me as I felt used and embarrassed and was fully expecting things to be awkward between us. I really needed this job, not only for myself as books were something I was truly passionate about but also for Ivy, I had to keep my enemies close to protect her. I wasn't particularly looking forward to seeing Jason either, id last seen him as I sarcastically waved him off at the front of Alex's building while goading about being his PA. I leaned forward and pressed my forehead to the table, how on earth was I going to get through this, not only today but for the foreseeable. I spent the next hour sulkily getting ready for work, showering, and then pulling on an old white chiffon shirt, a black side split pencil skirt and nude heels putting in minimum effort. I really wasn't feeling myself today but still made the effort to do my hair and makeup knowing I couldn't let Jason see any cracks, he would see it as a vulnerability and think he had the upper hand. I gave myself a once over in the mirror and fake smiled at myself, to anyone who didn't really know me I looked like any other person just going out to work, but I shuddered when I remembered how Jason could read me like a book. I needed to step up my game, applying slightly more makeup and replacing my outfit with a flattering orange sleeveless blouse and tight black skirt. I looked in the mirror again and smiled a genuine smile, my mask was well and truly in place, I looked confident and ready to take on the world.

I arrived at OSAR at 08:15 am, I didn't start until 9 but wanted to get there early to get settled in and find my way around a bit. The huge doors to the foyer opened and I walked across the marble floor to the back of the room. The last time I had been here I had fantasised as Alex guided me across the room, his hand resting at the small of my back, my heart racing as his skin connected with mine. Little did I know days later my fantasies would all come true. The large area was eerily empty, too early in the day for the hundreds of employees who worked here. There were various companies here, spread across multiple floors but it was OSAR who owned the top ten floors, the very top floor would be my workplace for the foreseeable. I spotted someone working at the back desk and quickly realised it was Tom. "Emily!" he exclaimed, gesturing me over with his hand. My face widened with a real genuine smile, I had misread Tom when we first met but could now clearly see he was a really likeable person, and I was actually happy to see him.

"Girl, that outfit!" he chimed, mock fanning himself, "you look amazing, I take it you got the job then, congratulations, you'll love it here." He smiled.

"Thanks, Tom, I'm really nervous if I'm being honest, this whole place is so intimidating, never mind my boss who is whole other level intimidating," I huffed back.

"Oh, babe, don't worry, you will be fine, I am only a phone call away if you need any advice or to vent, just push the front desk button on any phone and you'll get me, they are all programmed the same," he said while gesturing down at the button clearly stating front desk on his keypad.

"Perfect, I might take you up on that." I joked lightly but had a feeling I may be calling in this favour more than once.

"Have an amazing day, Em!" He shouted over his shoulder as I headed to the elevator, I decided in that moment that I actually really did like Tom before shouting back, "You too!"

I hopped in the elevator and pushed the top button which clearly stood out over all the rest, larger with delicate gold script reading OSAR Books. I smiled inside, so extra and over the top, all the other floors just had generic plain buttons with their floor number next to them. My tummy stayed on the ground floor as the elevator took me right to the top of the building, nerves and anticipation made my heartbeat faster and faster before I reached my destination and the doors pinged open. I walked confidently over to the main desk where a beautiful middle-aged woman with red hair and porcelain pale skin sat typing away at her computer. I guessed that she either wasn't from Miami or she had done a very good job of keeping covered as she had no hint of the blazing Florida sun ever touching her skin. "Hello, I'm June, welcome to OSAR Books." She smiled with a broad British accent. I smiled back; my guess mostly accurate.

"Hi, I'm Emily Moore, I'm here for my first day. I'm Mr Hutchinson's new PA," I chirped back.

"Ahh yes of course, he mentioned you were starting today, I'll show you to your office space, it's directly next to Mr Hutchinson's office, you'll be sharing your office space with Jason, he is his other PA, I'm sure he will show you the ropes, although you are slightly early so you may have to just see yourself around until 9ish," she said while glancing down at her watch.

"Yes of course, I've got a few bits to set up any way, do you have a cafeteria area for staff?"

"Yes, my dear, it's two doors along from your office, help yourself," she beamed back at me with a gentle smile.

"Thank you so much, I'll leave you to get on then," I replied heading towards the corridor that led to mine and Jason's office. I slowed as I approached the doorway to Alex's office, was he in there? The glass door that had been clear when I last went in was now smoked grey obscuring my view. I could tell that there were no lights on so presumed that he wasn't here yet. I continued on to the next door, it was already propped open, two large white desks sat in the back two corners slightly at an angle giving each person privacy, floor to ceiling windows at the very back flooded light into the small area behind where we would sit. The desk on the right was clearly mine, neat and tidy, not being used, a single monitor and an empty stationary rack was all that sat on the desk, the other one was littered with paperwork, and I could see the backs of numerous picture frames. Curiosity took over me as I headed over to Jason's desk, I felt like I was intruding, but this was our space, not his and this was a good opportunity to snoop for information, I scanned my eyes across the first couple of photo frames, a picture of his two nieces, they looked so grown up since I last saw them, guilt sniped at me as I remembered the good relationship I once had with them, going out for ice cream and laughing at the cinema together, the next one was Jason with his parents at a local fete, probably last summer, I hadn't always seen eye to eye with them, but nonetheless they were still nice people. I

35

moved along to see the final one and it floored me, my breathing stopped as I snatched the photo frame off the desk looking at it closely my heart beating out of my chest. It was Jason sat on a swing at the park around the corner from our old house in Wisconsin, and a girl we knew from town Chloe sat on his lap with her arms wrapped around his neck, planting a kiss on his cheek. Confusion swept over me, were they together now? I had once upon a time suspected Jason of having an affair with her but never had solid evidence and truth be told, at that time I was still a broken mess and the thought of knowing the truth wasn't something that deep down I could face so I had ignored it. Were my suspicions right, had Jason been having an affair or was this picture more recent? I tried not to let it bother me, but anger coursed through my veins, and I slammed the frame back on the desk. I stomped my way out of the office and into the cafeteria to make myself a cup of tea, a million questions running through my mind. I kept telling myself that it wasn't important, that even if he had of been seeing her while we were together, it didn't matter because he was nothing to me now but no matter how many times, I tried to convince myself, all I could feel was betrayal by a man I once loved and had planned on spending the rest of my life with. Once I had finished my cup of tea, I felt my nerves subside and my heart was beating at a less furious pace, I needed to get my head together, it was only day one and I hadn't yet faced Jason or Alex. I smoothed down my dress and headed back to my office space knowing that Jason was probably now in seeing as it was 9 am. I headed back over to our office and as I expected, Jason sat at his desk typing away, his face close to the screen squinting, I had always said he needed glasses, but he had shrugged it off saying he didn't want them as it would make him feel too old. The memory made me smile. He looked up for half a second as I entered the room and then went straight back to what he was doing.

"Morning," I chimed sweetly.

"Em," he replied blankly, still typing away engrossed in whatever he was doing. I sided around to my desk and began placing my personal items on it, a few stationary items, some hand cream and a snow globe that I had been given by a social worker on the day of Ivy's adoption. Her new family had asked her to pass it to me, it was a less traditional globe, a shiny silver base with a large globe on top, filled with dark liquid and small multi coloured flecks of glitter. Apparently, they had commented that when you shook it, it looked like the galaxy in deep outer space and as I watched it, every now and then a large grain of silver would flash through the liquid like stars shining out at me. Every time I saw those silver flecks when I shook it up, it reminded me of Ivy, my shining star in a dark place. I shook it up and placed it on the desk smiling, I glanced over at Jason, he had stopped typing and was now watching me through narrowed eyes. Shit, I hadn't even thought, he knew exactly what this globe meant to me, he huffed shaking his head and then looked away, continuing to type more furiously now. Keep it together I kept repeating over and over in my head. "So, what will we be doing today?" I directed over to Jason while logging into my computer.

"Whatever he wants us to," he replied sarcastically like I had just asked a stupid question.

"OK, so what time will Mr Hutchinson be here?" I snapped back.

"He's probably already here, in the morning meeting with all the editors and important people, we don't qualify as good enough for that gig," he sniped back.

"Do you not like working here or something, you don't seem very happy," I questioned genuinely.

He shoved his keyboard back across the desk and turned in his chair to face me. "I like working here, I just didn't anticipate having to spend every minute with you, you were supposed to have been down working with Alicia, not side by side with me all fucking day!" He spat back venomously.

Anger rose up in my chest and I stood up abruptly knocking my desk forward, spilling all my stationary I had just neatly lined up in its holder. "I'm not exactly fucking thrilled to be spending my days with you either, Jason, but maybe if you hadn't followed me all the way down here like some crazy person this wouldn't have happened, would it?" I fired back. He turned back to his computer screen and continued typing while laughing loudly. "What's so funny?" I snapped back.

"I didn't come here for you, and you know that," he replied with a sarcastic laugh.

Chapter 6

"I see you pair have broken the ice already, what's all the laughter about?" Alex beamed as he strode into our office moments later holding a takeaway coffee cup and a handful of paperwork. He looked impeccable, strolling over to my desk, avoiding my gaze, giving me ample opportunity to allow my eyes to wander. I glanced at Jason, his demeanour immediately changed, like a chameleon adapting his skin to suit his surroundings, he knew who the alpha was, and as much as he liked to act like it was him, when Alex was around, he shrunk into himself and allowed the reins to be taken freely. I smiled outwardly at his response, revelling in his uncomfortableness. I was so busy enjoying watching Jason's demise that I almost forgot it was now my turn to endure the awkwardness that I was fully expecting following our night of passion at the weekend.

"Tea white one by the way, Emily," he said lightly, raising his paper cup in the air and perching on the edge of my desk, taking a deep breath, and mentally telling myself it would be fine I looked up from my screen to meet his gaze, our eyes locking. I was surprised to see nothing more than a man speaking to one of his employers, no lust, no dark eyes, but in doing so I instantly felt at ease.

"Same as me, that shouldn't be too hard to remember then." I smiled back feeling genuinely relieved that our first meeting wasn't turning out as awkward as I had imagined.

"One? You took two sugars!" Jason scoffed from the other side of the room.

I felt both of their eyes on me at once as silence filled the room, "I, um, not anymore, I cut back," was all I could manage, my tone coming across slightly blunter than I intended. I watched Alex glance from me to Jason, then back again, more than likely assessing the situation and our relationship. I felt panic rise in my chest, my heart began to beat faster as I turned back to my computer screen to avoid making eye contact with either man. I couldn't allow Alex to know about our past, if he knew that me and Jason were once upon a time planning a life together, had history that would trump most people's entire life story, he would sack me immediately and my entire reasoning for being here would be ruined.

"It's been a long time since high school, Jason," I chimed back sweetly, pretending to look at something on my computer screen. "People change, along with their tea preferences also," I joked back lightly. Jason ignored me completely, choosing to instead turn to his computer and begin typing away loudly, clearly disappointed at his outburst.

Alex laughed lightly under his breath, "It would appear so, I remember a time when I didn't even drink hot drinks, the older I'm getting the more reliant I find myself depending on caffeine." I looked up to meet his gaze again, not wanting to be rude as Jason was clearly ignoring both of us now, "Anyway, Emily, I've got a few bits and pieces that need doing today," placing the papers he had come in with in front of me, he spun them on the desk so I could read them, clearly back in CEO mode and seemingly off my case. I relaxed instantly,

"These are the addresses and details you will need for a few of my places, and a couple of errands that I will need you to run, my gym, dry cleaners etc, every morning you will find one of these on your desk and it will outline what I need you to help me with each day." I looked down and skim read the first page, I briefly saw what looked like everyday requests, collect dry cleaning, check stationary stocks, things that I could manage easily, I flicked over the page and saw more of the same, collect special delivery post from foyer, check answer phone messages, when my gaze caught on the last entry, something I was unfamiliar with, "Fuego 7 pm?"

I looked up at Alex questioningly, I didn't need to look at Jason to know his gaze was now on me and I could no longer hear his furious typing. "Yes, Fuego at 7," Alex replied plainly, taking a sip of his tea and making his way over to the doorway, "I have a business meeting tonight at the Caribbean restaurant on main street, I am meeting with some clients who are potentially looking at investing in the company and offer us a printing contract." He stopped in the doorway and looked back at me, his eyes now dark and full of the lust he had been lacking earlier. "I need you to accompany me and deal with anything that may come up during the meeting." I thought I heard his voice wobble as he spoke, like he was almost trying to convince himself of what he was saying. I felt sure he could read the confusion on my face as he lingered slightly in the doorway awaiting my response, his eyes seeking approval, before turning and leaving without one, before I could say no.

My eyes lingered on the doorway even after he had left. Jason was back to his furious typing, completely ignoring the fact that I was in the room. I suddenly realised I had questions, questions that I wanted answers to. I couldn't work for Alex if he was going to blow hot and cold, I needed to know where I stood and address the weekend with him, let him know that it was a one off, that I was here to do a job, not to become his play thing that he could pick up and drop when he decided. I stood up abruptly, stomping after Alex. I felt Jason's eyes follow me as I left our office, him not saying a word, probably aware that I wasn't particularly happy. As I reached Alex's office, the smoked glass door was now clear, I could see him sitting at his desk holding a piece of paper, intently reading whatever it entailed. I swung the door open furiously, not bothering to knock and marched over to his desk. He immediately looked up from his paper, his eyes locking with mine as a took the last few steps towards him, I could see the confusion on his face as I slammed my hands down on his desk rattling his very expensive stationary and his paper cup, fortunately now empty rolled over onto its side, his mouth opened, clearly about to put me in my place.

"No!" I protested my hand now bridging the gap across his desk, my palm facing him. "Let me speak." I saw his eyes dance with delight as he leaned back in his chair, like he was amused with my little outburst, crossing his arms across his chest a smirk formed across his mouth, angering me more as he pointed his hand in my direction, clearly giving me the stage to have my say. I took a deep breath in, standing upright, folding my arms across my chest also matching his, and with his eyes watching me intently, I began, "Right Mr Fancy Pants, now I am very aware of who and what you are, and equally I am aware of my job roll and what I am here to do, but if you think that gives you the right to order me about with no thought that I may actually, in fact have a life and already have plans this evening, then you are not only deluded but also an awful person to work for." I watched his face soften as he listened to my protest, lifting his head up, he opened his mouth to begin to speak. "Ah, I'm not done yet!" I fired at him, raising my hand again to face him, a subtle nod as he unfolded his arms allowed me to carry on. "Not only do you need to learn some people skills, and how to speak to women without trying to get them eating out your hand, which for the record I am most definitely not here for, my hours are 9–4 and therefore a 7 pm meeting is outside of my working day, so I would suggest from now on, rather than demanding things of people, perhaps you should exercise some decorum and ask, then perhaps you'll get better results!" He leaned forward onto his desk, cradling his chin with his hands, a sarcastic smile stretching ear to ear, his eyes dark and full of excitement. "And while you're at it, look up the work professionalism and maybe you could learn a few pointers from it." Feeling better now id got a few things, albeit definitely not all, off my chest I stood confidently with my hands on my hips, staring, waiting for a response.

He continued to stare at me, his smile not wavering. "Hello, Emily," a soft lady's voice spoke from behind me. I spun around, shocked, to see a middle-aged lady, elegantly dressed, with warm, olive-skin and silky, dark hair twisted into a loose bun, was sitting in the room with us. Her legs were crossed over each other and she sat comfortably on a white leather sofa, paperwork strewn all at her side, a steaming coffee clasped in her hands, her face full of amusement. I immediately felt my cheeks flush and embarrassment sweep over me as I tried to find the words to explain my little show, I had nothing. I glanced back at Alex, who was clearly enjoying seeing me speechless and knowing full well how mortified I was that she had just witnessed my toddler tantrum.

Finally, Alex's voice broke the silence in the room. "Emily." He breathed softly, standing, and moving around from his desk towards me, I watched his face as he gently placed his hand between my shoulder blades, turning me to face the lady, her face still full of amusement also. As he did, his hand slid slowly down my back, stopping at the small of my back, sending shivers through me and igniting my body. It didn't matter what this man said or did, one touch was all it took to have me sated and at his mercy. Ignoring the fluttering feeling in my belly, I stared up at Alex's face as he spoke, "This is my mother, Isla. Mother, this is Emily, my new PA." A second wave of embarrassment ensued, truly horrified that this elegant lady had heard me speak to her son the way I just had. Thank goodness I hadn't continued with round two which was going to outline how I wasn't best pleased at him for fucking me then not bothering to call all weekend. I cringed at the thought. I stood glued to the spot, Alex now practically holding me up as his mother gently placed her mug on the side table and stood slowly, making her way over to me, her eyes not leaving mine. I struggled to read her expressions, a small smile and a glint in her eye were all I could focus on as she reached up to me and cupped my cheek with her hand, she lingered on my face admiring me before twisting a strand of my hair between her fingers and sliding downwards finally resting her hand on my upper arm squeezing gently.

"What a beautiful, strong woman." She breathed softly before pulling me into a tight hug. I felt cold as Alex's hand left my back, him stepping back to allow us to have a moment, but still warm as I embraced this lady I had only just met. I couldn't work out what was going on, why she was being so gentle and looking at me like she had known me a lifetime, but I hugged her back hard, not because I felt like I had to, but because I wanted to, and I felt safe and secure as all the anger and frustrations I had moments ago dissolved.

She took my hand and led me to where she was first sitting, shuffling all the papers she had been working on aside she gestured for me to sit down. Alex had made his way back over to his chair and was watching us both intently, as I stole a glance over at him, his eyes met mine, and all I saw was adoration, him clearly taking in this moment that seemed strange to me, but completely normal to him.

"Darling," Isla began, as she took a seat next to me and turned slightly to face me. "This man, my son, is one of the biggest pains in the backsides that I have ever known." I giggled lightly and listened watching her beautiful face light up as she spoke about her son. "He works hard, harder than anyone I know, and sometimes he can come across as being rude, or arrogant but I can assure you, his heart and morals are in exactly the right place, he just struggles to take a moment and give that extra minute or so to explain himself fully." I glanced over at Alex who was now looking down at his hands, obviously struggling with hearing his mother talk about him in such an endearing way. Looking back at Isla she continued, "I admire your tenacity, your fire and willingness to stand up for yourself, it makes you a strong and admirable lady but I can assure you, those walls are not needed around my son, he is a loving, caring and thoughtful man who always puts others before him, he cares for his employees and would never exploit or do bad by any of them. Just give him a chance." She smiled and squeezed my hand as she stood, looking over at Alex, she simply smiled, and he returned the same gesture as she left the room closing the door softly behind her.

"Sorry about her, she can be, well, umm, over the top," Alex muttered whist fiddling his watch strap and avoiding eye contact. I didn't know how to respond, yes, she was over the top, but I didn't mind, she gave me a sense of belonging that I didn't know I was missing until I met her. She also gave me more information about Alex than I had figured out by myself which I appreciated immensely. I believed what she said, every word, that Alex was a decent guy, that he had such an empire to run that he didn't always have time for the niceties in life and that things were more often than not, a hundred miles an hour. I suddenly realised that this guy probably just needed a break, that he was tired and lost in a world that was full of people, yet he was probably feeling very much alone. All the meetings and business propositions, partners, and staff, yet none of them were friends, always seeking something from him. I wondered if anyone actually asked him how he was and really meant it, I suddenly felt very sorry for this powerful man sitting in front of me, still adjusting his watch strap, clearly not sure how to act with me now that his mother had pulled me in that little bit closer, and in doing so had lowered mine and Alex's walls with each other simultaneously.

"I'm so sorry, Alex, I should never have shouted at you, especially in front of your mother, I had no idea she was sitting there."

"It's OK, Em," he replied plainly, still not looking at me. "You were right, I should never have just assumed that you would give up your evening for me, I'm just used to telling and getting, it won't happen again." I felt emotions rise up into my throat that I didn't know I had, to see his vulnerabilities laid bare just made me all the more intrigued, and although there was no denying that this guy was immensely hot, I found myself wanting to get to know the real him that little bit more. I walked round to his side of the desk, his eyes now on me as I edged myself into the small gap between him and the desk. His eyes watched me intently, him trying to assess my thoughts as he wheeled his chair back slightly, allowing me closer as I perched on his desk between his legs. His longing eyes now looking up at me, I leaned forward and gently placed my hands on either side of his face, I could see the emotion in his eyes, this man was lost and alone, I suddenly felt fiercely protective and I didn't know why, I had only known this man existed a mere week or so ago and yet here I was feeling drawn to him in all sorts of ways that out loud, sounded irrational and crazy, yet I couldn't help thinking by the way he was looking at me, that he felt the same. I pulled his head to my chest and he wrapped his arms tightly around my waist, my cheek resting on the top of his head, my fingers caressing his hair, he hummed in appreciation. We stayed this way for what felt like forever, no words spoken, just us holding each other. After a while, I was the one to break our hold, lowering my hands to his shoulders and gently easing him back, I felt his body stiffen again as he stood up and looked down on me, this time caressing my face, I felt my body ignite at his tenderness, like I needed his touch to keep me alive, he spoke no words at first, only smiling as he did.

"I really needed that, thank you, Emily," he finally said, the words heart felt and full of appreciation.

"I kind of thought you did." I smiled back at him moving gently out of his grip and slowly towards the door, aware that I needed to create some distance before I did something irrational and crazy at work. I felt his eyes on my back as I left and confusion swept over me, I had no idea what was going on, but I couldn't help feeling elated that I had seen a glimmer of the real him. I Knew deep down that I should ignore my feelings, that I should have stuck to my plan of keeping my distance, but it was becoming apparent that no matter what I did, we were drawn together every time.

Partly still feeling bad about my outburst, but secretly wanting to see him again tonight, I stopped in the doorway and looked over my shoulder. "Pick me up at 6:30?" The look on his face and the smile he gave me told me that he would be there.

Chapter 7

The morning had passed by fairly quickly, Jason had been mostly out of the office, ferrying a couple of Alex's cars to and from the garage having them washed and valeted, so I hadn't really seen him. He had already left our office by the time I got back from having a strop next door and I wondered if he had seen or heard anything. I was secretly hoping that he was doing more of the same this afternoon, so I didn't have to answer to him or explain myself. I had no explanation of what was going on between me and Alex other than I was drawn to him in a way I couldn't fathom, like our stars had aligned and brought us together. Jason was the last person I wanted to discuss it with. I knew at some point I was going to have to try and explain my day to Molly and Ali, how our master plan of remaining professional and calling the weekend a one off had been scuppered approximately ten minutes into my working day. I laughed as I imagined the next time I saw them, I would have some serious explaining to do, not knowing exactly what, if anything, was going on myself, never mind having to explain it to two gossip hungry girls. I mentally made a note to put off that meeting until I had more of an explanation for them. I had run a few errands for Alex during my morning, I had dropped off some parcels at the post office, bought, at his request a beautiful bunch of flowers, in his words, whatever I thought were pretty enough to go in his office, and then finally taken an array of clean clothes down to the gym, ready for his next workout. I cringed at the memory. I had stood at the reception desk watching people work out through the glass window separating the desk from the gym and my mind had wandered. I was imagining how Alex looked when he was in there, all hot and sweaty, breathless, and strong, and had blushed realising I had already seen him in that state on Saturday. The lady behind the desk looking at me like I was some kind of pervert, her repeatedly asking if she could help me, meanwhile, me ignoring her, all gooey eyed staring absent minded into the gym, her not knowing my mind was elsewhere. I had excused myself feeling embarrassed and hoped the next time I had to come back she wouldn't remember me, though I knew that wouldn't be the case. After that I headed back to OSAR and was lured by the smell of coffee, although I only drank tea myself, into the coffee shop next door where I purchased two teas to go, both white with one sugar and it had made me smile to know that we simply drank the same hot drink. I had a spring in my step as I walked back into the foyer, I could really get used to this job, I felt at home and even after a morning, felt that I could really fit in here. I waved at Tom as I passed him, obviously very busy, tapping away at his keyboard and talking to a lady who was standing at his desk, he made the time to shoot me a big smile as I made my way to the elevator. I had been feeling sick to my stomach only a few hours earlier taking this very same elevator ride to the top floor, I smiled thinking how much things had changed in such a short amount of time. As I walked back into the office, June on the front desk looked up and clapped with glee, "Ooooh those flowers are beautiful!" She exclaimed, delighted at my choice of an enormous bunch of orange lilies. I smiled back, grateful that she thought so. I had spent far too much time pondering up and down the aisles of the local florist with no idea what flowers to get a man, so I had just decided to just choose something what I liked and hoped for the best.

"You think he'll like them?" I replied, hopefully.

"Yes, dear I'm sure he will, what a beautiful colour, makes a change from boring white everywhere." She laughed as I walked down the corridor towards Alex's office. As I approached his office, I could see the door was already open, I walked in and saw Alex was sat at his desk, fingers entwined, elbows on the table with his chin resting on his knuckles, smile a mile wide, clearly awaiting my entrance.

"She's a cheeky little so and so," he joked, nodding his head in her direction, clearly beaming as I walked over to his desk, "I personally like white, it's classic and clean and doesn't clash with anything."

I smiled as I placed the flowers on their side in front of him. "I didn't really know what to get, so I just got what I liked, I hope you don't mind, they're quite bright and in your face," I whispered back, looking down at my feet, now worrying that I should have gone with my first choice of a bunch of white daisies.

"I got you tea as well," I offered up, trying to divert his attention from the flowers, placing his cup down on his desk.

"Thank you, just what I needed," he said before taking a big sip. "So, Lilies huh? I had you down as a rose's kind of girl." He winked. He was clearly in a

46

playful mood, and I felt instantly at ease as he gestured me to sit down, him taking the lilies and arranging them in a crystal vase at the side of his desk.

"Yes, they're my favourite, I was going to get you white ones but I love orange so..." I shrugged my shoulders apologetically.

"They are beautiful, thank you, perfect choice," he beamed back. I leaned back into the soft, white, leather sofa and circled my ankles; heels were not the best footwear for this job with all the running about I had been doing and I made a mental note to go shopping for some formal flats. I took a huge sip of my tea and felt my body relax for the first time all morning. My mind was mulling over how strange it was that in this moment we were casually chatting away, like normal colleagues on any given day, no tension or awkwardness, yet a few hours earlier, his head was resting on my breasts as I held him close, sharing a moment like we were the only people on earth. I couldn't explain how one moment I could be completely unaffected by him, then the next I would be imagining him ripping my clothes off. I started to prepare myself to ask Alex about the weekend, about what it meant for us and why he hadn't called me, but I didn't want to ruin the good mood that he seemed to be in, and besides, the awkwardness that I had been expecting hadn't materialised and it almost felt like it had never actually happened. I told myself that perhaps it was best to leave that conversation for another time and just enjoy how things were for now.

Tearing me away from my thoughts Alex chirped up, "Been a busy girl, have we?" he queried, clearly reading my body language correctly and noting my aching feet and audible sigh as I washed down my tea.

"Yes, but it's been good, I like getting out and about, I don't think sitting in an office all day is for me," I answered back honestly.

"Yeah, tell me about it, sometimes I just want to get up and go, explore, sit on the beach, it gets boring being cooped up all day with the beach on full view but rarely getting time to go down there." His gaze directed out of the window, admiring the stunning turquoise waters.

Remembering the times I'd walked down there on my own, the breeze whipping around my hair as I gathered my thoughts.

"I love to go down there either really early, or really late, there are less people around and the sun is amazing to watch also," I replied, wondering in my mind if one day I could take him down there and show him.

Alex was still looking down at the beach, "I wouldn't be able to go really early or late, I have things at home that I need to see to at those sorts of times you know." His answer was plain, like his mind was elsewhere.

"Like what?" I replied curious. His head shot round as he remembered where he was, seemingly regretting giving me too much information.

"Ahh, you know, just umm stuff," he quipped back, now rummaging in his drawer for something, but I guessed nothing in particular, just something to distract himself from our conversation.

"Oook," I replied as I stood to leave, Alex clearly not wanting to continue with our conversation. Not wanting to dull a good morning, instead I told him I had a few bits to get on with and excused myself, Alex nodding as a response and getting stuck into some paperwork he had on his desk. I felt confused as I settled down at my desk next door, why had he been so open and relaxed with me one minute, and then shut me off the next? This is what I had felt this morning about him blowing hot and cold, one minute us sharing a tender moment and the next him getting all weird when I asked him what he did in the mornings and evenings that took up so much of his time. I shook my head and sighed as I started opening mail that was addressed to Alex's PA, a job I was least looking forward to as it meant I would have to be in the same spot for a while, something I wasn't very good at doing. Most of it was just generic post, bills for his car valeting, thank you letters from a couple of charities thanking him for his generous donations, I smiled to know that his mother was being truthful, his heart was in the right place. I was grateful to get to the final letter, a crumpled brown envelope with Mr Hutchinson's PA scribbled on the front, the postage address of the building scribbled underneath and a singular blue stamp in the righthand corner. I noted that it looked a bit worse for wear, like it had been left in someone's bag, its owner continuously forgetting to post it. I peeled open the stuck down flap and pulled out a small piece of paper with an address neatly written across the middle, I stared at it confused wondering what it meant, I had no idea whose address this was, but my instincts were telling me this was not intended for Alex, it was intended for me. The address was here, in Miami, although I didn't recognise the street name or area, my heart began to pound as I wiggled my computer mouse bringing the screen to life. Typing in the address on the paper my hands shook, my foot tapping on the floor impatiently as the results loaded. The search took me to a small town a few miles out of Miami, I cocked my head to the side trying to make sense of what I was looking at, it was a small gathering of houses, seemingly normal, nothing that made any sense to me. I clicked on street view and the image of the house I had just typed in came flashing into view, as it did, I felt every hair on my body stand on end and I gasped loudly, my hand flying to cover my mouth. The house was small but homely, the masonry had been painted a light blue colour, and small baskets of bright flowers hung under the windows. In typical Florida style, small palms scattered the front and side of the house, and browning grass, clearly lacking some TLC covered the space between the sidewalk and front door. The thing that was most notable, and the reason my body was now surged with adrenaline, were the children's toys littering the front driveway. A few ride on cars, a toy stroller with a doll strapped in, albeit upside down on its head but still, I smiled at the image. A small number of building blocks and a bright pink football completed the scene, a dark-haired toddler stood next to it, a pretty yellow dress flowed at her sides, her back to the camera and her arms stretched out towards the blurry image of a lady sat in the doorway with big brown curly hair. My eyes welled and a sob caught in my throat as I grabbed the computer screen at either side and pulled it towards me in a subconscious attempt to get close, closer to Ivy.

I stared in disbelief at the small, pixelated image on the screen, tracing my finger lightly over the little girl's hair, tears now welling up in my eyes. I minimised the screen and began furiously researching anything I could about the address and its owners, I had come up with nothing. Could that little girl in the picture actually be her? I had no other explanation as to why this address had found its way to me, but I was also aware that it could be Jason playing cruel games. If this was Ivy's new home, I was pleased to know that the owners were private, not allowing their personal details to be placed on the address database that was available to the general public, a clever move for a family of a child they had potentially adopted. I smiled, grateful that the family that were now possibly caring for my daughter seemed to be taking sensible precautions but frustrated at the same time, that I had no more information. After some time prowling the internet, searching social media, local groups, and telephone directories, I leaned back in my chair defeated and picked the note up, running my fingers over the faded ink. Who had sent this? Was it Jason, letting me know that he had found Ivy, an indirect threat without speaking a word? I admired the handwriting on the front of the envelope, it didn't look like his writing, although it wouldn't be hard to disguise it, knowing that I would recognise it if he didn't. I shook my head, not convinced, but at the same time, aware that no one else, other than myself, Jason and now Molly and Ali knew about my adoption. It had to be Jason. I didn't want to directly confront him about it, he would then know I had her address, information I didn't want him to know if it wasn't actually him behind it. I mulled over a few ideas before settling with a plan to gage his reaction, I stuffed the empty envelope into my desk drawer, and with the address safely hidden in the bottom of my handbag, I logged off and headed down to the foyer for my lunch break. My heart heavy, full of worry, worry that if this was Jason and he had Ivy's address, this afternoon would turn out to be very interesting indeed.

Chapter 8

I wasn't sure what I wanted to eat, my appetite had someone wavered in the last half hour, but I needed to get away and gather my thoughts away from OSAR. I pulled my phone from my bag to catch up on anything from that morning, as expected I had a few texts, an early morning message from Molly wishing me good luck and telling me not to worry, a message from Ali joking about making sure I wear my hottest outfit, I shook my head and smiled, it was typical Ali. Then two messages from Molly mid-morning, the first one a polite, how's it going text, the next one 20 minutes later, in screamy capitals and followed by a hoard of explanation marks requesting me to text back as she was going mad not knowing how things had gone. I sighed loudly, I couldn't believe how much had happened in just one morning here, so much that I had to figure out. I was now engaging in some sort of strange relationship with my boss, a relationship that I had no title to give it. All I knew was that I was so drawn to him in a way I couldn't explain, that when he touched me, we created a moment so full of fire and passion, that it wouldn't be long before people around us started to notice and I knew deep down, that staying away for either of us was not an option. I was now working alongside my ex, who I still fully believed had murdered someone, but I had absolutely zero evidence to prove it, and he was now trying to manipulate me, by threatening to harm my daughter to buy my silence. Then, to make matters worse, neither man knew of my relationship with the other. This was such a mess. I thought about the brown envelope, the address I had discovered earlier and decided this was the first and most important thing I needed to get to the bottom of for now. Once I had discovered if it was Jason who has sent it, which I was almost certain of that it was, I could decide my next move, one thing I was certain of though, is that I needed to go to the address, I didn't know what I would say, but I had to see for myself. If Ivy was in danger, I would need to phone the police straight away, I shook my head in frustration, that wouldn't work, I had absolutely no information to give them other than he gave me an envelope with an address on it, and that three years or so ago, I woke up in the middle of the night feeling drugged up and he was acting strange, but it's OK because I now work with him and our boss is now my sort of lover. It sounded crazy and I knew it wouldn't be enough to erase Jason from the equation, it would only anger him and perhaps cause him to do something hasty. I needed to get to the bottom of this before I went to the police, I needed solid evidence and the answers as to what was going on. I typed out a quick reply to the girls saying everything was going well, that I was super busy and would call them tonight before slipping my phone back into my bag and headed across the foyer feeling defeated and completely out of my depth.

"Emily, wait up!" I heard a familiar voice call from behind me. I turned around to see Tom slinging a bag over his shoulder, speed walking towards me.

"You going to lunch?" He asked, throwing his arm across my shoulder, and guiding me towards the exit.

"Yeah, well I mean I'm going out for my lunch break, but I don't know where or if I'm going to bother getting any food," I replied, feeling a bit sorry for myself now I'd said that out loud.

"Oh honey, you can come with me if you like, I'm just going to the Thai place on the sea front, excellent food and if we can get a window seat, you get a prime view of all the guys on the beach!" He chuckled loudly, taking my hand, and easing us through the doors onto the street. Feeling like I didn't have much of a choice in the matter, he pulled me with him up the sidewalk. I upped my pace, now matching his strides as we walked side by side heading towards the beach, grateful to be able to forget about all the drama going on, have some normality and seemingly finding a friend in Tom. As we walked Tom told me a bit about himself, he was originally from New York and came down here for the sun and men, as he told me, I had laughed telling him my story had been much the same, obviously leaving out the finer details. He was now living in an apartment a few miles away, renting a room from the woman who owned it, her away for long periods of time as she worked on construction contracts around the world. I felt at ease walking along with Tom sharing our stories, and I could tell he was a genuinely nice guy. I could feel the sea breeze on my face as we approached a break in the buildings leading us down towards the water, it was a welcome addition as it was a hot, muggy day, something I still hadn't quite got used to since moving here. The midday sun was beaming down on us and as expected, the beach was full of people. Some were people doing the same as us, on their lunch break, sat on benches eating their sandwiches, others were clearly tourists, slathered in sun cream enjoying the warm waters. I loved the beach and the feeling I got being down here, the turquoise waters and white sand were beyond beautiful, and seeing people enjoying themselves down there made me smile.

"It's just up here, hopefully they've got a seat inside, I'm absolutely sweating." Tom was now wafting his face animatedly with his spare hand, still holding mine with his other.

"Table for two please, Jess," Tom chirped cheerfully at the lady working the desk in the foyer of Enchanted Thai, a beautiful quaint restaurant that I was disappointed I'd never noticed before.

"Window seat?" The young pretty waitress replied laughing, grabbing a couple of menus, and gesturing us towards the large windows that reached floor to ceiling, allowing the sun to flood in, illuminating all the mahogany furniture a fiery orange colour. I laughed as Tom nodded smirking, clearly a creature of habit.

"Feel free to join us, I spotted a group of lads playing volleyball on the way in, should make for a good lunchtime viewing," Tom offered, raising his eyebrows suggestively.

"Ahh I'm going to be far too busy for that," she added shaking her head smiling as we took our seats, placing the menus in front of us.

"This is Emily by the way," Tom said looking up at Jess, gesturing over to me, "Jess, Emily." He waved his hand between the two off us absent-mindedly while diverting his attention to the menu.

"Emily, nice to meet you, do you work with Tom?" she asked, her face welcoming and polite.

"Yes, it's my first day," I replied shyly, although I wasn't sure why.

"Oh amazing! You'll have to talk to Tom and come along at the weekend for drinks, we are all meeting at the Yacht Club, it's a swanky bar up the other end of the promenade, super cool vibe, lots of hot men, you get the picture," she responded enthusiastically.

"OH MY GOD YES!" Tom shouted, now dismissing his menu, and slamming his hand onto the table outdoing Jess's enthusiasm. I jumped, not expecting his over-the-top outburst, but smiled at the same time. "I almost forgot that was this week, I love the scene there, we can get all dressed up and pretend we fit in!" Tom added clapping. Jess and Tom laughed at the same time. "Yeah, like all those snooty bitches have anything on me," Tom said while swishing an imaginary S mid-air between us.

"Sounds good, I'm in," I responded, though lacking their excitedness. "Is it an open invitation?" I asked hopefully, thinking of Molly and Ali.

"Oh my god yes, the more the merrier!" Jess offered up smiling.

"Perfect," I grinned back.

"Now what can I get you both to drink?" Jess asked.

Thirty minutes later, we were both sat back in our chairs sated, my stomach content and full after my giant bowl of chicken and vegetable noodles, Tom had demolished a huge bowl of green curry and rice and we had shared a large plate of spring rolls followed by a bowl of ice cream each. We were now laughing about how we were going to manage the waddle back to work, full to the brim and in the searing heat. "I really shouldn't have eaten that, I've got to go to a business meeting with Alex tonight, a meal at Fuego or something, I don't think I have any more room for food today!" I said jokingly, my skirt unbuttoned and my hand resting in my waistband.

"Wait what?" Tom fired back, now practically laying his top half across the table, his face full of delight.

"A work meal, for work, with my boss, with other people there also," I droned back smiling, knowing his train of thought.

"Have you been before?" he shot back, like he knew something I didn't.

"No, I'd never heard of it until earlier, why?" I sat forward, now concerned he was about to tell me it was a gentleman's club or some sort of seedy equivalent.

"It's theeee most exclusive place in Miami," he whispered across the table like it was a secret. "It's usually by invitation only, I've never been obviously, but I'm dying to hear all about it, I'm so jealous," he sunk back into his chair pouting.

"I'm sure it's not going to be all that, I mean it's a business meeting after all, it's bound to be boring and dull," I offered back, hoping to dull the sting of his disappointment.

"Wait, what are you going to wear?" Tom added, cocking his head to the side.

"Umm," I replied, looking down at myself and using my hands to illustrate I hand intended on just wearing my work clothes.

"No, no, no, honey!" He shot back his hands now running through his hair in dismay. "Please tell me you have some form of formal dress, something classy but with a bit of something extra, something sexy?" He was worrying me, his face now full of genuine concern.

"I mean, I have some plain work dresses, tight fitting, curves on show and all that," I offered shrugging my shoulders.

"Oh god no," he fired back, now heading toward the door, dragging me behind him. "Money's on the table, Jess, thank you!" He shouted, blowing an air kiss, her waving at us both and smiling at me being dragged out of the restaurant.

"Where are we going!" I giggled, now managing to keep up with his fast pace, him seemingly on a mission.

"You'll see," he shot back. We got almost back to OSAR when he crossed us over the road and came to a stop at a stunning clothing boutique that sat opposite OSAR, we had passed it on the way here, but I had seemingly not noticed. We stood on the sidewalk peering in through the big glass windows, beautiful dresses lined up on mannequins, the sun glinting off the glass embroidery trailing down most of them.

"Meet me here after work, I'll help you pick, you should be able to find something stunning." Tom smiled at me like he had solved the puzzle as I glanced up at the beautiful dresses.

I would no doubt be able to find something in here, my gaze dropped to the price tag at the bottom of a black lace dress that had first caught my eye and my heart sank, "189 dollars, Tom, I can't afford that, this place is way over my budget," I whispered, embarrassed. Tom shuffled foot to foot, thinking for a moment, hand at his chin, clearly coming up with another master plan.

After some time, he clapped his hands together in delight, his face beaming.

"Ah hah!" he chimed, as he looked me up and down and twizzled his finger in a circle, gesturing me to spin around.

"Tom what are we doing?" I questioned as I turned around on the spot.

"Going back to work," he chirped back, grabbing my hand, and now heading back over the road towards OSAR.

"I am so confused, what's going on?" I asked.

"Meet me here after work, 4 pm," Tom replied, pointing at the pavement directly outside the front doors to OSAR, people were coming through them and now having to maneuverer around us as we stood there. I shook my head and waved my hands at him, asking a silent question about what on earth was going on. "4 pm." He nodded, before disappearing though the revolving doors, leaving me standing there wondering what on earth he had planned.

Chapter 9

I headed back up to the office wondering what Tom had in store for me. I had really enjoyed my lunch with him, he was exciting and full of life, and I found I enjoyed being around him. I found him refreshing in a time that my life was chaotic and full of drama, a welcome distraction that I needed right now. I sighed as I reached the top floor, knowing that I was more than likely going to be spending my afternoon with Jason. I still hadn't been able to work him out and it bothered me. For a man that I previously dated for many years, it should have been easy to read him, suss him out and be one step ahead, but he was portraying such a demure character, something that I wasn't familiar with, like he was a completely different person. Yes, he had been slightly off and had the odd snipe at me, but when my mind cast back to the night he had strangled me, all those years ago, and the verbal abuse that followed in the years after, I didn't feel like I was looking at the same man from back then. I felt sure those traits were perhaps still a part of him, especially since he had hinted that he hadn't come to Florida for me. I knew I just needed to push him to see if I could entice the real him to the surface. I knew I needed to do it on safe territory, and where safer than here, with Alex next door if I needed him. The office was mostly empty when I got back, most of the staff still at lunch. As I headed to my office, I noticed Alex's door open, I popped my head in and waved, seeing him deep in conversation on the phone, reeling off figures and statistics that meant nothing to me, he immediately lowered the phone and offered me a smouldering look, I waggled my finger at him and made a quick exit as he grinned getting back to his phone call. I was grateful to find mine and Jason's office empty, perhaps he had already made a start to get finished up with the car job from this morning. I dumped my handbag on my chair and hesitated at the space between our desks, noticing that the drawers on his were not fully closed. Looking over my shoulder towards the door my heart started beating as I took my opportunity, I moved over towards the desk and slowly took a seat in his chair. I felt intrusive and scared, my body spiking as the adrenaline took over, but this was too good of an opportunity to miss out on, after seeing him lock them before leaving this morning, I knew I had to take this chance now. I ran my hand over the surface of his desk, rubbing the dust between my fingers. I took a deep breath as I opened his top drawer, casting my gaze across its contents, nothing jumped out at me. A few pieces of paper mostly invoices and to do lists for Alex. I slowly closed it and moved down to the next. A small pill bottle was the first thing I noticed as it rolled towards me, I reached in and held it up, twisting it around to read the faded, torn label. The words Diazepam, wrapped around the bottle in barely readable black ink with the instructions to take two, three times a day, I pouted wondering what he was taking them for. I turned the bottle around again, the back of the label now visible, my heart stopped, and fear rose up in my chest, the name Emily Moore splayed across the remainder of the label. I dropped the bottle back into the draw in shock, my hand covering my mouth. Why the hell did he have a prescription for me in his drawer? A prescription I had never seen before, a medicine I had never taken. I dropped to the floor on my knees, and in a panicked rage, began rummaging further in the drawer, my hands froze as I saw another two pill bottles stuffed at the back of the drawer. I slowly reached in and grabbed both bottles, bringing them up into my view, knowing that I wasn't going to like what I saw. Pure fear engulfed me as I saw two different women's names on the bottles, one a name I didn't recognise, the other, Chloe Lopez. I jumped up, throwing the bottles back into the drawers, slamming it shut, not wanting to touch them, like I knew they were poison and that he was up to something, something I wanted no part of. I sat back slowly into Jason's chair, my eyes wide and heart still beating out of my chest. I spotted the photo that I had seen earlier, the photo of him and Chloe at the park, I leaned over and picked up the photo, my finger traced across Chloe's face. What on earth was she doing with a man like Jason? She was a nice girl from what I remembered, I hadn't had much to do with her when we arrived in Michigan, but I often saw her around town, she tended to keep herself to herself, worked a successful job as a dental nurse and owned a nice home a few streets over. Other than my suspicions of her and Jason, that were never addressed, choosing to ignore it rather than knowing the truth, choosing not to be hurt over again, she seemed a pretty decent person. I had left all that in the past, I was no longer angry, hurt or seeking answers, all I could think was how I was now gravely worried for her, worried that she had fallen into Jason's grasp, unable to escape, a victim like I had become. I needed to find Chloe, find her and warn her, before it was too late.

"What the fuck are you doing?" Jason whispered through gritted teeth. My head whipped up to meet his gaze, him closing the door quietly behind him. Fear coursed through my veins as all the hair on my body stood on end. I opened my mouth to scream but nothing came out as I watched him move across the room towards me, his eyes dark and angry, not leaving mine. "I asked you a fucking question," he spat, his face now inches from mine, leaning over his desk.

"I, umm…"

"Shush!" he soothed, pushing a single finger to my lips, my hands shook as he reached down and took the photo frame I was still holding. "What's this?" He laughed as he turned it around to see I had been holding the photo of him and Chloe. "Ahh yes, beautiful Chloe, heads and shoulders above *you*!" His eyes glazed as he spoke, placing it back on his desk delicately as I sat frozen, unable to move or speak. My heart dropped to my stomach as he stalked around to join me, his eyes dancing as they wandered over my body. He perched on the desk between my legs, the same way I had done with Alex earlier, bile rose in my throat as I he slipped his hand between my thighs, snaking it up higher as he breathed heavily in my ear. I wanted to scream, to push him off me and get as far away from him as possible, but my body betrayed me as I sat frozen to the spot, a single tear falling into my lap as my breathing stopped.

"Enough!" I spat venomously into his ear, my body going into survival mode, slapping his hand away and standing abruptly. I saw the shock on his face, as he rocked backwards into his desk, forced to stand as I shoved him up, him stumbling backwards off me.

"Brave girl." He laughed quietly as I rushed over to my desk, seeking as much distance as I could but knowing I still had a lot to say to him.

"Why do you have prescriptions in multiple women's names, Jason, including fucking mine!" I hissed back at him, finding my confidence, and remembering he couldn't hurt me here. His eyes shot to his desk and back to mine, full of fury, I watched his jaw tense as he moved towards me again. Standing my ground, I stood tall and looked him right in the eyes as he moved within an inch of mine, his stale breath filling my nose. Suddenly, out of nowhere, I felt his hand around my throat, lifting me so that my toes barely touched the ground. I choked for breath and grabbed at his hands as I tried to free myself.

"Keep your fucking mouth shut, you utter one word, one god damn word and I swear, you'll regret it for the rest of your life," he spoke through gritted teeth, his face rigid as he slammed me back into my chair. I gasped for breath, my eyes watering as the realisation of what had just happened dawned on me. He slowly began moving away, his back to me, before pausing between our desks. I jumped, shocked, tears now streaming down my face as he swung around swiping the contents of my desk to the floor, my snow globe hitting the tiles and smashing into tiny pieces, glitter flowing across the tiles as the water carried it away. I felt my soul leave my body as my heart shattered along with it. He knew the sentiment of that snow globe and knew that it would cut deeper than anything physical he could do to me. He laughed as I rushed over, falling to my knees desperately trying to save what I knew was impossible as he took his seat and began typing away at his computer. My hands bled as I began gathering up the glass, tears now falling into the glittered water, when the door suddenly swung violently open, banging on the wall behind it, Alex's face, eyes wide bolting from me to Jason and then back again.

"What the hell happened; I heard a huge crash!" He shouted, I watched his face drop, as his attention focused on the mess in front of me. I saw his eyes fill with pain as he dropped down onto his knees in front of me, pulling my hands to his, enclosing them entirely inside as uncontrollable sobs began to take over my body.

"Well? Is anyone going to explain to me what the hell just happened?" Alex's voice boomed across the office, his face rigid with anger as he helped me to my feet, guiding me down to sit on the small sofa that sat near the doorway, his gaze cutting across the room at Jason. Taking a seat next to me, Alex pulled me to him and caressed my hair gently, soothing me instantly, making me feel protected and safe. I looked over at Jason who was now wide eyed, watching me intently, his face panicked and scared.

"I have no idea!" Jason blurted out, words shaky and uncertain, "one minute she was sat there, and next the globe went flying off her desk and she burst out in tears trying to pick it all up, it all happened so fast!" Jason spoke quickly, his face softening as he spoke, feeling more relaxed as he went on, believing his own lie. I felt Alex exhale deeply next to me as he assessed the situation. I couldn't believe Jason was doing this, I desperately wanted to scream at the top of my lungs, tell the whole building what a liar he was, how he was abusive and controlling, for Alex to grab him by the scruff off his neck and throw him to the

60

curb. I felt Alex's hand tuck a lock of my hair behind my ear, lifting my chin to face him as he did.

"Em?" He questioned, his eyes longing me to speak out, like he knew something wasn't quite right, but he wanted me to have my say first to confirm it.

I hesitated for a moment, and took a deep breath, "I tripped," I whispered quietly, glancing over at Jason whose face immediately relaxed as I spoke, a small smirk forming on the corner of his mouth. Alex's face screwed up as he shook his head, asking a silent question. I sat upright, Alex arm falling from my shoulders, and turned confidently to speak to him, "Yeah, I…um…tripped…tripped over the corner of my desk, my globe fell and smashed, it's, umm, very sentimental to me, probably the most important thing I own, so I dove straight down to try and catch it, but it was too late." I turned my hands palm up, the blood now drying, small grazes dotted them where the glass had cut me, the pain of my smashed globe, a thousand times more painful. I watched Alex intently as he tried to process what I was saying, his eyes darting from Jason to me and then the mess on the floor. I needed to convince him, I couldn't out Jason just yet, it was too soon, I had too much that I still needed to figure out first, to get my head around. If Jason wasn't around, I wouldn't be able to dig for information, get the answers I needed, and besides, I wanted him close, where I could keep an eye on him, and absolutely nowhere near Ivy. In that moment, my protective instincts rose to the surface, fuelled by the knowledge of Jason's abilities, willing to put myself in harm's way to keep her safe, I rubbed my hands together and winced, a light sigh at the end doing just the trick.

Alex's eyes darted back to me. "Come, let's get you cleaned up," he spoke gently, lightly taking my elbow and helping me to stand, leading me towards the door, "and, Jason, get this cleaned up please," he spoke curtly, not bothering to turn to look at him, his eyes focused on me the entire time as he led me next door to his office. We never spoke, as he led me through, and he never broke our touch, a connection flowing between us constantly, warming me from the inside out, igniting my senses. He closed the glass door behind us, the smoked glass giving me the privacy I needed right now, before leading me to a corridor at the back of his office. I stared up at his face as we walked, his hand resting gently on my hip, the other lightly gripping my inner elbow, encasing me in a protective bubble, safe under his arm, dwarfing me with his masculine body. I could see that he wasn't happy, that he was deeply troubled by what he had just seen, and

I knew deep down that he didn't believe what I said. We reached the bottom of the corridor and I gasped as he pushed open the huge door and let me walk in alone, him hesitating in the doorway as I admired the room. I moved slowly into the huge bathroom, bigger than my entire apartment, and fitted out to an impeccable standard. The entire room basked in a white glow, marble counter tops and two gleaming white basins lined the left side of the room, a huge mirror flowing up from the backs of them, meeting the ceiling, fully covering the entire space.

A walk-in shower big enough for at least ten people, ran the length of the other side of the room, multiple shower heads dotted above the area, the mirrors above the basins reflecting the entire shower space back at me. I felt my belly flutter as I imagined Alex showering there, being able to see his reflection as he ran his hands over his body. I Looked back at him, still waiting in the doorway, his eyes watching me as I admired the space, his eyes dark and full of lust. I smiled as I looked away, making my way slowly past the showers, towards the back of the room, my eyes darting around, taking in the magnificent room. I ran my hand along the edge of the giant free-standing bathtub that looked lost against the huge floor to ceiling windows that stood behind it, the blue waters and white sands creating a backdrop that didn't look as if it could be real. As I got to the other side, I paused at the basins and glanced in the mirror, my face streamed with mascara, my eyes puffy and red, and my hair all ruffled where Alex had been soothing me. I shrunk inside, knowing that Alex had seen me in such a state, embarrassed. I looked away quickly and turned the taps on, placing my stinging hands under the flowing water, hearing the door click quietly shut as I did. My breathing quickened as I felt his presence nearing, my body longing for him to be close to me, and my heart stopped as his face came into view behind me, his eyes drinking up my body as he looked me up and down. My body sprang into life as he stroked his fingers gently up the back of my naked thighs, my skin prickling at his touch, his eyes locked on mine. My hands stilled as I held his gaze while he trailed his fingers lightly up by behind, helping himself to my body as he made his way to my hips, grabbing me tightly, before continuing his trail up my sides and slowly to my shoulders. My body was now screaming with desire, alert and wanting and I leaned my body back into his, my head falling backwards. I could hear his breathing, heavy and deep as he leaned forward and kissed me lightly on my neck, his excitement obvious as he pushed into my backside. I closed my eyes as he moved his mouth further down my neck, his fingers now lightly moving down my arms towards my hands, taking them in his, rubbing his palms lightly against mine, cleaning them gently with his own. I lifted my head slowly, watching his face intently as his gaze focused down on my hands, checking all the glass was gone, cleaning them delicately, ensuring he didn't hurt me. I held my breath, forgetting to breath, completely infatuated with him, unable to look away as I watched him tenderly take care of me. As he finished, he reached over and switched off the water, turning me round to face him slowly. His eyes locked on mine as he reached up and used his thumb to wipe away the makeup smeared on my face, I turned my head into his hand, placing mine over the top of his, a small smile forming on the corner of his mouth. His hands dropped down to my chest, slowly unbuttoning my blouse, his fingers brushing the delicate skin on my breasts as he went, before pushing it over my shoulders, and onto the floor. My hands mirrored his, helping myself to his shirt, and dropping it to the floor with mine, before making my way to his trousers. He slid the zip down on the back of my skirt as I unbuttoned his trousers, my body now aching and craving his touch. I watched his eyes as he slowly dropped them over my body, taking in every curve, his fingers running under the strap of my bra, undoing it easily and tossing it aside. His eyes filled with fire, as he slid my underwear down slowly, allowing them to drop to the floor, me now completely naked in front of him. He hummed in appreciation as I allowed my hands to explore, grabbing his hard length and squeezing, and pushing his black boxers over his hips and down onto the floor. He closed his eyes tightly, his breath hissing out between his teeth as he grabbed my hand, stopping me, and instead lead me over to the shower. I watched in awe as he switched the shower on, water and steam filling the area immediately, him guiding me under the stream of water and joining me. He stepped in behind me, squirting a generous amount of wash from a black bottle in his palm, he began running his hands slowly down my body, washing me as he did. His hands circled over my breasts, my nipples responding favourably, desperate for more. I looked up and noticed our reflection in the mirror and my pulse raced, he was watching our reflections too, his eyes full of passion, his face watching over my shoulder, taking in every inch of me as he explored my body, his hands slipping lower. He swept gently over where I wanted it the most, my body arching forward, desperate for more, yet he continued his slow onslaught. I could feel him, hard, his hips circling into my behind, as his hand trailed up my spine to the back of my head, grabbing a hand full of hair, he twisted it around his wrist and pulled it back tightly, nipping at my neck. My body had never wanted anything more than it wanted him in this moment, my breathing now uncontrollable, desire burning through my veins. My body whined as he broke our connection, leaving me alone and wanting under the water, my eyes stalking his body as he walked across the bathroom, dripping water off his hard, rigid body. I furrowed my brow, sulking, as I watched him wrap a towel around himself, before coming back and turning the water off. He stepped back in with me and wrapped the huge soft white towel around me, before kissing me softly on the lips, I pushed my lips harder on to his, still desperate for more, he pulled back smiling. Looking down at me, he spoke for the first time since we had entered the room, stroking the side of my face. "Not here," he spoke softly, kissing me gently on the top of my head. "You mean too much to me," he added, turning my world upside down as he did. My eyes filled with tears at his admission, my body choking with emotion, as he pulled me close. He felt it too, and I knew from that moment onward, no matter what happened, and who tried to come between us, we wouldn't be able to keep away from each other.

Chapter 10

I spent the afternoon out of the way, tucked in my office, sorting out invoices and other bits and pieces for Alex. He had spent most of it in and out, trying to get me to go home for the hundredth time, insisting that I didn't have to stay if I wasn't feeling up to it. Of course, I protested and stayed anyway, partly because of my stubborn nature, and partly because I felt safer being close to him. He had now resorted to bringing me endless cups of tea, and repeatedly asking me if I needed anything or if he could do anything for me. I found the irony amusing, our roles had seemed to reverse, my job was to wait on him, yet he was being overly attentive towards me, and I had no doubt that he would have done anything I asked of him. I would be lying if I didn't say I enjoyed it, I had found great amusement watching him place my cup in front of me, eyes dancing with anticipation, waiting for me to take that first sip, to see his expression change to pure delight as I hummed my appreciation at a job well done. His demeanour was almost childlike, like he was desperately seeking my approval and enjoyed being praised. It was a far cry away from the hard-faced mogul I had presumed he would be, and I was even more surprised at how quickly our relationship had developed. I felt like I knew this man on a deep level, like old friends from a past life. There was no doubting our physical attraction to each other was overpowering, my heart still raced whenever he came near me, and his eyes would mist over with lust when he admired my body, but I couldn't help feeling there was something more there. It seemed incredulous that after such a short amount of time, our relationship had taken off with such force, but I also knew in my heart that everything about it felt right. We hadn't discussed what we were, or what exactly was going on, presumably too soon to put a label on it, but I knew that I enjoyed being in his company and I was sure he felt the same way also. All I was certain of, was that I was happy and content to just continue how we were. I hadn't seen Jason at all since our earlier drama, he had gone by the time I had got cleaned up, and I was grateful for his absence. I guessed he was still working on the car job, but the memory of Alex's face when he had walked in on us earlier flashed to my mind, his eyes dark and full of anger as I hopelessly tried to gather up the broken glass, made me wonder if he had been told to leave. It wasn't a question I wanted to ask, actively avoiding going over what happened, knowing that it could spark up further questions from Alex about what had gone on. I shuddered as I remembered Jason's hand wandering between my thighs, his vile breath as he spat venomously into my ear. I had initially wondered if perhaps he could have changed, that our relationship had just been a toxic one off, and that he had the means to be a nice guy, but after what happened earlier, I was now more certain than ever that he had dark secrets. Dark secrets that I needed to figure out before I made my move to be rid of him for good. I made a mental note of the things I needed to explore, and I felt overwhelmed when I realised the extent of them. I needed to go to the address that was given to me anonymously, I didn't know what I was going to say or do when I got there, but it felt urgent, especially as I suspected Jason was behind it. I needed to try and get hold of Chloe, perhaps suggesting we meet up for a coffee and gage her reaction, I was sure if he was treating her badly, I would recognise the signs and be able to offer her help and advice, whether or not she would take it would be another thing. An ex-girlfriend reaching out and offering relationship tips wasn't exactly the norm. I also needed to figure out what the prescriptions in multiple women's names was about, including mine, but I hadn't yet worked out how I was going to approach that situation, I had a feeling it would be dark territory that once I had stepped over the line, it would be hard to come back from. I leaned forward and placed my head in my hands, sighing deeply, I was so out of my depth, so deep in a messed-up situation that I saw no end to. I stared down at the phone on my desk, mulling over calling the cops, wondering what I would say. There were to many elements to explain, and no definitive reason for me to call them. Sure, I could say that he had assaulted me earlier, but it would be my word against his, certain he would play the angle that I had just started a new job and I was lying to get him out of the picture as he was my ex. I considered going to Alex, coming clean and explaining everything, I was sure a man of his power had the connections to make this all go away, but I felt guilty at the same time at potentially bringing him into a situation that he had no idea of the true gravity of, never mind the chance that he could want nothing more to do with me once he knew my real past. I couldn't risk it, I was completely on my own, trying to take down this monster who had turned up here when I thought I had left him behind. "Em, what's wrong?" Alex's concerned voice broke me from my thoughts as he hurried over to my desk, carrying yet another cup of tea, my lukewarm one still half full beside me. He perched up against my side of the desk, his legs brushing against mine as he reached over and smoothed my hair away from my face. My body warmed from the inside out as his hand touched my skin and I leaned into his touch.

"Nothing, I'm fine, it's just been a crazy morning you know." I was being genuine, while leaving out all the finer details.

"Go home, please." Alex looked down at me, his face etched with concern. "And don't worry about tonight, I can manage the meeting on my own," he added, with a hint of disappointment. My heart dropped, I had completely forgotten about tonight, I was meant to be meeting Tom out the front after work for some crazy dress solution that I hadn't yet worked out. I looked up at Alex's face, awaiting my response, eyes glinting, a forced smile. Sure, I could really do with going home, closing the door and forgetting the world like I often did when things went wrong, but looking up at his face now I couldn't bear to be the one to let him down.

"Absolutely not!" I chirped back, "I could do with the company, plus, I've already sorted a dress out now," I lied, taking a sip of my drink. "I'll be ready by 6, OK?"

I watched his face light up, as he jumped up, "Only if you're sure, I'll be there, at yours, at 6, you know, like you just said." I smiled, he was stuttering now as he left the room, trying to hide his glee and acting casual. I loved this dorky, awkward side of him, it was endearing and made him look about six years old, a side I didn't imagine many people got to see, I felt honoured and special that he felt he could be like that with me. I just wished I could offer him the same back, but my walls were still sky high, protecting him from myself, protecting him from Jason.

Tom was already waiting for me when I got off work, I felt at ease straight away, like I could finally relax and breathe after a crazy day. Part of me wanted to go home, kick back and forget about it all, but I had things I needed to see to. I couldn't let Alex down, he had been so supportive all afternoon and Tom was super excited for whatever he had planned for us, so I was glad I made the effort and came. "Come, it's this way," Tom gleamed, grabbing my hand, and pulling me up the sidewalk, much like he had done at lunch time, but in the opposite direction to earlier. I giggled and imagined Tom was perhaps a little bit used to being sassy and getting his own way, not that it bothered me, I had no energy to protest and was happy for him to take the lead. "You're crazy." I laughed.

Tom laughed back, "Yep, but you will thank me for it." After a couple of minutes, we arrived at a cute apartment block situated on a popular corner of town. It was busy, with lots of people finishing up their day, heading home or out for the evening, and I liked the vibe I got from it.

"You live here?" I queried, taking in the expensive looking building in front of me.

"Yes, well like I said earlier, I'm renting a room from Mrs Megabucks, so technically I'm just the lodger but she's never here, so I feel like it's pretty much mine." He laughed, winking as he led me through the glass doors and to the elevators. The apartment was beautiful, not huge, but classy and decorated to a high standard, a big step up from where I was staying, a middleclass home for middleclass people. I would never fit that demographic. I felt sad for my predicament but happy for Tom, nonetheless. We made our way through the apartment, my attention constantly drawn to the extravagance of it all, before we reached a beautiful light, feminine bedroom. "There you go, take your pick." Tom gestured towards a huge walk-in closet, lined with rows and rows of expensive looking clothing, smile a mile wide. I looked back at Tom confused, before realisation set in.

"Oh god, Tom, no, I can't wear someone else's clothes!" I shouted, backing out of the room at the same time. This was clearly Mrs Megabucks' wardrobe, there was no way I could intrude like that and wear her dresses.

"Oh, come on, don't worry about it, she will never know, Cindy's been out of the country for four months now, we will have it back before she knows it, she's pretty much the same body type as you, plus you want to make a good impression, right?" Tom was now looking at me with an exasperated look on his face, his head cocked to one side like he was mocking me. "And I'm not taking no for an answer," he added smirking. Mt thoughts transitioned between what was right and wrong as I glanced over the stunning looking dresses hanging in rows upon rows. I was slightly disappointed in myself but felt my heart race as I gave in far too quickly.

"OK, OK, I give in," hands up in surrender. "But nothing too fancy, just something classy and elegant." I smiled back, a little bit excited, feeling like I was in a private boutique not having to worry about the price tags.

"After you." Tom waved his arm into the huge wardrobe space, his face beaming with joy at having won. After half an hour, and six dresses later, we had settled on a stunning deep burgundy satin dress with spaghetti straps and edged in delicate lace. It skimmed all my curves in the right places and finished just below my knee, making me feel a million dollars as I twirled around in the mirror, Tom clapping his hands in glee as he admired me.

An hour later I was giving myself a once over in my apartment mirror, Tom had seen me off in cab and insisted I call him as soon as I got back to give him the gossip on what Fuego was all about. I had thanked him a hundred times, him playing it down each time like he was doing the tiniest favour, yet to me it spoke volumes about the person he was, genuine and kind. I had washed and blow dried my hair into a wavy do, slicked on some sultry make up, and I felt confident that I looked the part. I skimmed my hands down my body as I toyed with the idea of putting underwear on, I had ended up having to forgo it due to the dreaded pantie lines, but as my hands explored, I enjoyed the endless line the silky satin created, my nipples straining against the fabric as my own touch elicited something inside me. I jumped as I heard a car horn from outside my apartment, tearing me away from myself. I steadied my breathing, took a deep breath, and made my way down to the foyer, nerves now fizzing to the surface. My heels clicked on the wooden floor drawing attention, and I suddenly realised I felt self-conscious. I could feel eyes on me as I passed elegantly through the open space and onto the street, the warm evening air hitting me as I made my escape from the cool foyer.

My breath caught in my throat as I clocked Alex standing on the sidewalk, holding the passenger door open to a stunning black tinted sports car. He looked impeccable, wearing a black tailored suit, with an equally as appealing black shirt and tie, his dark hair and stubble completing the picture, he oozed sex appeal and I felt my pulse rise instantly. I saw him double take as I headed over to him, watching his eyes drink my body in as he greedily looked me from head to toe. I smiled as the look on his face changed, and the heat in his eyes ramped up. His reaction to me sparked a confidence inside that I didn't know I had, my hips subconsciously swayed more, my strides became more elegant, and I smiled confidently.

As I reached him, I made a note to thank Tom again. "Wow," was all he said as I reached the car, his tone breathy and low as his outstretched hand allowed me to slide in the passenger seat with ease. My heart raced as he walked around the car and slid in next to me, my body desperately pining for him to be near me.

I couldn't look away as he joined me, his hand entwining with mine as he lifted them to rest on my thigh, sliding it along the silky fabric and getting comfortable for the ride as he put the car into drive.

"You look, just, wow, stunning, Emily," Alex whispered, taking in every inch of me as he spoke.

"Thank you," I spoke back softly, looking at my feet embarrassed, my newfound confidence bubble deflated as I struggled to take his compliment.

"Why do you do that?" He pulled my chin up to meet his gaze. "Speak like you don't believe me when I say that?"

My mind raced as I realised he could read me like a book, "I just, I don't know," I offered back honestly, "I guess I don't really hear compliments that often, so I don't know how to react to them." I felt pathetic at my admission, like I was seeking sympathy unintentionally.

"I never want you to feel like that, like you are anything less than worthy, you've done amazing things in your life, Emily, and you deserve to be cherished." He was now staring forward, speaking curtly like he was chastising me but couldn't look me in the eye as he did it.

I forced a fake laugh, "Really, like what? I've never done anything noble, or courageous to deserve that."

Alex turned his head to look at me, his eyes sad at my admission, before speaking softly, "Not even bringing a new life into the world?"

Chapter 11

My heart pounded as I watched the buildings and cars move past me in slow-motion, I wondered how long I had been sat here speechless, unable to articulate any words. I stole a glance at Alex, his expression was unfazed, he was concentrating on the traffic, his hand still entwined with mine, I couldn't read him, and I began to doubt what I had just heard him say. How could he possibly know about Ivy? This was a part of my life that I wasn't willing to share, I was still hurt and ebbed with regret, ashamed of the choice I had made. My mind pondered the possible reasons that he would have that information and part of me wondered if him and Jason were working together, instantly seeing the worst in people, used to disappointment and betrayal from people in my life. It would be the ultimate revenge, allowing me to believe that my life had finally started to pan out, dream job, dream man, I chastised myself as everything began to make sense. It was all too perfect, nothing like this ever happened to someone like me, I didn't deserve it. Of course, Jason would seek out the help of someone like Alex, powerful and influential with plenty of connections to the right people. I didn't want to believe that I had been fooled so easily, and that Alex was a bad guy, but I saw no other logical explanation and couldn't risk being around anyone who was a potential threat to Ivy or myself, he knew too much, a distraction. My fingers straightened, pulling away urgently like his touch had just burned me, my hands clammy and shaking, as his head whipped round to meet my gaze, his expression full of concern. "Em?" he spoke softly, his voice edged with regret. My eyes blurred as I fought back the tears that were threatening to spill over, desperately wishing to be anywhere but here as I realised, we had come to a stop, the lights on Fuego's sign glowing across the parking lot. Alex reached out for me; his face pained with the realisation that perhaps he had said too much.

"No!" I shouted, desperately seeking my escape as I opened the car door and jumped out, my legs wobbly and beginning to give in on me, I knew this was it for me and Alex. I stood froze to the spot as he rushed around to my side of the car, his face looked panicked as he looked me up and down, seeing the state I was in. His arms reached out to me tenderly, asking a silent question, his expression panicked and sad. I instinctually took a step back, knowing that if I allowed him to touch me, that connection that I had been drawn into so falsely would hinder my thoughts and I would make a rash decision. I slowly took another two steps back, distancing us further, my eyes locked on Alex's as sadness instantly washed over his face, the realisation that I was denying him. I could see that he had a million thoughts rushing through his mind, he was confused and scared, but at the same time he knew that he needed to allow me to have my moment and I wouldn't allow him to impede on my personal space right now. I closed my eyes tightly, knowing that if I couldn't see him my mind would be clearer, the tears I was holding back now spilling down my cheeks, I took a deep breath in, knowing what I needed to do. Alex spoke as I opened my eyes,

"Emily, I'm so sorry I didn't mean to."

"Goodbye, Alex," I spoke softly, cutting of his apology, as I turned and walked away, my heart shattering as I did.

I wasn't sure how I had got home, my mind numb and defeated, my walls remaining high until I got into my safe place, and I could remove my mask. Finally, home, and able to relax, I stripped off my dress and curled into my bed, now safe from the world I could finally breathe and let go. I pulled the covers over my head, my mind too exhausted to comprehend what had just happened, tears streaming my face as uncontrollable sobs took over my body and I passed out physically, and mentally drained. I woke still sleepy, confused, my eyes hurt, puffy and sore from the endless tears after crying myself to sleep. I wasn't sure how long I had been here for, but the clock read 2:15 am, I rolled over and grabbed my phone from my bag, it was on silent, and I hadn't looked at it since I got home.

I sighed as I saw 16 missed calls and 12 texts. I opened my inbox and saw numerous names, Molly, Ali, a number I hadn't got saved, but the preview of the message saying "Hi it's Tom" told me who it was, but my heart raced as I saw the remainder were from Alex. I sighed as I opened the messages, they started off with polite "Where are you?" messages, then it moved over to him profusely apologising for him prying into my private life and upsetting me before I reached the final one which struck me to the core. My heartbeat faster as I read it slowly, the realisation of what I had done dawning on me.

"Emily, I am so sorry for earlier, please know that it wasn't my intention to hurt you, nor was I prying into your personal life. I have checks made on all my employees before they start, and your daughter was something that came up. After you left earlier, I chased after you, but I was too late. I saw you get into a cab on the main street, and I couldn't run fast enough to catch up to you. It was watching that cab drive away that I realised my true feelings for you; it's crazy, fast and completely irrational seeing as we have only known each other a couple of weeks but there is something about you that draws me to you. I feel immensely protective and my body aches when I'm not around you. I'm not sure what we are, or what we were, but just know that you are special to me in a way I cannot explain. I have called you so many times, but you are not answering, and despite protesting and pleading, your door man will not let me up to see you. I know you don't want to see me, and I am reluctantly taking your silence and avoidance as a goodbye. As much as it pains me, and I know my night will not be the same without you, I will respect your wishes for tonight and leave you be, but just know that my feelings for you are genuine, I meant everything, and I won't give up on us." I hugged my phone to my body, and threw my head back into my pillow, tears flowing yet again, I wanted to believe what he was saying, his actions had spoken nothing but being genuine, but my mind was telling me to steer clear, that it was too risky to have this man in my life if it meant Jason came with him too. I deleted the message and blocked his number, knowing that If I continued to read messages like that, it would hinder my thought process and I could go back on my decision, a decision that had broken me completely, but I knew I had to stand by. First light was dawning by the time I had managed to get back to sleep after hours of tossing and turning, my mind trying to comprehend what was going on in my life and what everything meant, I hadn't managed to make sense of anything and eventually my body finally gave in, a deep sleep I had needed to recover. The sun was now blazing through my window and the air was muggy and warm. I reached over for my phone, 10:40 am, I had no texts or missed calls and sighed with relief that I hadn't got anything else to add to my already complicated life today. I was an already reclusive person typically, choosing to shut out the world rather than burden anyone with my problems when things got tough and today was no different. I wanted nothing more than to close the curtains, lock the door, put on my comfy pjs and settle down in front of the tv for the day, this was my way of coping and how I felt safe. I knew now wasn't the time to hide, and I had things I still needed to figure out. I headed to the shower and stood under the scalding water, I instantly felt better as I washed off the previous day and by the time I had slicked on some make up and dried my hair I was ready to face the world. I pulled on some jean shorts and a light tank top and decided to head down to the beach to clear my mind, I didn't like going in the middle of the day as it was usually far too busy but I knew I needed it, it was one of my favourite places to be and I knew that if I didn't go out now, I would end up falling into a dark hole, locking myself away from the world. I had taken a slow walk to the beach, the warm sun prickling my skin as I meandered up the sidewalk, people passing me by absentmindedly, no clue of the inner turmoil I was going through, my fake smile fully in place. I had crossed over the road as I reached OSAR, not wanting to be seen, but I had found my pace slowing as I crept by and I couldn't help but pause and look up at the vast building, wondering what Alex was doing in that moment. Sadness took over me and I was in a daze by the time I reached the beach, now hot and thirsty. I found a small stall at the sea front and ordered myself a peach iced tea, the girl gave me a sympathetic smile as she served me, and I wondered if my heart break was written all over my face. I settled on a patch of sand just past the greenery that split the walkway from the beach, it was a nice quiet area, secluded and away from the hustle of the water, and away from the busy flow of people walking up and down the front. It was a beautiful day, leaves on the huge beach palms danced as the warm breeze tousled them, seagulls chirped as they flew above, circling people waiting for any scraps as the water gently rolled in and out on the shoreline peacefully. I sat and watched the people on the beach, there were couples walking hand in hand, deep in love, enjoying each other's company, sunbathers, slathered in cream, their bodies baking in the boiling sun. I felt a pang of guilt as I watched the families, their children splashing in the waves while their parents looked on smiling and proud. A sadness washed over me as I realised, I could have had that, I could have been a proud parent watching Ivy build sandcastles and run in the shallow water, if only I had not been so broken, I could have made things work. I'd have worked endless jobs; I'd have gone without just to ensure that my baby had everything in the world that she desired. I scooped up a handful of sand and let it slowly fall through the cracks in my fingers, the breeze scattering it back onto the beach. I envisioned each grain as my dreams, my hopes, and aspirations in life, escaping hopelessly through my fingers and blowing away forever. I felt an urgency wash over me as I snapped my fingers closed desperately and squeezed the tiny amount of soft sand remaining firmly in my palm, it was cold and hard, but I held on tightly, like my life depended on protecting the few things in life I still needed to achieve. I grasped my fist to my chest, covering it with my other hand protectively, not wanting to spill another grain, another dream, the sand warming in my palm, no longer cold or lifeless, but changing at my touch as the realisation that I could still make a difference engulfed me.

30 minutes later I was almost at my destination, I was staring down at the crumpled piece of paper with the address scribbled on it from the day before, my hands shaking, nerves and anticipation taking over my body. I had held on to the paper the entire bus journey, watching in surprise as the big apartments of the city slowly whizzed past the windows, shrinking in size the further out we went, eventually turning into small quaint homes owned by local people living real lives. My heart raced as the bus came to a stop at the side of the road, I willed my legs to carry me as I slowly made my way off and onto the warm concrete sidewalk, the smell of fresh flowers and warm air filling my nose. I wasn't quite where I needed to be, the address was a few streets over, but I wanted time to gather my thoughts and make my way there slowly, not yet having any idea of what I was going to do. I began heading to the end of the street, it was alive with laughter, children playing on their bikes, dog walkers, people watering their gardens, a real sense of family and community oozed here, and I smiled at the homely feel of the place. Part of me thought I was best to just slowly walk by, and try to gauge what I could see, but I didn't know how I was going to react at what I could potentially come across. If I saw Ivy, I knew I would have an overwhelming need to hold her, be near her, which would be highly inappropriate for a stranger just walking off the street to be doing and I would need to keep my distance. My senses spiked as I finally rounded the corner, the small blue house that I had seen on my tiny computer screen, now real as it came into my view. It looked prettier than I had seen, the flowers and lawn clearly had been tended to as cascades of bright flowers flowed from the baskets under the windows and the lawn was lush and green. I felt my pace slow as I got closer, my heart beating fast and my curiosity running wild. As I reached the house, I could see the garage door was wide open, I crouched down to tie my already tied shoelace, giving me longer to investigate, I could see children's toys, much like I had seen before, paint tins, laundry appliances, a typical household in a typical neighbourhood. I sighed deeply, the disappointment of not seeing anything sweeping over me as I stood up. I was about to move on, admitting defeat when

suddenly I felt my breathing stop, all my hair stood on end and my world became instantly brighter as a small dark-haired girl ran excitedly into the garage from inside the house carrying a small pink ball, her white summer dress dancing around her as her giggles filled the air. I stared, transfixed on the little girl as she skipped onto the driveway, unable to process what I was seeing, her little ball escaping her grip as it rolled down the driveway towards the road, towards me. I heard her shriek as her eyes followed the path of the ball, seeing it rush towards the road, presumably into territory she wasn't meant to venture, panic washing over her face. I lifted my foot as the ball dashed towards me and stopped it firmly with perfection, saving it from certain death on a busy street. The little girl stopped in her tracks, clutching the hem of her dress nervously, her playful mood diminished, cautious of the stranger watching her intently. I reached down and grabbed the ball, my eyes never leaving her as I did, offering it out to her, mid-air, adding a smile to alleviate her fear, she took a few timid steps towards me holding her hands out, trying to maintain some distance. I studied her face, she was beautiful, olive skin and round cheeks, a typical cheeky young girl. As she took the ball from my hands, I felt my heart skink and emotions wash deeply within me as I locked eyes closely with her, big beautiful green eyes stared back at me, they were unfamiliar, scared, and wary. They weren't the eyes I remembered so vividly; it wasn't Ivy. I dropped to my knees feeling the same pain as I did the day I lost her, feeling like it was happening all over again, tears numbly falling down my face as I watched her run hurriedly back up to the house shouting 'Mommy' in a panicked tone, I was broken and incomplete. All of a sudden, a lady's voice broke me from my meltdown. I whipped my head up to face her, her expression confused, angry.

"Hello, I said can I help you?" She shot curtly, the little girl cowering behind her legs, looking at me with scared eyes. It was the lady I had seen in the photos, her big brown hair exactly the same. I choked on my words as nothing came, holding up the crumpled paper with her address on it instead as she snatched it from my hand, fear washing over her face as she realised what it was. "What the hell is this?" she spoke through gritted teeth, now clearly concerned at the situation.

I looked up at her, my eyes blurry and hurt, "I'm sorry, I didn't mean to scare you," my voice was shaky and weak, "my name is Emily Moore, I thought…I thought that…" My gaze moved to the little girl as more tears came. I watched the lady glance from me to her child and then back to me again, confused, before her eyes widened, clearly realising something and she dropped to her knees in front of me, her face full of sorrow, as she pulled me into her arms.

"Oh my god, Emily, you're Emily Moore?" she offered shocked, as confusion washed over me. She pulled me up onto my feet with her as I saw her quickly look left and then right up the street, concerned. "You better come inside," she offered, pulling me quickly up the driveway with her.

Chapter 12

Confusion continued to flood over me as I followed tentatively behind the lady, she led me cautiously into her house before looking up the street multiple times as we went, the little girl skipping playfully and unfazed behind us. The fear and apprehension that had taken over her face as she had discovered my name sent chills up my spine, my mind was working overtime, trying to figure out multiple possible scenarios, each one, inevitably leading back to Jason. As we stepped into the house, I was wary, looking around for any clues, walking lightly, expecting the worst in every situation, my senses spiking. I berated myself for being so silly, so easily drawn in off the street by some unknown lady, immediately wanting to leave, feeling unsafe and out of my comfort zone, but equally drawn in by how the lady had reacted. I was unable to walk away, unable to leave without pursuing this, without finding out more. I took a deep breath and shook off the feelings of uncertainty, I had to do this. The young girl joined us as we entered the kitchen, it was a pretty, quaint little room, south facing, the light pouring into the area making it feel light and airy. The little girl settled down to finish a half-completed puzzle on the floor, humming away to herself as her mother filled a water pot and placed it on the stove putting me slightly at ease at the normality of the Situation. "My name is Erica, this is Louisa, my daughter." She gestured towards the young girl as she smiled proudly, she was completely oblivious to our presence, deep in puzzle mode as Erica continued. "Tea, coffee?" She smiled at me setting two mugs on the side as I took a seat at the small table in the middle of the room.

"Umm tea, white one please," I whispered back politely, still slightly on edge.

"I wouldn't ordinarily invite strangers off the street into my house," Erica looked over her shoulder as she spoke, adding sugar and tea bags to the mugs, her voice was kind and gentle. "But I can see the confusion, and as a mother I understand your pain also, but I need you to know from the beginning that I am bound under law, I can offer you an ear to listen, but I will not breach my licence in any way shape or form, OK?" She looked at me sternly as she placed our mugs on the table and took a seat opposite me.

"I…I don't understand," I replied, my brow furrowed deeply as I shook my head, trying to work out what exactly she was saying.

"Emily, I'm an adoption councillor, I have been for the past 15 years, here in Miami, I remember your case," she spoke sympathetically, watching my face as the realisation of what she was saying hit me, the blood draining from my face instantly and my heartbeat quickening.

"An adoption councillor?" My voice was barely audible as I whispered back, my eyes wide. Suddenly an overwhelming rush of emotion came over me as I stood quickly, grabbing both of Erica's hands in mine, my thighs knocking the table and spilling our drinks as I reached over at her.

"So, you know where Ivy is?" My voice was now loud, urgent, as I saw Louisa cower into herself and look wearily at her mother, scared. Not caring about my outburst, and how crazy I looked in that moment, I continued on, desperate, needing any information I could get.

"Please, you have to help me, I'm worried she's in danger, I don't know who sent me your address, but I feel like it was a warning, I'm scared." I rambled on, my face pleading with her, as she pulled her hands aggressively from mine.

"Emily, enough, sit down." Her voice was stern, her eyes angry, as she looked towards Louisa, smiling, enough to put the little girl at ease as her gaze shot back to mine. I sank back into my seat, embarrassed, offering a fake smile to the little girl by way of an apology for my behaviour, after no doubt scaring her. She lingered on my face before going back to her puzzle, my heart sinking as I realised, I had probably said too much to this stranger I had just met, who no doubt had questions that I would have to answer to now, questions about my past and Jason.

"Why would you feel she is in danger, Emily?" her tone was now calm, concerned as she focused on my face, trying to read me. I didn't want to give too much away, but I knew I would have to give her something to work from, something to know that I was being serious.

"Look, I know you can't give me information on where she is, and I know you can't tell me anything about her, I just need to know, as a parent, that she is safe." I looked across to her Louisa as I spoke the final words, her gaze mirroring mine as she watched over her daughter proudly. "There is someone from my past, who isn't fond of me anymore, that I fear could do something to Ivy in order to hurt me, I have no proof, other than my gut feeling and my previous experience of him." I could see the torment in her eyes as she mulled over the information, I was feeding her, concern for me and Ivy.

"I see," she rose from her seat and stood at the kitchen sink, looking out into the garden, her hands on either side of her face as she thought. "You can't tell anyone that you were here." She slid back into her chair, taking my hands urgently in mine as she glared deep into my eyes, her face stern, serious. "You need to phone the police, and make an anonymous tip off about a child in danger." My head shook aggressively as I opened my mouth to protest. "Ahh hear me out," she carried on, silencing my thoughts as she saw my hesitation, "the social services will have to take it seriously and look into it. I know who her adoptive family is, and there is no way that they would allow anything to happen to her, they are an amazing family, protective, close, and I feel that with a small bit of information from the police, it would make a world of difference to her safety." She studied my face, waiting for my response as I tried to process all my thoughts.

"You know her family?" I whispered back, emotion now rising in my chest at the thought of her calling someone else Mom.

"Yes, I do, but Emily, you have to understand I cannot tell you anything, part of a closed adoption is that that information is forfeited by you the moment you sign the papers," she offered a weak smile, attempting to soften the blow, but it stung all the same.

"I understand," I replied weakly, knowing that I wasn't going to be able to find out any more about her, but feeling better knowing I now had a way to keep her safe. Erica picked up the crumpled paper from of the table in front of her, she looked concerned, worried as she studied it intently.

"I just don't understand this?" she huffed, handing it back to me. "Why would someone who you think wants to hurt your daughter, lead you to me, surely, they would give you her address, not mine?" She shrugged her shoulders waiting for my input.

"I'm not sure, the only thing I can think of is that he doesn't actually know where she is, and he knew that…" My blood ran cold as I realised Jason's game plan.

"He knew that I would come here, knew that by using me, I would lead him right to Ivy with your information, information you would only give to me, not to him."

I stared at Erica, wide-eyed as she ushered me up out of the kitchen and towards the front door, "You need to leave, do not contact me, I will contact you if I need to, this is too much, too close to crossing the professional boundaries I abide by. I will look into her file, make sure she is safe, but you must call the police Emily, I cannot do anything else without that do you understand?"

I nodded my head as she guided me urgently out of her house, checking the street for anyone watching. "Good luck, Emily, I hope you find what you are looking for." She smiled bleakly before closing the door, leaving me standing there even more confused than when I arrived here, wondering what on earth was going on and what I was going to do.

I walked to the furthest bus stop I knew of, giving me plenty of time to process what had just happened and what was going on. I felt disappointed that I hadn't found Ivy but also a sense of reprieve that I had inched slightly into her world, more than I had ever had since the day I had given birth to her. I knew what I needed to do, I wasn't keen on involving the police, but Erica made herself clear, without that snippet of information, she had no reason to contact her family and it was the only way that I could keep her safe for now. I clenched my fists as I thought of Jason, playing me so easily, me giving him exactly what he wanted as I fled to the address. My only positive was that Erica had remained professional, she hadn't given me the information on where Ivy was, thus giving Jason no information either as he would have no doubt followed me there if I had of found out. I felt a shiver roll over my spine as I looked around the street paranoid, suddenly aware that he could possibly have followed me today, already putting his plan into action. Panic washed over me as I began running, running as fast as I could, to get away, I didn't know if he was there or not, but my senses were telling me to run anyway, to distance myself from this man as much as I could. I couldn't carry on like this, I was sinking back into the old Emily, scared, and living in fear knowing this man was back in my life. I needed to end this, before it ended me. I was sweating by the time I reached the stop; I had been running in the muggy heat for what felt like eternity, and the air-conditioned bus was a welcome escape as I slumped down onto a seat, exhausted and breathless. I relaxed as my breathing returned to normal, I opened my eyes and rubbed them, suddenly aware that I more than likely looked a state after my traumatic morning.

I glanced around, the people on the bus preoccupied with their own business, not a care in the world for me or mine. I sighed deeply as I pulled my phone out of my bag, my mind wandering to Alex, my instincts wanting me to call him and tell him all about my crazy emotional day, knowing that he would know exactly what to say and how to soothe me. My heart sank as I had nothing from him, no texts, and no calls as the realisation that I had left him hit me. I knew in my head that I had done the right thing by leaving him, but I couldn't help but feel like my heart was slowly caving in on me at his absence. I felt my eyes prick with tears as I moved on, I had numerous texts from Molly and could tell by her wording that she was getting annoyed with me, I had been meaning to call and text over the last few days but had ended up reading her messages and leaving them on read, not really knowing how to explain how my life had taken a crazy turn and not sure if I was emotionally able to say the words out loud. Guilt poked at me as I realised, I was being a shitty friend and that I needed her right now, that's what friends were for. I took a deep breath as I dialled her number ready for the onslaught. "Oh, you are alive then?" Molly shot sarcastically, my feeling that she was mad at me on point.

"Molly, I'm so sorry, it's…it's been a few crazy days. I…I don't even know where to begin." My voice broke as I realised, I'd been holding so much in and that hearing Molly's voice threatened to let it all come flooding out right here on the bus in front of everyone.

A long silence hung between us before Molly eventually spoke, clearly sensing my imminent breakdown, "Oh, Em, you know I'm here for you always, I just wish you would pick up your phone once in a while," she spoke softly, so as to not hurt my feelings as I scrunched my eyes closed feeling awful.

"I'm so sorry," I whispered back.

I heard her sigh deeply at the end of the phone. "Movie and takeout at yours tonight?" I nodded, not speaking any words. "Em, you there?" she added, concerned.

I straightened up in my seat wiping my eyes, "6 pm?" I managed bleakly.

"I'll be there, see you later on, OK," she replied before hanging up. I needed this more than I realised as I mentally prepared myself to relive the torture that I had been enduring over the last few days all over again.

Chapter 13

"Wow, just wow," Ali gasped with her hands over her mouth. Her and Molly had been at mine for the last hour, and we were still going over in depth all the gritty details of the last few days. I needn't have worried about feeling bad for not keeping in contact, it was like we had never been apart as they walked in and hugged me tightly, bags full of chocolate and snacks, the minimum requirements for a girl's night in when one of us was going through something awful. We had done this many times during the girl's breakups or when one of them had a bad day at work, and I kind of felt like perhaps it was my turn to have a wobbly moment but as soon as I started explaining what had been going on, the silent looks they shared between each other as I spoke, told me this was heads and shoulders above any drama we had previously gone through together, but I still knew I would feel better for sharing it with them nonetheless.

"So, are you sure it was Jason who sent the note?" Molly asked quietly, she was sat across from me in her comfortable tracksuit, hair scraped up into a bun, she had been fairly quiet during the whole story, as if she was trying to figure out in her head what was going on, rationalising all the information, and trying to make sense of it all. Ali on the other hand, offered a more irrational approach of running him off the road or throwing him into a canal with rocks in his pockets, I had laughed at the thought as she gestured with her hands the sizes of the rocks, we needed to find to make it work but we all knew that we needed a more logical plan that didn't involve killing him.

"I mean, I think so, I don't see who else would have sent it, it has to be him, no one else here knows about Ivy other than both of you, and him." I shrugged my shoulders as I leant back on the sofa stuffing more chocolate in my mouth, hoping it would make me feel better.

"I thought you said that Alex mentioned that he knew, and that's why you freaked out and left him." Ali was shoving handfuls of crisps into her mouth and was chiming in between chews.

I shook my head while jumping straight to Alex's defence.

"No, it's definitely not Alex, he only stumbled across the information during my security checks he had to do, what with working so closely with a man of importance, I can rule him out completely," I spoke confidently, knowing that Alex would never dangle that kind of information over my head, I just wasn't ready for the hundred questions that would be bound to follow suit, answers that I didn't even have yet.

"It just seems a bit strange that Jason would do that knowing full well that it would be obvious that it was him, it seems too sloppy, something doesn't add up." Molly was now pacing the length of the living area one arm folded across her chest while the other rested on her chin.

"And they definitely don't know about one another, Alex has no idea that Jason is your ex?" She added stopping in her tracks as she questioned me.

"No, I don't think so, he knows that we are both from Wisconsin and that we were old school friends, but he doesn't know the ins and outs of our relationship, I never lied to him but I also never told him the full truth." I forced the corner of my mouth into a fake smile, trying to soften the mood, worrying that I had put too much onto the girls.

"Jason, does he know about what has happened with Alex recently?" Molly was firing the questions off rapidly now, seeking more and more information.

"He knows me, better than probably anyone I know, we spent many, many years together, I would say that he can read me like a book and knows that there is something going on, he just hasn't directly asked me or mentioned it, nor does he know the true extent of it all." I felt sad as the realisation of what we once were and how badly things had turned out hit me. Ali took a break between her crisp marathon before chirping up sarcastically,

"True extent? You mean the minor situation that you are fucking your super-hot millionaire boss's brains out on the regular, who is kind of your boyfriend but is also your ex's boss as well, and said ex is now torturing you in front of new lover boys face?" She laughed before raising her hand for a high five.

"I'd say you've done well for yourself girl, I mean, beats any boring day to day crap that normal people have going on, and anyway, the best way to get over someone is to go out and find someone else to distract you, what do you say?"

I smiled at Ali's way of thinking, how not much fazed her, how she could be so carefree and positive in almost any situation. I matched her high five with a genuine smile. "Funny you say that, I've been invited out on Saturday to the

Yacht Club with a guy Tom from work and his mate Jess, they said you are both more than welcome to come along if you fancied it, I could do with a good night out?" I winked, knowing where her train of thought was going.

"Hmmmm, older rich men, champagne, swanky boats, let me think about it." She grabbed her chin sarcastically as she pretended to think, "Yes, I'm in, like you had to ask!" We laughed together as she jumped up and began testing out her best dance moves, humming to some unknown beat that she completely mismatched to her dancing, looking like some sort of crazy feral person as I clapped along encouraging her.

"Mol, you in?" I spoke over my shoulder between claps, as she came and joined me on the sofa, laughing at her younger sister and shaking her head.

"Sit down, Ali, you can't dance." Molly gestured down at the sofa laughing as Ali gasped, placing her hand theatrically over her chest as if her feelings had been hurt, before taking a seat, a fake pout firmly in place.

"Yes, of course I will be there, I just want you to be safe and careful that's all, you've got a lot going on at the moment and there are so many elements of it that we don't understand yet, I just think you should keep your wits about you while we figure this all out you know." Molly was facing me now and playing with a loose strand of my hair, genuinely concerned for me. It felt good to know that I had such good friends in Ali and Molly, and it meant the world to me that they were so supportive of everything that I had going on.

"I will, don't worry, I just don't think I can go back to that place, I can't stand the sight of Jason, and if I am around Alex, I just know that I won't be able to keep away from him, it's too risky and I don't want them knowing too much while I'm trying to get my head around this all, I'm going to call M and see if I can have my old job back."

I looked at my feet, embarrassed at how my life had gone full circle in the last few weeks, and I was now going all the way back to square one, but now with the added stress of Jason in my life. I wished things could go back to being how happy and simple it was a mere couple of weeks ago, but as the realisation that I didn't have Alex in my life back then washed over me, I knew I would face it over and over again if it meant I could keep him by my side, but now wasn't the right time for us. I forced a smile at Molly and gave her a serious look before she pulled me into her arms and hugged me tightly. "Now how about we get this Chinese food ordered," Molly added laughing.

"Oh god I think I'm going to pop." Ali rubbed her belly while reaching for another prawn cracker, not one to admit defeat when it came to food. We all laid back on the sofa stuffed after ordering way too much food and having our own mini buffet, there was tons of food left over and I knew we would all be eating it in the days to come.

"Stop then!" Molly shot at her sister, berating her for still going at the crackers.

"I can't, they are so good," Ali was talking with her mouth full, her words barely audible as she tried to swallow her food.

Molly shook her head, "Honestly, Ali." Ali stuck up her middle finger and forced a smile telling her sister to mind her own business. I laughed at them both, close as anything but tearing each other apart the next.

"So anyway, what's the dress code for a place like, the Yacht Club?" Molly looked at me and quoted inverted commas as she said the name of the club, and I could tell she wasn't sure about the place.

"I don't really know; I think it's smart casual I guess." I rolled my bottom lip out and shrugged my shoulders not wanting to make the place sound to intimidating but having a slight idea that it was a high-end club, not really feeling myself getting too dressed up for it, and equally knowing that the same thing was going through her head as well.

"Uh, uh." Ali was shaking her head and trying to chew her food quickly to add her input, she swallowed before adding her thoughts. "We are absolutely getting dressed up, it's a fancy place, not some local bar, we need to look the part." She was nodding as she looked at me and Molly, waiting for our reaction, as I saw the look spread across Molly's face. Molly was older, a mother, and was more of a jeans and nice top type of girl, I typically usually followed in suit, not often wanting to draw attention to myself and I felt myself having to defend ourselves against our outfit choices that we hadn't even chosen yet, knowing that Ali would disapprove and have other ideas for us.

I rolled my eyes and Molly sighed as Ali jumped up, gesturing us to follow her. "Come on," she chimed excitedly, us both knowing what was about to ensue, a fashion show after eating our body weight in Chinese food was definitely not the one.

"Urgh, Ali no, I feel so bloated, I don't want to try clothes on." I protested, grumbling as she took my hand and tried to pull me up off the sofa. "I'll pick something nice I promise," I faked, trying to get her off my case.

"Not a chance, come on, we all know your fashion sense is a bit, umm off." She smiled and coked her head to the side as she said the word off, I gasped as I jumped up and stomped through to my bedroom, aware that I was giving her what she wanted but wanting to prove her wrong all the same. Molly huffed as she dragged her heels behind us, not wanting to be left alone as me and Ali played dress up. A short while later I had held up five different outfits, starting with skinny jeans and a camisole, before upping the ante and I was now holding a white fitted dress.

"Better, but no, let me look." Ali jumped up off my bed and began rifling through my wardrobe.

"I know, I know." Molly held her hands up in defeat. "She's a nightmare." I laughed as I laid back on my bed and folded my arms behind my head while Molly played a game on her phone, clearly not wanting to get involved with Ali's plan. I could hear Ali chuntering to herself, adding the odd "Urgh" or a sarcastic "Wow" as she slid my clothes across on the hangers, clearly disapproving with most of them before I heard her stop, I looked over at her as she pulled out a knee length fitted black dress. The entire material was sheer with a built in modestly panel for a skirt and a separate black vest to go under the top part. I had bought it cheap in a sale and had never actually worn it but didn't completely disapprove of it.

"This," Ali held it up, swishing it around on the hanger.

I tilted my head left to right giving the impression that it wasn't a no but also wouldn't be my first choice either before she smiled and pulled the small vest top out from the inside of the hanger and tossed it on the floor. "Like this." She was now smiling cheekily as she still held the hanger up, I realised that she wanted me to wear it with no top underneath.

"Ali, no! Everyone will see everything!" I protested shaking my head.

"Oh, come on, you need to find a super sexy black bra, with the sheer material over the top, it's super fashionable and you will look amazing," Ali argued back.

"Molly?" I questioned, seeking some assistance with taking her sister down. She looked up from her game at the dress and smiled before looking at me, "You have to admit, Em, that would look super-hot," she offered back, placing her phone on the bedside table and getting up and taking the dress from Ali.

"Yeah, I really like it, you've got the boobs to pull this off, it's classy but sexy, go for it," she added.

"Are you serious?" I shot back laughing, "you are the first person to go for the safe option of jeans and now you're saying a see-through dress is a good choice?" I rolled my eyes and put on my most convincing sarcastic tone. "And I thought you were my friend." They both laughed at my non-Oscar winning performance as I took the dress from molly and faced the mirror while holding it up against me, pulling it tightly around my waist.

It was fitted and I knew it would show off all my curves, but it left just enough to the imagination and I felt I needed a confidence boost after the week I had just gone through. "OK, I'll do it," I offered confidently. Molly and Ali both shrieked in unison as I did. "But…" they immediately stopped as I spoke, holding a single finger up at them, "…on one condition." They were hanging onto my every word as I spoke, awaiting my response, "You're wearing a dress too," I fired back, pointing at Molly.

She smirked at my condition but didn't protest as I could see her mind already agreeing. "Done."

She locked eyes with mine, accepting my challenge, "Well we best get going then, we've got another fashion show to attend to." Ali laughed as she dragged Molly towards the front door rolling her eyes as she went.

Chapter 14

The rest of the week had passed by uneventfully, M had offered me my job back with open arms and had been genuinely sad for me that my new venture hadn't worked out as planned, giving me a huge hug and telling me that I always had a job there if I needed it. I felt emotional as I realised how much of a mother figure, she had become over the short time I had been here, and also extremely fortunate to have someone like her to look out for me. I had made the anonymous phone call to the police as Erica had requested the morning after Molly and Ali had come round, giving them the small amount of information that I had in the hope it would make a difference. I knew I still needed to do some digging with Chloe, but I had so much more on my plate right now that I had asked the girls to see what they could find out while I got my head around everything else that was going on. Since then, I had desperately tried to draw a line under the week and look forward to our night out, but I couldn't help but feel numb, a failure. I hadn't heard from Alex all week, every time my phone went off, I found myself rushing to pick it up, followed by a pang of disappointment when it wasn't him, desperately wanting him to reach out to me, my pride not allowing me to be the one to text first. I felt lost and alone, not knowing where my life was going to take me now that I had lost my dream job, Alex and my daughter, my life was a mess. A lump formed in the back of my throat as tears blurred my vision, the shop was, as expected, empty, it was Saturday and we only had 20 minutes left until closing time, but I knew I needed to let everything out in order to get through the night. I rushed over to the entrance and turned the sign on the door to closed before bolting it firmly shut, dimming the lights, I sank to the ground behind the till to have my moment, private and away from prying eyes I let the weeks emotions spill out as I sobbed into my hands until I was cold and empty. I used my sleeve to dry my eyes and stood up slowly before taking a seat at the till, preparing to cash up and finish the day. I felt better after my emotional outburst, like it would be easier to hide my feelings and paint on a brave face with less bundled up inside of me, tormenting me and choking my personality, forcing me to be someone who I wasn't. I sighed a breath of relief as I finished cashing up, determined to have good night with my friends, and headed home, I had always enjoyed the walk home of the evening, the humidity of the day easing as the sun set, a small reprieve as the temperature very slowly dropped turning the hot day into a warm night, it was a time that I could think, watch the world pass by, oblivious to my demons. By the time I got home, a light sheen of sweat blanketed my skin, glistening, a cool shower was a welcome, needed addition as I stepped into the frosty water shivering as the water stung my skin. I closed my eyes as the water cascaded gently over me, washing away all of the negativity that had been suffocating me all day, like a therapeutic spa, it was one of the ways I coped with my demons and began to breathe again, forcing them all down the plughole and giving my body the fresh start, it needed to carry on. Refreshed emotionally and physically, I turned my stereo on, music loud, an instant spirit lifter as I bopped around my room trying to get in the mood. I pulled my black dress out of the wardrobe hesitantly and laid it on the bed with a pair of high, strappy black stilettos and grimaced, as if I had agreed to wear this, I flopped down on the bed in my towel with my hands over my face before sitting bolt upright and slamming my hands down on the mattress either side of my thighs mentally giving myself a pep talk, telling myself to stop being dramatic and get on with it. I turned my music up louder and went to the kitchen to get myself and pink gin and lemonade, double of course, and began the perilous task of turning myself into something sassy, confident and ready to take on the world.

An hour later and the task was complete, I stood in the mirror and admired my reflection, I looked like a newer version of myself, confident and sexy, no hint of the inner turmoil as my sultry makeup created a mask firmly in place to protect me. I skimmed my hands down my body as they outlined my curves, the dress hugging my skin, complementing its full shape and womanly features. The sheer top clung to my pert breasts, full and covered completely with a balcony black lace bra, it was sexy but classy, just like Ali had said as I twisted to the side to give myself an all-round view. I smiled, pleased with what a saw, feeling ready to take on the world as I gulped down the last of my drink, the concentrated gin at the bottom of my glass scorching my throat as I grimaced before heading down to the foyer to wait for the cab I had called. I held my head high as I crossed the foyer of the building, my stride strengthening in force as I felt the confidence flood my veins, curious eyes trailing behind me as I approached the doors. "You look beautiful, Emily, off somewhere nice?"

Rodrigues, the middle-aged door man who wasn't used to seeing me all dressed up passed comment as he held the door wide open for me smiling genuinely. "Rodrigues, hi," I spoke back cheerfully, I had grown fond of him since I had lived here and had stopped for many a conversation with him, learning of his family and children. "Yes, I'm off to the Yacht Club up by the marina with a few friends, should be a good night," I added with a smile as I passed through, spotting my cab at the curb side.

"Sounds nice, have a lovely night, I'll be here when you get back, stay safe," he said as he waved me off, me smiling as I waved back enthusiastically.

I felt excited as I arrived at Tom's place, the gin and music had done the trick and I felt ready to dance until the sun came, up even more so as Molly scooped me into her arms the second, I walked through the door. "Emily, you look, wow, amazing!" She was holding me at arm's length admiring my dress as she nodded with approval. I tilted my head to the side and smirked. "I'm going to need a few more drinks to pull this off." I laughed.

"Come on," she whispered as she led me through to the kitchen. My skin prickled in the heat as the alcohol flowed, pre-drinks at Toms was going down a treat and I laughed as Ali and Jess danced together in the middle of the kitchen, music blaring as Tom, Molly and I watched on, downing yet more Malibu orange juices. They had been taken aback when I arrived, the wolf whistles and comments on my attire had been well appreciated along with a cheeky boob grope from Tom who naughtily asked what the puppies names where. I blushed as I laughed at him while shaking my head before returning their compliments, Ali and Molly had gone to town on their outfits, Molly was wearing a one shouldered cream and gold Grecian style dress with gold heels, her long blonde hair cascading in ringlets down her back making her look like a beautiful Greek goddess. Ali was looking equally as amazing, wearing a black fitted pencil skirt and silver silk camisole showing off way too much side boob but amazing all the same.

Tom was wearing some tailored black trousers, a white linen shirt tucked in with an expensive looking belt and shoes to finish, he looked handsome and chiselled. Jess stunned in a red lace midi dress and nude heels, complimenting her dark hair and long legs as she swayed her hips to the music, I smiled as I looked on proud realising that we all scrubbed up pretty well and needn't have worried about the Yacht Club being high end, we all looked a million dollars and would have no problem at all fitting in. They had all clearly been drinking plenty before I arrived and they seemed to be getting on like a house on fire, giggling away, the alcohol helping new friends to drop their inhibitions and get to know each other on a fun and real level. I hadn't really thought about how they would all get on and me playing the middle woman, but I felt relived all the same that they all seemed to be getting on so amazingly with no divide to worry about.

"Come on girls, the cab is here," Tom beamed, gesturing us all to the door impatiently as Ali was desperately trying to slick on a final coat of colour onto her lips, Jess fighting for mirror space as she fixed her hair. "Girls, seriously, you look hot, let's go." He was shaking his head and rolling his eyes now as me and Molly giggled, passing under his arm and into the hallway. The bar was around 20 minutes away, Tom, Ali and Jess sat in the back seat talking way too loudly and laughing away at anything and everything as the bottle of wine they snuck out was being passed between them, adding fuel to the volume levels.

"Honestly, it's like I've got the kids with me." Molly laughed, pointing her nose to the back seat.

"Ahh they're having fun, it's nice to just get out and have a laugh for a change you know." I smiled back, meaning every word.

She pursed her lip into a firm line, before forcing a smile, "How have you been coping? I can't believe Alex hasn't bothered messaging you." She shook her head frowning, like she was expecting a reasonable excuse from me for his lack of trying.

"I mean, I haven't bothered messaging him either, so he's not completely to blame, I just..." my thoughts trailed off, wondering what he had been doing in the last week and if he had even thought of me once, then realising that I was probably just another one to fall under his spell. "I just wish I hadn't have freaked out and left, but at the same time, I'm OK, I'm getting there, this really helps." I used my hand to gesture to everyone in the cab.

"Of course, it does, friends are always the medicine for a break up, well, that and someone else to keep your mind of them." She winked and raised her eye brows suggestively.

"Oh, Mol, I don't think I could, I just want to have one drama free night and enjoy it with you guys." I laughed shaking my head.

"No more boys," I chanted, waving my hand in the air.

"I'll drink to that!" Tom's voice boomed behind me, followed by the giggles of Jess and Ali, as he tipped the bottle back draining it dry.

By the time we got to the club, I was ready for another drink, and I sighed as I saw a huge que trailing way back from the entrance. "Oh really?" I moaned, "we will be lucky to get in there by tomorrow never mind tonight."

"Little lady, do you not know a single thing about me?" Tom was being all theatrical as he spoke, swishing his hair to the side as he took my hand and placed it in the crook of his elbow. "Girls, this way!" he shouted over his shoulder and began making his way towards the entrance, past the huge que and under the rolling eyes and stares of those patiently waiting.

"Tom, we can't just…" I began, realising what he was doing before being cut off with a sharp hush.

"I got this, don't worry," he beamed, adding a wink. The two huge bouncers clocked us before we reached the front, one leaning into to whisper something to the other, eyes on us as we came to a stop in front of them.

"Sir, sir." Tom nodded confidently towards each of them individually before clearing his throat. "My ladies and I have a reservation under the name Tom Alvenor if you wouldn't mind, please." He smiled and held their gaze confidently. The girls had quietened down now, taking in what was going on, huddled together nervously, and I was relieved the alcohol hadn't hindered their ability to identify a tense situation.

"Do you have any identification, Sir?" one of them questioned, him still assessing and glancing at us girls practically hiding behind Tom.

Tom whipped out his wallet and presented his driver's licence proudly. The bouncer took it from him before studying it intently, and then handing it back to him. "Mr Alvenor, ladies, this way please, you will be seated in the VIP area, all drinks are on the house this evening." I whipped my head round and shot Molly a wide-eyed look, she shrugged her shoulders and smiled as I heard Ali and Jess shriek behind us, the attempt to do so quietly went out the window completely.

"The limo will be waiting around the back for whenever you are ready to leave." Silent, excited glances between each other ensued before Molly's quiet whisper broke it,

"Limo? Like an actual limo just for us?" Tom simply smiled and raised his eyebrows telling us that was exactly what we had before the excited shrieking and bouncing began again. I rolled my eyes and giggled at how jovial and inexperienced we all were at these fancy extras. We all beamed; eyes unable to keep up with our surroundings as he led us in through the huge glass doors into the venue. I struggled to contain my excitement any longer as I squeezed Tom's hand tightly and shot him the biggest smile letting him know that this was beyond amazing. The atmosphere swirled as we passed the hordes of people gathered around the bar, equally matched by the number of people dancing on the central floor. The entire place was shrouded in wood panelling and white features, lit up by extravagant over lighting creating an ambient glow throughout. The area was bordered by small private booths, a huge centre table encased and cream tweed sofas surrounding them finished each area off to a high standard. Every single one was full, people laughing and talking, the table tops full of glasses as they enjoyed their night. I wondered where we would be seated as it seemed all the VIP booths were filled, before my attention was diverted as we reached a big silver velvet curtain with two equally as scary looking bouncers either side. "This is the regular area." He gestured back towards the bar and dance floor that we had just passed through, "Obviously you have full access to this area but be sure to make use of the VIP area tonight." He smiled for the first time, making his features seem less aggressive as he pulled back the curtain and allowed us to all pass through. I stopped dead in my tracks and felt the hair on my arms stand up as I took in the vast view in front of me, the shrieks from the girls even louder than before.

"Oh my god," was all I could manage. A huge open plan area with beige marble floors shined brightly as the moonlight cascaded in through the floor to ceiling windows that bordered three walls of the room. The glass gave us prime view of the rear harbour and all the awfully expensive boats that lined up below, bobbing gracefully with the seas current. A huge silver and glass circular bar dominated the left-hand area of the room, tiers of alcohol bottles stacked up in the centre of it as waitresses circled the inside ring creating drinks for the handful of people waiting at the bar. The other side gave way to a crystal white dance floor encased with splattering's of quartz that glittered under the spotlights like distant stars, beyond that were more private booths, far larger and more superior that those we had just seen in the other room, and finished with lush cream velvet. The entire place screamed class and I suddenly felt very self-conscious as a young blonde led us through to one of the booths gesturing us to take a seat.

"Hi, guys, my name is India and I will be your server for the evening, if you need anything at all please just use the panel to order and I will bring your drinks over, restrooms are down the corridor to the right and be sure to make use of the downstairs promenade area in front of the marina through those doors at the top, anything else I can help you with, don't hesitate." She smiled before heading back towards the bar area.

"Tom?" I whispered questioningly, "how?"

He laughed loudly while tapping away at the smart screen ordering us some drinks. "Let's just say that I have an ex that works here, and said ex owed me a very, very big favour." He winked before turning his attention back to the screen.

"This is amazing!" Ali clapped her hands before grabbing Jess's hand urgently. "Come on let's go dance." She gleamed as they both headed towards the dance floor.

"Seriously this is amazing, Tom, thank you so much!" Molly shouted excitedly over her shoulder as she followed the girls. Tom laughed and waved his hand through the air as if it was nothing before handing me the tablet to order my drinks, tonight was going to be amazing.

My feet burned and my legs ached as the song we had all been dancing too came to an end, the next one slowly fading in. "I need some fresh air!" I shouted over the loudening music as I gestured to the outside promenade area. Molly was still dancing away with Jess, clearly both still full of stamina as I wavered.

"Want us to come?" Jess mouthed, getting into the next song as she swayed to the music elegantly.

"No, no, you both stay, I'll only be a couple of minutes, I'll be right back," I promised as I headed off towards the doors. The room swirled as I made my way to the doors, a wall of warm fresh air hit me violently as I passed through onto the wooden promenade making me realise just how much I had drank this evening. I teetered over to the railings and held on tightly as I took in the breath-taking view, inky black sky caped the glittering water, the moon and the stars, full and bright reflecting back in the waves as they tumbled towards the shoreline, rocking the yachts, resting peacefully in the harbour. I smiled gratefully, grateful for my friends who had been more than supportive this evening, who I had laughed with until my sides hurt and danced with until my legs gave in. I had had such an amazing time, the VIP area had been more than I could imagine as we had spent the night making the most of the open bar and glamourous surroundings, fitting in nicely at the best of times but the odd moment giving away our true social status, but caring less and less as the drinks flowed.

Molly and Jess had been inseparable all night, dancing and laughing away while Ali and Tom had scouted the area, wing-manning each other as they found cute guys to flirt with. I had laughed when I saw Ali, getting cosy with a middle-aged guy with salt and pepper hair, his hand resting possessively over her bare knee as they giggled and whispered into each other's ears. This was exactly what I had needed, what my mind needed to help me heal. I glanced around me, the promenade dark and empty as I stood alone, the fairy lights bordering the railings warmed me as I wrapped my arms protectively around my body absorbing fully this serene moment, tranquil, restful, and sated, I sighed deeply and closed my eyes before tilting my head back allowing the breeze to gently caress my neck. I suddenly felt a pleasant chill trail up my spine as my senses heightened and my heart began to beat faster, I whipped my eyes open, before taking two steps backwards, away from the railings, like something was drawing me away from the darkness of the sea and pulling me back into the light. I spun round urgently, rushing to return inside before my body froze, my feet anchoring me heavily to the spot, my blood hot and raging as I took in the image in front of me that I could barely comprehend. A tall dark handsome man dressed casually in dark jeans, a white shirt and fitted blazer stood beyond the doorway, his face anguished, in pain, his eyes questioning. He slowly closed the distance between us, my skin igniting as his presence neared, my body refusing to move, my heartbeat pounding in my ears. His face softened as he reached out and stroked a warm finger down my face, and in that moment, I felt everything I knew, everything I thought that I needed and wanted in life crumble into oblivion as our connection was made, a connection I knew would end me if it was ever broken again. "Emily." He breathed softly, as Alex pulled me into his arms firmly.

Chapter 15

My skin ran cold the moment Alex released me and held me at arm's length, his eyes greedily looking me up and down slowly, a slight smirk forming on the corner of his mouth as he drank me in. I blushed, looking down at the floor before he gripped my chin possessively, guiding my gaze back up to meet him, "Don't," he whispered as his face hardened, "don't deny me," his demeanour was serious, like I had done something unforgiveable, my mind still trying to make sense of what he was doing here and how he was being with me.

"How? What are you doing here, Alex?" I stammered, pulling away as I took the railings as support, anger and hurt still dancing around in the back of my mind. The disconnection between us allowed my brain to function in a more logical manner, not hindered by his aura as I prepared myself to grill him on his absence, wanting an explanation for his behaviour, even though it was my doing. I could hear the pain in his voice as he began to speak, him clearly sensing my apprehension as I turned my back to him and stared out towards the water.

"Emily, I'm here for you." His words came out as a whisper as he joined me, his hand pressed lightly at the small of my back, his body facing mine completely as I angled my face away from him.

"How did you know I was here?" I shot back, turning to face him fully, the remainder of the alcohol now deciding to give me the bite that I needed to air my frustrations.

"You haven't called or texted all week, and now you think you can just show up and sweep me off my feet?" I forced a fake giggle as I shook my head, moving away abruptly.

I didn't manage more than two steps as Alex shot around me blocking my exit, his hands against his chest, palms facing towards me in surrender. "Please, just hear me out, I will explain everything I promise, just walk with me?" His eyes glittered with hope as his head tilted to the side, slowly turning my anger into dust as I sighed deeply and nodded.

"OK," I whispered gently as his face gleamed, my strength and willpower evaporating pathetically as I allowed myself to be drawn in by him so easily. I rolled my eyes and huffed loudly as he took my hand in his, admitting defeat as he began leading us towards the far end of the promenade and down the steep wooden stairs that cascaded down to the marina. The breeze was stronger down here, the wooden walkway cut across the shoreline, housing giant boats tied safely to the wooden harbour, the wind whipping through my hair as it broke viscously between each boat.

"Are you cold?" Alex questioned nervously, seemingly reading my mind as goose bumps covered my skin.

"A little," I answered honestly as he shrugged off his blazer and placed it loosely over my shoulders, giving my arm a tight squeeze and rub warming me from the inside.

"Better?" he looked at me hopefully, like a timid puppy seeking approval from its owner, desperate for love and affection, my heart fluttered as I realised, he truly needed that approval, truly needed that reciprocation from me as it had been me who left him, standing in the street as I rushed off, giving him no explanation or reason behind my irrational behaviour.

"Alex, I'm so sorry, I'm sorry I left you, I just, I panicked, I didn't know what to say," my words came out rushed, like I needed him to realise what was going on in my head as soon as I possibly could. Alex didn't speak, he simply took my hand and squeezed it tight, tugging me roughly to face him, I could see the darkness and desire in his eyes, like something feral had envenomated him as he forced me backwards, using his huge presence against my body. I subconsciously stepped backwards, the back of my legs struck the cold stone wall behind me forcing me into a seated position, Alex closed in, his eyes fixated on mine before his gaze stalked slowly down my body while he sank to the floor by my feet. A small grin escaped the corner of his mouth as my heart began beating frantically, like my body knew the mood he was in and it was desperate to be used by him, a furious pulse beginning to ache in my centre.

"This is not talking, Alex," I whispered, his eyes piercing mine with his dark desires spilling into my consciousness, he smirked as he placed his hands gently on my knees sending a shiver straight up my spine, his grip tightening as he forced them apart aggressively. I giggled nervously as my breathing quickened and the pulse throbbed deeper, becoming more urgent as he leaned in towards me, planting a soft kiss on my inner thigh, my fingers running through his soft hair as I guided his head. I felt him smile as my hips bowed outwards, desperately seeking more as his tongue swirled against my skin, moving slowly down my inner leg, his fingertips caressing me gently as he made his way to my feet, I leaned back using my arms for support and let my head fall backwards, my veins flooding with ecstasy as he explored me. I writhed on the spot as he grabbed my ankle firmly and rested it outstretched on his shoulder, his fingers slowly untying the staps on my stilettos as he slipped them off and used his fingers to gently massage the soles of my feet, the achy burn subsiding gratefully as his fingers made deft work of the hours of dancing. I felt his warm wet lips against my ankle bone as he slowly made his way back up my leg, nipping and kissing every inch as he went, I slowly lifted my head back up and locked eyes with his as he approached me where I needed it most, his fingers brushing the edge of my panties as my body practically convulsed. His breath was warm against my skin, and his breathing was ragged as he planted a painfully slow, delicate kiss through my panties, directly against my throbbing as my body begged for more. Suddenly I felt like someone had snapped an elastic band against my skin as his contact broke away fiercely, and he stood up abruptly, my stilettos swinging from his hand, his arousal obvious through his tight jeans as I eyed him aggressively shaking my head in question.

"What?" Alex teased smiling as I sat panting on the side wall, legs still wide, confusion clearly all over my face, "you can't exactly walk on the sand in these," he winked holding my shoes up high as they dangled in the air, him stepping down onto the sand, satisfaction oozing from every pore.

"Are you serious?" I pouted, trying to be angry but not wanting to dampen his unusual playful mood, before getting to my feet and tugging my dress hem back into place. Alex was on the sand now and I rushed to catch up with him as he looked over his shoulder and winked. "Why, why would you do that?"

I was lightly jogging to keep up with his long strides.

"Frustrating right?" He threw my shoes down onto the sand and glared at me coolly, I felt my skin blush at his chastising, knowing he was referencing my recent behaviour as I avoided his gaze.

"You don't get it, do you?" his tone was sarcastic but sympathetic, as he tilted my chin up to meet his eye, "I'm falling for you, Emily," he whispered as he pulled me close, resting his chin on the top of my head. I felt my heart constrict and my blood run faster as I took in his words, unable to give a response as my body processed and analysed what he was saying.

"When you left me standing in that car park, running away because I knew about your daughter, it devastated me, devastated me that you couldn't allow me in just a little bit, that you didn't trust me, that you closed up and shut me out." Silence filled the air as the mention of my daughter panicked me, the questions I wanted to ask jammed tightly in my throat, not wanting to hear them out loud through fear of my past being laid bare in front of me leaving me vulnerable and exposed. He knew about Ivy, but did he know about Jason? I forced myself to speak as I prepared myself to be revealed, my entire past, his for the taking.

"How did you find out about Ivy?" My words were barely a whisper as I felt Alex tense around me, his jaw becoming even more rigid as it rested on the top of my head. He released me slowly, taking a seat on the sand, pulling me down gently with him and snuggling me in closely to his side.

"I have security checks taken out on all of my employees who work closely with me." He nodded nervously as he spoke, like he was trying to convince us both.

"And?" I spoke louder, more confidently as I probed him further, sensing his apprehension to share.

"And it really hurt my feelings, Emily." His voice was low and pained as he spoke now, my regret cutting deep as I realised, he was hurting just as much as me. I had left him confused and in the dark, but I was also relieved that Ivy seemed to be all he knew about. Silence filled the air as I struggled to find the words to sooth him but feeling more relaxed now I had taken back the upper hand. The cool breeze blanketed my skin in goose bumps as a shiver convulsed up my spine, Alex pulled me in tighter, his fingers twirling strands of my hair, his touch easing me enough to lower my walls ever so slightly as I took a deep breath and prepared to let him in.

"She was really beautiful, I can still see her face now," I whispered my words, ashamed, worried what he would think. I felt his body tense as he turned to face me, pulling my hands into his lap but saying nothing, my emotions waved through me as I struggled to continue, "8lb 4oz, dark hair, piercing brown eyes, I loved her the moment I held her, she was my everything, and I knew in that very moment I had made the biggest mistake of my life." I began to choke on my words as I spoke out loud the thoughts that had been haunting my mind for years, the words that out loud seemed more real and painful than buried deep inside, safe from the outside world. I began smoothing the cool sand under my palm nervously beside us, before Alex moved gently to sit in front of me; our knees touching as he leaned in closely hanging onto my every word, his hands reached out tentatively for mine as he gently prized my fingers open, brushing the sand away softly, bringing my focus back between us, "Don't stop, I'm listening."

I forced my gaze up, meeting his blurred, painful eyes, his emotions seemingly matching mine, my own betraying me as a single tear rolled down my cheek. Alex brushed it away with his thumb as he eased me gently into his lap, his huge arms protecting me, warming me gently, his touch subconsciously fooling my body into surrender as I felt my muscles ease, my head resting comfortably into his shoulder.

"I always felt I couldn't give her enough, my entire pregnancy I tortured myself into believing that I couldn't be a good-enough parent, I had no money, no job, no family. I was in no position to give her the world and that was the very least that she deserved." My tears burned my cheeks as I stopped holding them back and I felt Alex's hold tighten as I went on.

"That very moment I held her and looked into her eyes I realised that I wanted to keep her, that no matter what life presented to us, I would move heaven and earth to ensure that baby girl had everything, that she would feel loved and cherished, protected and safe, but it was too late, I had already signed the papers, her new family were waiting, she wasn't mine." My body heaved as I spoke the last words, the pain I felt on that day cutting me as deep now as it did then, the wounds real and raw.

"I regret it every day of my life, every moment I go on I wish I could have her by my side where she belongs, I wonder where she is and what she looks like now and it pains me, pains me to think that she has another family that isn't me. I never speak of her out loud because it hurts too much, it's my deepest and most painful secret, and to know that you knew." I shook my head in shame as I pulled back to look Alex directly in the eyes, grabbing his face to hold his gaze, "It was never, never that I didn't trust you, I was embarrassed and ashamed, shocked and confused that you knew, and I did what I always do when I can't handle something, I fled, and you didn't deserve that." He opened his mouth to speak as I saw his eyes fill with tears. "Wait, I'm not done." I cut him off before he could speak, "I'm nothing, a nobody, I have nothing to give to you, I'm just a mother who gave up on her child way to soon, and to have you, someone so successful, endearing, handsome and perfect look my way, showering me with such affection and understanding, it's not something I'm used to, not something that

I've learned to accept, I don't think I ever will…" I eased backwards onto the sand as I looked down at my feet, "you're too good for me, I don't think this could ever work." My voice broke as my last words were barely audible, pushing him away yet again.

Suddenly Alex's hands were in my hair as he planted a firm kiss on my forehead, his warm tears dampened my skin as he leaned back onto his feet, "Emily, I admire you, you have nothing to be ashamed about, and I never, ever want to hear you speak otherwise. You as a mother, gave the ultimate sacrifice, you allowed your daughter to be placed for adoption in order to give her a better life, and while I believe you would have done everything in your power to give her what you could, you knew deep down it would be better for her to be placed with another family, I don't know of anything in this world that could be more painful or selfless that what you did for her that day, I'm in complete awe of you."

I stared at his pained face as he spoke passionately, I felt the passion and sincerity in every word he spoke as they soothed my dark thoughts slightly, hearing for the first time someone explain it from another point of view, something I could tell he meant genuinely as he blinked back tears. "As for me," he shrugged his shoulders and shook his head, "I'm as normal as normal can be, behind all the cars and businesses, I'm just a normal guy. I'm not looking for someone fancy, perfect or with everything to give me. I don't need all of that, I want someone who can make me laugh, who makes my heart beat faster when they are near, someone who I can grow old with and sit on the beach in the middle of the night and bear my soul to." He cocked his head to the side and looked at me with a smirk, a small giggle escaped my throat as he eyed me sarcastically.

"Emily, I don't care about your past, or what you have or don't have, it's only about you, you and you only, and all I know is that when I'm with you, I feel complete, and when we're apart, I need you here again so I can breathe, it's as simple as that." My mind swirled at his words, him laying it bare like that even after everything I had told him, my heart beating faster as I realised I was falling for him too, that I needed him as well in order to function, that I wanted him permanently in my life.

I smiled up at him. "So, what do we do?"

His mood had begun to lighten, and I saw his face glow at my acceptance. "I think we should date, take it slow." He eyed me intently waiting for my reaction. I thought for a second as the word date processed in my mind, we had taken things far too fast to begin with, I had jumped into bed with him at the first opportunity, before I knew him and although my body craved him at every moment, I knew that taking it slow meant something serious, that I wasn't just another girl to fall under his spell, my heart swelled at the thought.

"Date, so like start from the beginning?" I shrugged my shoulders as I goaded him to explain more.

"Yes, like date, meals out, shopping, all the things that people in a new relationship do, a fresh start, no secrets," he was excited and speaking quickly as he thought of us as a couple, but I winced at his last comment as I thought of Jason and our past together. I wasn't ready to share that, not yet, and I lied as I nodded my head in agreeance, one small secret wasn't going to make a difference, not now he knew my deepest one.

"I'm keeping my job at the card shop though, I don't think it's wise for us to work together, it's not professional or healthy," my comments were truthful, but the motive was more to distance myself from Jason as much as I could, trying to keep things less complicated.

I saw the hesitance all over his face as he agreed reluctantly, "As much as I was hoping you would come back, and as much as I selfishly want you around all the time, I respect your choice, and I think it's probably for best, well for now any way." He winked at me before a deep throaty laugh made me smile, I narrowed my eyes at him and folded my arms over my chest in a pretend huff letting him know that I wore the trousers in this relationship.

He jumped up onto his feet enthusiastically before reaching down for me and helping me up off the sand. "Clothes, off," he ordered as he began taking his own off slowly and throwing them to the side.

"Wait, what?" I shook my head as I questioned him, he smiled as wide as I had ever seen before as he dropped his boxers to the sand revealing his toned and chiselled physique, smattered in a dark stubble, my stomach twisting as I drank him in greedily before he headed down to the water.

"You once told me that this was your favourite place to be, sunrise and sunset on the beach, and as much as I would love to spend forever sat here talking to you, the sun will be coming up soon and I would very much like to kiss every inch of you in the waves as it does, do you care to join me?"

My eyes widened in shock at his admission, "What happened to taking it slow?"

I laughed as he screwed his nose up, him realising that he was contradicting what he had just said, trying to think of something witty, "Uhh, we can start tomorrow, today your all mine." He laughed as the waves began lapping around his ankles. I smiled, completely besotted, feeling loved and dreamy, as I stripped off completely, joining him in the warm turquoise water.

Chapter 16

I swirled my pen around in circles absentmindedly, doodling dark ovals across the paper on the desk, my mind still fixated on the amazing weekend I had just had. Alex and I had agreed to take things slow, and although every fibre of my being wanted him intimately, my heart felt fuller knowing he was more content in owning that, than pursuing me for sex. The cracks that had formed over our week apart had been eased slightly as we watched the sun rise up over the horizon, spilling warm, orange light across the water as he held me tightly, whispering sweet nothings into my ear as the waves swirled around us. Although, we had already been through so much in the short time we had known each other, it felt like the beginning, like it was how things were supposed to be from the start, pure, innocent and full of lust, I smiled contently at how things had turned around before a shrill voice pulled me from my thoughts. "Hello, can you hear me?" the lady's tone was sarcastic as she waved a banner in the air from across the shop, "I said how much is this?" her rudeness irked me as she held it in the air waiting for my response.

"The price tag is on it, if you look," I shot back bluntly, forgetting my customer courtesy as I realised where I was. I jumped up from the till dropping my pen onto my scribbled paper as I forced an apologetic smile, heading over to her in a desperate attempt to redeem my rudeness, her face shooting me a look that clearly questioned who the hell I thought I was speaking to.

"It's probably one of those really small ones though, you might not have spotted it," I added cheerfully, hoping to put the blame onto me and not her being arrogant at not bothering to check. She eyed me though narrow eyes as I lifted the end of the banner up, an obvious bright orange sticker glowing against the black packaging clearly displaying the price. I smiled sweetly as she met my gaze, realising her stupidity and seemingly forgetting my outburst as she pulled it back and placed it in her basket.

"Do you have the matching balloons as well please?" She smiled back, letting me know that all was forgotten.

"Yes, right this way, I'll show you," I gestured towards the back of the shop, as she followed me down the aisle.

I visibly relaxed as I waved her goodbye and told her to have a good day, inside I was mentally pouring myself a cup of tea and snuggling down into bed to watch a good movie, wishing the day to be over. Alex was away on a business trip in New York for three days, and although he was only at the end of the phone if I needed him, I felt hesitant to contact him while he was working and was missing the excitement that surrounded the time I spent with him. We had exchanged the odd text during the day, but I was keen to get home and call him once he had wrapped up his busy day, to hear his voice and help bring me out of my gloomy mood, but he had already let me know it was going to be a late one.

As much as I was super grateful for Mary giving me my job back at the card shop, I had been finding it mundane and boring since my brief time at OSAR Books, finding myself drifting off into more favourable memories or creating fantasies in my head of a more enticing scenario than I was currently in, sitting at the desk helping people pick out celebratory cards and faking a smile. I sighed deeply, it was only mid-afternoon, and the shop didn't shut until 6, I had a few hours until I could switch off. I pulled my phone out of my bag and sent a text to the group chat that Molly, Ali, and I shared seeing if they fancied meeting up for a coffee when I got off work. I immediately got a reply from Ali, excitedly telling me that she had loads to tell me about Eric, the guy she had met on Saturday night, I smiled genuinely, happy for her to be finally having some luck in the male department. Molly added that she would be there as soon as Lee, her husband got home from work and could take over from the kids and that she was excited to see me. I felt happier instantly at the thought of a natter with the girls and being able to give them both a full explanation for my sudden disappearance the night before last. I had giggled when I checked my phone after we had got out of the water and headed back up to the beach, seeing a single message from Molly simply saying "Alex?" and a shocked emoji. I simply replied with a winking face before she responded saying she would catch up with me soon, I had yet to give them the full downlow on the night, knowing they would be greedy for all the details, but also relieved that they didn't seem to be judging me and my confusing rocky relationship. I plodded through the next couple of hours, grateful that the shop hadn't been too busy, and I had been able to cash up and get locked up bang on my finish time. I switched out the lights and set the alarm before locking up and heading the short walk around to the agreed coffee place. It was still stickily hot and although it was 6 pm the sun still blared down, prickling my skin as I walked slowly on the sidewalk the smell of freshly brewed coffee already wafting through the air. The girls were already there when I arrived, and I was pleased to see my favourite mug of tea waiting for me at the table as I sat down.

"Oh, you girls are the best, this is just what I needed," I moaned as I took the mug in my hands and blew the steam from the top as I got comfortable. Ali was beaming and I could tell she was bursting to tell me everything, I glanced at Molly and smiled, a questioning look furrowing my brow as I looked at her, she laughed loudly before realising I was querying what Ali was so excited about, knowing I was teasing her, dragging out her excitedness.

"Don't, honestly, I don't think I can hear this story for the twentieth time."

Molly rolled her eyes sarcastically, but smiled widely, clearly pleased for her sister, but keeping up the role of pretend irritation anyway. "Oh, give over, Mol, you love it!" Ali giggled before clasping her hands together under her chin, elbows un lady like on the table as she settled in for the long haul. "So, his name's Eric, and he has a boat, like an actual boat!" She gleamed, speaking as if she was telling the story for the first time, I nodded, wide eyed showing my approval but saying nothing, knowing that she was about to go into full blown story mode, and it wasn't worth trying to get a word in. Sometime later, and with Ali swooning after filling me in on the night, I felt genuinely pleased for my friend. Eric was 42, single, no children, and worked in real estate flipping property across the country, making his millions in savvy agreements and engineered deals.

They had spent the night together after I had left, flirting at the club and getting to know one another into the early hours as everyone else in the club went about their business. I would have ordinarily worried for any girl seeking out a man of such wealth and importance but knowing Ali, and her matter-of-fact approach to life, I knew she had this handled, especially after her explaining to us that he was only after some fun, someone lively and exciting to spend time with, along with someone who was happy to be spoiled and let him lavish them with the finer things in life. I knew Ali fitted the bill perfectly and that she had no problems in having the no strings attached type of relationship he was offering to her, it's all she knew, and I was genuinely happy for her to have a bit of excitement and fun she craved.

"So, when are you seeing him next?" I asked Ali.

"Tomorrow night, he's taking me to a wine bar, I've never heard of it, but he assures me it's top class, I actually can't wait." Ali clapped her hands together and squeezed her shoulders up to her chin, swaying in her seat smiling.

"Ooh very fancy." I winked back at her, only fuelling her excitement further.

"Maybe I'll get drunk and put out, who knows," Ali chimed sweetly, a wicked look in her eye telling us that she most certainly would do.

Molly closed her eyes and shook her head in disapproval. "Ali, just please be careful, I know you go about things in a casual way and of course it's your life but I do worry about you, you hardly know the man." She stared Ali down in a caring but stern manner.

"Oh, Molly, I'm fine please, I'm not a baby, I can handle myself, I'm just having fun you know, before I settle down and have responsibilities I have to attend to." She cocked her head at Molly at the last comment and I could tell that it stung slightly.

"I'm envious of both of you," I chirped in with an over-the-top tone, desperate to dissipate the tension, Molly and Ali both turned to look at me at the same time, seemingly not understanding my comment.

"Yeah, I mean, Ali, your positive outlook to life, relationships and having fun is amazing, I would love to be able to have that sort of attitude and live life on the edge." I saw her smirk, lapping up my compliments confidently. "And, Molly, you have the most content life, happily married, two gorgeous children, an amazing home for you all, you have it all figured out, most people take years to achieve that and you found it so early on with Lee, you're so lucky," I spoke genuinely, but more to bring Ali down a peg and get her to lay off her sister, and also to boost Molly's confidence, I know she often felt like the older Momsy one, but my comment seemed to do the trick as she sat more upright in her seat dominantly, smiling at me gratefully as she did.

"So, now for the juicy stuff, Alex?" Ali was staring straight at me rubbing her hands together, a sarcastic tone as she said his name told me she was playfully mocking my company that night.

"Yeah, what on earth happened, we came up to find you on the promenade as you were taking forever, and when we got up there, we saw you out there with him chatting." Molly was smirking at me as she spoke, so I know she didn't disapprove, she just had a cheeky, Told-you-so look on her face that made me smile.

"I honestly had no idea he was there, he just appeared from nowhere," I spoke softly, remembering my shock from seeing him there that night as my mind drifted off. "We sorted everything out, decided to take things slow, start from the beginning." My gaze snapped back up to the girls, "yes, like proper you know, how it should be," I said confidently, like I was trying to convince myself that our relationship could ever be normal, desperately wanting it to be, but knowing it couldn't ever be.

"As long as your happy that's the main thing." Molly took my hands in hers as she spoke, that motherly instinct kicking in fiercely wanting to protect me.

I smiled and nodded, "I am, I really am."

She released my hands gently and nodded before picking up the menu. "Now who wants cake?" She playfully suggested, knowing that we all were a sucker for a sweet treat, as we geared up for the full uncensored run down of our night out.

I felt content and happy by the time I had got home, catching up with the girls had been fun and I was still reeling from the fact Alex, and I had sorted things out and were now official. I couldn't quite believe that I had bagged myself a man like him, and desperately pushed away the creeping thoughts that I wasn't good enough for him. Alex had text me saying he would be back at the hotel by around 11 so If I was still awake, he would face time me then, I had replied letting him know that I was going to have a bath and chill for a bit but that I would definitely be awake to take his call, I was far too excited to speak to him to even consider missing it. I had taken an extra-long soak, allowing the hot water and bubbles to ease my muscles after a busy day, and after slipping into a white vest top and panties, I clambered into bed with a cup of tea, flicking through my phone absentmindedly waiting for it to ring. My heart soared as I saw Alex's facetime request flash up on my phone and I found myself straightening my top and fixing my hair slightly as I sat up to take his call, although my effort was in vain as I was wearing no makeup and my damp hair clung to my face, but I made an attempt anyway.

"Hey, baby." His voice was grizzly and deep, clearly tired after a long day as he laid topless on his bed, obviously just out of the shower as his silky, dark wet hair framed his face shaggily.

"You just out of the shower?" I asked nervously, wincing inside as I realised, I'd asked a dumb question as it was plainly obvious that he was.

"Mmm hhmmm," he replied lazily, angling the camera down his torso to confirm my question, a white towel fixed low around his waist, a stubbly V-shape angling down below the fabric. I felt my insides clench as I drank up his toned damp skin before he swung the camera back up to his face.

"Me too!" I exclaimed a little too enthusiastically as I too lowered the camera to show my minimal attire, not really knowing what else to do or say as somehow his ability to turn my brain to mush, even through a phone and miles apart he still prevailed. I watched his eyes light up as he repositioned himself into a more upright position on the bed, his face seemingly now more awake than before.

"Show me again," he whispered, his voice husky and sexy as his eyes pierced mine. I didn't say a word, I just simply lowered the phone down again, but with a slower and intended speed, reading his thoughts accurately.

"Mmmm, I can see your nipples though your vest, are you excited about something, Emily?" He added cheekily with a wink.

I glanced down and saw my breasts straining against the white fabric, still slightly damp from my bath, giving him a prime view. "Maybe," I spoke softly.

"Show me again and we'll find out."

I felt my pulse quicken and my skin flush as he lowered the camera to his waist, pulling the towel loose around his hips barely covering him as he slid his hand down below the fabric and groaned lightly.

"I'm so tense and frustrated," he whispered as I watched his hand explore where I couldn't see, my heart pounding at the unexpected road our call had immediately taken. He brought the camera back up to his face before smirking, knowing exactly what he was doing. I huffed loudly and pouted, making it clear that I was enjoying the show, "Oh, baby, don't pout, you only have to ask, ask nicely and I'll show you more." He raised his eyebrows suggestively as a lustful look filled my eyes.

My blood flowed faster, and my core twisted with want as I desperately craved this man, his presence and size not dwindled in the slightest by his physical absence as a playful idea washed over me. "So how was your day?" I asked plainly, ignoring his proposal, much to his surprise as he glared at me questioningly.

"Uhh? Yeah, it was busy, boring business stuff you know, I missed you though," he added, desperately trying to bring me back, confused by my sudden change of mood.

"Definitely sounds boring," I whispered as I reached into my bedside draw and pulled out my bullet vibrator out of his view.

"You?" he added nonchalantly, his mind still elsewhere, my thoughts trailed back to my day, starting off with the rude lady from the shop. "I had a boring morning, frustrating really, I really needed to blow off some steam," I spoke quietly, suggestively, as I angled the camera to my breasts, my free hand running lightly over my top, pulling my nipples into firmer peaks. I watched with delight as I got the reaction I was hoping for, attention all on me, his face speaking a million words as I saw the want and lust in his eyes for my body, wanting me so desperately, yet he couldn't touch me. I smiled naughtily as I placed my phone on my bedside table, leaning against my lamp, my bed with me laying on it displayed perfectly in the frame. I watched as his breathing quickened, his shoulders moving up and down at a slightly faster pace than before, his eyes completely focused on me, dark and feral.

"Yeah, then when I finished work, it was so, so, hot outside, too hot for covers." I pushed the covers slowly down the bed before pulling my vest up to rest on top of my breasts, just the right amount of under boob giving him a peek before picking up my bullet and nuzzling it gently against my throbbing centre, pulling my lacey underwear to the side giving him primal view.

"Choose a number between one and five." I asked through whispered breaths.

"Four," he shot back before I had barely finished asking him, greedily hurrying me along.

"Hhmm, four OK," I replied happily before pushing the button on the end of it four times, a strong buzz thrumming through my groin as my back arched off the bed and I murmured out a groan. I felt like a goddess as the pleasure washed through me, the pulses unwinding my core slowly as I writhed, watching him watch me, ignited me further as the jerky motions of his camera told me he was pleasuring himself. I watched his jaw harden as I continued, "Then I went to a coffee shop, had something super sweet," my words came out between deep breaths, barely audible as I allowed my body further, "I know I should have resisted, but I wanted it so, so badly, I needed it," my last words came out as a whine, desperate, seeking my release.

"What next?" Alex growled through laboured breaths, clearly loving story time, I smirked to myself, loving what I was doing to him.

"I came home and had a really hot bath, I parted my legs and let the jets massage my ache, but it only made me want more." I felt my ache swell harder and faster, closing in on my desire. Alex's head tilted back lightly as the veins in his neck hardened, the muscles in his shoulders contracting firmly as his body began to quiver.

Seeing his closeness and feeling mine, I shot my finale piece to him, "Then I laid on my bed and pleasured myself whilst imagining my man tying me down onto his bed and fucking me within an inch of my life until I came loudly." My words blanketed both of our visions as I watched him push himself over the edge, his groans rumbling through gritted teeth as I moaned loudly with him, my inner frustrations crashing into pieces as I reached my own climax.

Sated, and satisfied I laid breathless on the bed before turning over to look into the camera, Alex clearly breathless himself, a light sheen of sweat covering his body, smirked, and looked at me cheekily, "Wow, what a day you've had."

Chapter 17

I tapped my feet impatiently as the clock drew closer to midday, my shift was due to finish and Cory the new guy, young and carefree, still hadn't shown face to relive me, my body now anxious as my stomach twisted nervously. Alex had got home late last night from New York, and we were meeting for lunch once I knocked off and it couldn't come sooner. The last few days had been hell as I craved his touch and company, like a petulant teenager with their first crush, I unashamedly had let Alex know my feelings as he confessed to needing me just as much and I was beyond excited to see him today. My heart lurched as I saw Cory swan through the door casually, like he was in no rush, holding up my day. I jumped up from the counter grabbing my bag as I quickly rambled off a pathetic handover while heading towards the door. Cory looked up confused as he stopped in his tracks and stared at me, eyes wide like he didn't know what on earth was going on as he pulled his ear buds from his ears, the dull sound of music whispering lightly from them as he held them in his palm. "What?" he murmured quietly, in his typical slug like demeanour, still a teenager at heart even though he was in his early twenties.

"There is an order out back, I've re stocked most of it, you just need to do the anniversary cards." I smiled as I snaked past him into the doorway and out onto the street, leaving him standing on the spot wondering why my behaviour was so off.

"See ya!" I yelled over my shoulder as I headed off, not waiting for a response, my mind clocking off from card duty, and in on Alex. My breathing was heavy as I reached OSAR, my fast pace and the hot air leaving me out of breath. I stopped briefly looking up at the vast building towering over the rest, dwarfing them in size as a feeling of sadness that this was no longer my place of work overcame me, my dream job that I had left because of one man who failed to leave our past behind. I shivered as I thought of Jason and the likely hood that he was probably here. I hadn't seen him since the day he lost it with me in the office, swiping my most loved possession onto the floor, smashing my snow globe I had received from Ivy's adoptive parents into pieces, breaking my heart as it did, and although that day was still painful in my mind, like he always managed to back when we were together, I began to doubt I believed it ever happened, his hold over me guilting me into believing it was all my fault and that I was in the wrong. I shook off the sickly feeling that washed through me and stepped into the cool foyer, determined to leave my past where it was.

No sooner had I stepped foot through the door, a familiar voice bellowed into the air, "Em, oh my god, where have you been?" Tom was now standing at his desk, completely ignoring the looks of everyone who had turned to look at the culprit of the over-the-top outburst. My cheeks flushed as people looked from him, to me, clearly wondering what was going on as I shuffled my feet towards his desk, giving him a forced smile that told him to sit down and let us blend into the background again. By the time I had reached him at his desk, everyone in the foyer had carried on going about their business and we were no longer the focal point, much to my gratitude but to the dismay of Tom who loved being the centre of attention.

"Tom, oh my god, was that loud enough?" I whispered to him, side eyeing the room for onlookers.

He laughed and swatted the desk playfully. "Ahh ignore them, how are you girl? I haven't seen you for ages, where have you been?" He forced a pretend pout as he sat back down in his chair, resting his chin in his hands as he propped them up on the desk, clearly waiting for some amazing story.

"Oh, Tom, it's been a crazy week, I'm so sorry I haven't messaged after the weekend, we will have to catch up and I'll tell you all about it." I felt guilty after everything he had done for us girls that night and I hadn't made the effort to message. His eyes lit up knowing there was some gossip to be told but also frowned as he realised, he would need to wait for it. I laughed and rolled my eyes as he sulked, but my mood lifted being in his presence, like being wrapped in a comfort blanket cosy and warm, he gave off brotherly vibes that I cherished during our short friendship.

He nodded as I headed towards the elevator. "Don't sweat it, I'll text you," he chimed winking cheekily at me. My stomach was in knots as I made my way up to the top floor, I grinned inside remembering the familiar feeling I felt not so long ago making my journey up here for my first interview, and now I was going to meet the same man, but a man I now called my boyfriend. So much had changed so fast, but I wasn't regretful, my life now had colour, and although the pace had made my head spin, I was eternally grateful for fate bringing us together. I loved this man, I hadn't ever felt anything like it and for reasons unknown, we were one. The ping of the elevator pulled me from my thoughts making me jump, the doors opening suddenly, my body betraying me as I forgot to breathe. Alex was standing there, waiting for me with the biggest bunch of lilies I had ever seen, a grin a mile wide as we stood silent, smiling at each other like lovesick puppies. I lurched forward urgently, his big arms scooping me up as the flowers swayed behind my back, petals dropping to the floor unforgivingly. I could feel his heart beating fast against my chest, mine mimicking his and becoming one as I absorbed in his warmth and smell not wanting to let go.

My heart swelled as he kissed my forehead and whispered the two words that always got me, "My, Emily," he hushed against my skin. He pulled back and held me at arm's length while looking me up and down, not in a lustful way but a protective way, like he was searching for anything broken or amiss. After his visual check he smiled contently and grabbed my hand, pulling me towards his office. I felt eyes follow us as we swanned along the corridor and my self-consciousness bubbled to the surface momentarily, wondering what the staff must think of me after working there for such a short period of time before becoming the boss's lover. I winced inside before a wolf whistle from the back of the main foyer drew my attention back over my shoulder, all I saw was beaming smiles from familiar faces, faces who had been my work colleagues not so long ago eyeing our every move followed by a flurry of giggles.

"Back to work you lot," Alex moaned sarcastically with a cheeky smile as he looked down at me and rolled his eyes, louder giggles from his team ensued as I beamed back at him shaking my head. I was on cloud nine as Alex whispered gently in my ear, "They like you," as he playfully tickled my side, I giggled as I squirmed away from him, his eyes lighting up like he had discovered a new button he could push.

"Oh, like that, is it?" He teased as I twisted away from him.

"No don't, Alex." I giggled loudly while trying to evade his nimble fingers poking my ribs, backing into his office as his eyes stalked my every move. He laughed loudly as he slung the flowers aside and made a grab for my waist, swirling me around into the air as I squealed playfully.

115

"Alex, I'm really ticklish, please," I was now uncontrollably giggling as he nuzzled my neck before a gruff cough snapped us both out of our playtime. Piercing eyes met mine from across the room as Alex continued to hold me, not bothered that Jason had just seen our display. I could see the anger wash over his face as he took in our show, disgust and fury flooding his emotions as I suddenly felt like he owned me again.

"Sorry, Jase, I didn't know you were in here," Alex spoke casually, like he wasn't reading the same person that I was, as he set me back straight on my feet, his arm snaked protectively around my waist as I pulled myself tightly into his side, wanting to feel safe, not bothered if our closeness provoked Jason further. I watched intently as the switch flicked over in Jason's brain as he snapped into fake him, pulling his mask firmly back into place, fooling everyone but me.

"No problem, I just thought I'd check the paperwork against the contract that has just come in for the linear deal, but I couldn't find it here." His hand gestured to the filing cabinet he was standing next to, his demeanour now professional and unaffected by our presence as he avoided my eye, knowing that I knew, knowing that I was the only one who could dislodge his mask.

"It's here," Alex broke our touch as he headed coolly over to his desk reaching out for the mound of paperwork stacked neatly on the edge. Fear rose into my chest as my heart began beating faster, he left me, left me standing here, vulnerable and alone where Jason could get to me. Even though Alex was a mere few steps away, I felt isolated and in danger as my eyes subconsciously glanced across towards Jason, needing to assess the threat. My breathing stopped as I locked eyes with him, his mask fully off, a sarcastic smirk on the corner of his mouth as he took control over me with a look, we both knew it, and it empowered him to see my reaction. The battle for dominance was over as I cowered into myself letting him win pathetically. Jason stepped towards Alex's desk, his back still to us as he flicked through the files, unaware of the tension that bubbled behind him as I stood rooted to the spot, unable to move.

"Ahh cheers, I didn't think to look there," Jason chimed as he took the files from Alex, "I'll go over these and get back you."

Alex smiled, as he turned to lean back on his desk, his arms folding casually over his chest, "Thanks, bud," he shot back confidently before his gaze met mine, a look of concern and query awash his face as he stood rooted to the spot, not coming to me even though he could sense something was wrong. I felt a sob betray me as my eyes glistened, tears threatening to spill over as Jason headed towards me, his face beaming as he saw me crumble, taking back the power as he watched my breathing labour as he closed in.

The glee on his face as he placed his hand firmly on my shoulder and squeezed too tightly was electric, holding his grip painfully as a single tear rolled down my cheek, he spoke loudly, "It's so good to see you back, Emily." He smiled sickly as he released his grip, my body jerked at his firm release as a feeling of nausea washed over me as I watched him swan off up the corridor whistling triumphantly. I glanced up panickily at Alex who was still in the same position propped up against his desk, eying me intently with a look on his face I struggled to read. I quickly remembered where I was, and my secrets I needed to keep as I stood up straighter wiping my cheek with the back of my hand and forcing a smile in his direction. He stood still, not returning my smile before sighing loudly and dropping his hands into his front pockets before pushing himself off the desk closing the gap between us in a few long strides.

My heart pounded as he stopped in front of me, his eyes washing over me before giving me a tiny frown as he leaned slowly over me, closing the door gently, before whispering sternly, "I thought so. I think we need to talk." Alex led me silently over to the seating area, my clammy hand engulfed in his as we took a seat on the white leather couches. My mind felt numb as I knew exactly what was coming, it was obvious he knew. I had made damn sure of that with my pathetic display moments ago. I chastised myself silently at yet again, allowing Jason to grip hold of me and ruin everything I had worked so hard for. This was it, bubble burst, there was no way that Alex would want me now, not now he knew about Jason and I. I mentally prepared myself for the disappointment and heartbreak that I knew was always going to come, and accepted the fate that happiness wasn't something I was destined to have. His body angled towards mine as he gripped my chin gently, raising my gaze to meet his.

"Why didn't you say anything?" He huffed disappointedly as he spoke his words. I choked on my explanation as I tried to think of what to say, how to explain yet another lie I had kept, another deceitful thing I had kept from him. I took a deep breath as I began my excuses.

"Oh it was just a brief thing; I didn't think it was worth mentioning you know." I smiled sweetly as my voiced chimed confidently, desperate to alleviate some of the tension that was bubbling between us. Alex's jaw hardened as he stood slowly and walked over to the glass table that separated his work area from his more casual space that I was sitting in. My breathing quickened at the distance he was putting between us, my mind panicking as I felt myself losing him my senses telling me that he was not OK. A huge smash echoed around the room, pulling me from my thoughts with a jump, a huge shiver running over my skin as Alex's fists slammed hard into the table, his back rigid and tense as he leaned over it, his head hanging forward between his shoulders. My eyes widened in horror at the new Alex I was seeing, the aggression oozing forming from his pores as I watched his back rise and fall with each deep breath. I couldn't move, my body frozen to the spot as desperately tried to figure out what was going on. "I, umm…Alex," I began to whisper.

"Enough!" Alex's deep stern voice reverberated through me as he swiped my flowers that he had just got me off the table, unforgivingly onto the floor, the petals scattering the marble.

"Enough with the fucking lies! Did you think I wouldn't find out, or that I wouldn't notice?" He turned around to face me as the anger and torment in his eyes became more obvious, piercing my gaze with his. I struggled to find any words as he continued. "That" – he gestured to the corridor that Jason had just left down – "was not something casual," he sarcastically air quoted as he spat the word casual. "I gave you plenty of opportunities to come clean, to tell me the truth but time after time you feed me the bullshit of no secrets, fresh start to continue lying to my face at every given moment." Alex leaned back against the table, his head lowering to the floor as he spoke the words that stung me deep, that cut deeper than any word he had spoken to me since we met. "This is why you can't be a mother."

I sat rooted to the spot as uncontrollable sobs took over my body, my mind in complete disbelief at what had just been said, any feeling of inadequacy smashed to pieces by the venom that had just been spoken out loud by the person who was supposed to love me. I was angry, angry at me for not defending myself, yet knowing that the words he spoke were only hurting so much because they were true. What felt like forever and a moment passed between us in uncomfortable silence. I had mentally blocked out his bitter comment, knowing that my heart couldn't defend myself, his cutthroat words stung yet I had no words to say. My quiet sobs subdued into deep breathing and anger at yet again, my past and Jason ruining everything I had going for me. It was becoming a bitter pattern of one good day, followed by an absolute tirade of lies and arguments the next as my past caught up with me quicker each time, even more monumental and damaging than the last. I knew something had to give, he already knew my deepest darkest secret about Ivy, surely nothing could be worse than that. I sighed loudly as I prepared myself to yet again wipe the slate clean, re-invent a fresh start and promise that this would be the last lie I told, in the hope of pulling Alex back to me, giving me yet another chance.

"Jason and I were together for many years." My voice was quiet, soft, apologetic. Alex looked up from where he was sat, the look on his face told me that even though he knew, he still didn't expect to hear it out loud.

"Years?" Alex's eyes were wide with shock as he processed the fact this wasn't going to be an easy hear.

"Years," I repeated, not filtering anything now as I knew the whole truth had to come out. "We were childhood sweethearts; he was my first and we were madly in love." My mind eased as I remembered the good days, Alex's jaw hardening at my admission. I closed my eyes as I went on "Life was, perfect, great, and it was for many years." I shook my head and opened my eyes, Alex was staring straight at me, enveloped by my every word, taking in every ounce, whether it hurt him or not, desperate to make some sense of what I can only imagine being complete and utter turmoil for him as he tried to figure out what was going on right in front of him this whole time.

"What changed?" his voice was softer than I expected, his brow furrowed as he spoke. A shiver ran down my spine as I remembered that terrifying night, the one that had sealed our fate and changed both of our lives forever.

"I think he hurt someone. Badly." I rubbed my hands over my face at the memory. Jason disappearing in the middle of the night and returning covered in blood, my blurry recollection as my drugged-up conscience caught up with me that strange night. "I think he drugged me." I shook my head and shot my gaze over to Alex, like I was asking him a question and waiting for him to confirm it.

"Hold on a minute," Alex shot loudly, "what do you mean hurt someone, and drugged you?" he screwed his face up as his thoughts yet again processed.

"You're not explaining this properly." He clearly didn't know what he was in for as confusion and fear washed over him. I arched my hand over my eyes and closed them as I thought of the best way to explain the whole situation to him.

"OK, this is what we are going to do, I will tell you everything, the whole lot, no interruptions, then you can ask questions at the end. OK?"

He simply nodded and leaned back into his chair as he let out a deep breath. I sat up straight as I started again.

"So, we were perfectly fine, until this one strange night, I was really, really tired and had gone to bed early, we both had. We had fallen asleep together when I remember waking up early that morning feeling strange, like drunk but worse, and the room smelled of fuel." Even though no words were spoken, I could tell from the look on Alex's face that anger was his current emotion.

"It was so bleary, I just remember him being in the shower one minute, women's blood-stained clothes were on the floor at the end of the bed, then he heard me and came flying out of the shower." Alex's face was so focused on mine as I spoke, my face confused even to this day as I spoke the words out loud.

"Yeah, then he strangled me until me until I passed out on the bed, and when I woke, it was like nothing had happened, like I had dreamt it. Our bags were packed, and we moved states that very day, left everything behind, nothing was ever spoken of it. I was too scared. It took me a year to pluck up the courage to leave him, but after a year of abuse from him, I finally did it." My voice trembled as I went on.

"I thought I'd escaped, I moved all the way to Miami, but he followed me. I had no idea he worked for you I swear."

I looked up just in time to see Alex throw his chair backwards as rage enfolded him. "I'll kill the fucker." He darted towards the door, pure and utter malice washed his entire face.

"No, please don't!" I screamed as I darted up and blocked the doorway, panic pulsing through me. "Not here," I soothed as I reached up towards his face, a slight glint of hope shone through as after what felt like forever, his face turned gently into my hand. He was on my side. I felt a new fight in me as I realised, we were still one, that he was with me, through thick and thin, that after an admission like that he was still willing to fight my corner. I thought I could take Jason down by myself, but now I had Alex on board, I knew this was a certainty. That everything I had been trying to figure out on my own was now halved as he took on my burdens with me, willing to fight for me to protect me. We would do this together, but we would do this right. My number one priority had to come first.

"I think he is going to hurt Ivy to get to me." I breathed softly as I spoke the words out loud to my worst nightmare, the visible quiver that washed over Alex as he took in what I said only fuelled me more, as he slammed his fist into the door above my head, the thought haunting him just as much as it me.

"Over my dead body," Alex spat through gritted teeth.

Chapter 18

"The Mercedes?" I could sense his heartbreak just by the tone of his voice. It was my day off, but I was shamelessly hanging out with Alex at his office while he worked, like a lovesick puppy that couldn't get enough. "Ahh, man, OK, I'll have to see if I can get it to the garage to be seen to." He ran his hand through his gorgeous silky hair as he spoke, his white shirt unbuttoned just enough that I could see the splatter of hair peeking though at his throat, his two-day old stubble framing his perfect face. This man was a god. Not a clean cut, crisp suit kind of guy, but the rugged, manly type, the type that looked just as hot wearing his sweats around the house as he did suited and booted. A wide-eyed glance locked in on me as I smirked from the corner of my mouth. Busted. He repaid me with a smirk of his own through his quiet chatter, still on the phone with Mr whoever sorting out Mercedes gate, knowing exactly what I was doing. A subtle eye roll and shake of his head confirmed it, he leaned back into his chair casually, his body relaxing, but giving me even more of a view. He knew what he was doing, putting on a show, a minimal effort show nonetheless, but that's all it took when it came to him.

The phone was still tucked neatly under his shoulder as he spoke, yet his gaze never left mine, our eyes piercing through each other, daring the other one to break the contact, no words exchanged yet a million vaults might as well have been passing between us as the tension fizzled. He felt it, I felt it. It was a connection that had buzzed under the surface since the day I met him, a connection that at first thrummed with lust, passion, and desire, yet as the weeks went on, although that desire was still very prevalent in our relationship, a new underlying tone had made its way to the surface by means of trust, friendship, and affection. It was a change that I enjoyed, something that I hadn't expected from Mr mogul, the seemingly got it all together guy with the world at his fingertips. Yet here he sat, in front of me, with eyes like dreams as he looked at me the same way I looked at him, reciprocating everything I offered right back at me, but in a degree I just didn't understand. My subconscious slapped me hard in the face, my confidence de throned as my anxiety took over. Damn it. I looked down at my feet, cutting the tension in the room with a knife as I felt unworthy of him.

"Thanks again for letting me know, Mark, it's much appreciated. See you." Alex placed the handset back into its holder before folding his arms across his chest, his face unimpressed as he eyed me questioningly. "What was that?" He shook his head as he spoke.

I glanced up to meet his gaze. "What was what?" I meekly replied, my acting skills failing me as I pretended, I didn't know what he was on about. He forced a sarcastic laugh as he got up from his chair, heading over towards me.

"Oh, Em, don't. One minute you're eyeing me up like I'm your next meal, which, for your information, was welcomely received, then it's like someone threw your plate on the floor and you're no longer hungry." I huffed loudly as he scooted next to me on the sofa, pulling me neatly into his side affectionately. A moment silence passed between us as I took in his huge presence, firmly and possessively holding my body with his, dwarfing me in size as his thumb stroked the small of my back.

"You're beautiful you know," Alex spoke with such tenderness, betraying the demeanour his physicality portrayed. A soft kiss on the top of my head told me that his 'what was that about' question was rhetorical, as he knew exactly what was going through my head in that moment. That I was tormenting myself into a turmoil of self-pity, not feeling worthy enough for this man, or for anyone in this world to love me in any sense or way. He rocked me gently as I took in his warmth and scent, feeling safe and protected, like his touch and words were medicine to my messed-up head, a constant battle of guilt and self-consciousness quashed down into my soul, only temporarily, but deeper and more permanent at learning his words spoken, were actually true.

"I'm so sorry he hurt you, Emily." His voice was a whisper against the top of my head as he spoke, my body tensing slightly at the mention of Jason. My heart began to slowly beat faster, like the mere thought of my past clicked my body into a sense of heightened alert to protect myself.

"I knew there was something off from the start when I first saw you together. I just couldn't put my finger on it." He was procrastinating, opening up without me asking or prompting. I sat in silence, taking in his every word as he spoke, my heart matching his as he still held me close, grateful that he could not see my face, burrowed into his chest.

"I mean, what are the chances, old school friends bumping into each other unknowingly halfway across the country, never mind working for the same company, for the same person, in the same department." I felt him shake his head and sigh gently, clearly kicking himself for not seeing the obvious on day one.

"What kind of weirdo follows someone that far, that secretively, obsessively, when all they have done is hurt them." My body was rigid now against him, I was sure he could tell, yet he just held me tighter as my emotions swirled dangerous close to the surface.

"Emily, I promise you we will get to the bottom of this, and that man will never, ever hurt you again. You and your daughter will always be completely safe with me. I will protect you both until my last breath." His words broke me, broke me beyond the barriers of normal, as warm tears spilled over onto my cheeks and onto his shirt unapologetically.

"And this." He squeezed me gently and pulled me back to look at my face before nodding up and down, gesturing his eyes over my body, "I'll fix too," he pulled me back close again.

"It will take time, patience and a lot of love, but I will prove to you that you are only worthy of no less than the entire world, that only a gentle touch means love, and everything you are, is mine to cherish." I knew right then, in that very moment. I loved this man.

"So, Mr Elliot has full knowledge of Miss Moore's daughter who was placed for adoption?" The kind faced man in the brown suit that I now knew to be Sergeant Will Green, spoke gently across the table to Alex.

"Yes, that's correct, he knew of her only after the adoption however Emily and him were, were in a relationship together for some time," the slight pause as he spoke the last part out loud was obvious, as well as the speed in which he spat the unsightly words out, bitter in his mouth. It had taken me by surprise when Alex had told me we had a meeting together, even more so when I found out he was a local police sergeant, taking time out of his busy schedule to assist Alex in digging dirt on Jason, off the book. I shuddered at how many numbers must have been on that cheque to get him here.

"OK, so Miss Moore, what makes you believe that your daughter might be in danger, in particular from Mr Elliot?" I shifted uncomfortable in my seat, unsure how I was going to explain to this man I had just met, the drama that had beheld my life for the past few years leading up until now.

"I understand that your, um…relationship with Mr Elliot was tumultuous in the time leading up to your relocation here, what I'm after is specifics that can link him to your daughter, more so now than back then." I gazed over to Alex, questioningly, but knowing full well that the detective had clearly had a brief before the meeting today. I shirked off the slight annoyance at the realisation that this man obviously knew all my business, knowing that of course that's what he was here for, and in a way, relived that I didn't have to go over it all again out loud now. I hesitated as I thought of the proof I had, nothing other than just hunches, spiteful words spat out by Jason slyly, a mother's intuition wouldn't be enough to anchor this detective right now. Suddenly, my skin pricked and the hair on my arms stood on end as I remembered something, my eyes scrunched tightly as the air forced out of my lungs. I was pretty sure that this wasn't going to go down well, yet another secret I hadn't give up to Alex, but it was all I had. I reached down into my bag and rummaged deep until I found what I was looking for. I placed the piece of paper down in front on me and smoothed it out flat. The address written on it still smudged, but clear. I felt Alex's gaze snap to the paper, and then back to me before he broke the silence in the room.

"What is that?" He snatched it up from the table eyeing it intently, a slight hint of annoyance in his tone, less than I actually expected.

"I received it while I was working here for you, anonymously." I turned to face Alex as I spoke, to cool his no doubt impending mood that was rolling in at the thought of not knowing everything.

"I see and do you know who's address this is my dear?" Mr Green was jotting notes down in his small black notebook as he spoke.

"Yes, I do actually, I went there," I might as well have jumped up and down on the table and got a better reaction that I did at that moment.

"You did what!" Alex had now screeched his chair loudly sideways to face me in its entirety. Mr Greens note writing would have to wait as he jolted his head upright, Alex's outburst clearly more important at this moment.

"Relax," I hushed at Alex, shooting the sergeant an apologetic smile as he propped his chin into his palms on the desk, awaiting some form of explanation.

"It was fine, I came back in one piece." I forced a laugh to dissipate the tension that was not unmistakeably dampening the mood in the room, to be met with silence. And staring eyes from both men. "Oh honestly," I huffed, "It was just a lady and her child, no scary monsters, no one crazy." I sat back in my seat and folded my arms across my chest, like a chastised child admitted defeat.

"I see, and did you know these people personally?" Mr Green had gone back to his notebook now, scribbling on the pages with scruffy handwriting. Alex was still staring at me, awaiting a mega explanation as I rolled my eyes away from his gaze.

"No, I mean, well not really. The lady was the one who dealt with my adoption, I don't remember her though, apparently, she dealt with her new family, and the little girl was her daughter. I thought." My memory darted back to the disappointment I felt, the hurt that the little girl was in fact, not my Ivy.

"I thought it might have been Ivy's new home, but it wasn't." Mr Green's brow furrowed deeply as he took in the information that I had given him before he spoke again, his words dragging out slowly as he tried to piece together my story.

"So, who do you imagine gave you this anonymous tip off, and what would be the purpose of having you find this lady?" It was obvious that he knew the answer I was going to give, the puzzle slotting seemingly into place in his mind, my confirmation was all he needed to solidify it.

"Jason," I quipped back bluntly. "I think he gave me this address as he knew it was the only way to find my daughter, he knew I would go there, he knew I wanted to find her, and the information on her location would only be given to me, not him, so he sent me on a wild goose chase."

I had barely spoken my last word before Alex chipped in aggressively, "And what information did she give you about her?" He was staring me down now, the anger inside him no longer subtle or discreet as he made no attempt to hide it.

"Nothing," I shot back defensively, "She wouldn't tell me a thing." I shrugged my shoulders towards Mr Green who had now closed his notebook.

"She told me that she was bound by her licencing law to retain the adoption information and that all she could tell me was that she had a good family who would protect her indefinitely." I could hear Alex's breathing heavy beside me now, I ignored him and continued to address Mr Green instead.

"She suggested that I make an anonymous tip off to the police about a child in danger, which I did, in an attempt to protect her, it's all I could do, she wouldn't budge."

I jumped as Alex stood bolt upright next to me, "That was you?" He shot at me in disbelief. "Wow, just wow," he muttered as he walked over towards the door, allowing it to bang shut loudly as he left.

"Oh, dear," Mr Green chirped lightly as he gathered his belongings, Alex's departure clearly calling the end of the meeting early. He made his way over to the door as I scurried over to see him out. "Miss Moore, all of the information you have given has been more than helpful, I can assure you that we will endeavour to do all we can to protect your daughter, and in the meantime if you learn anything new, or think of anything more, please call me." He handed me his business card before placing a friendly hand on my shoulder and squeezing it gently, "Take care, my love." He smiled before seeing himself out.

Yet again, confusion washed over me as I sat back down at the table in the meeting room, attempting to gather my thoughts and process what I now knew from this get together. One thing I did know, was that Alex was pissed, beyond pissed. More than likely at the fact that I had kept the address from him, and more so that I had gone there alone. I sighed loudly as I kind of understood his point. We were at a different stage then, in fact we weren't even together, I had just left him standing in a car park the night before after discovering he even knew about Ivy, what did he expect me to do? God things had got complicated. I shoved back my annoyance and went to find Alex, knowing that I probably had some grovelling to do. I shuffled sulkily along the corridor to his office, not bothering to knock as I snuck in tentatively.

"Yeah, she fucking went there." Alex was on the phone to someone, his back to the door, perched on the edge of his desk. The door banged loudly behind me as it swung back on its hinges, Alex spun round sharply before meeting my glaring gaze.

"Look, Mom, I've got to go, I'll catch up with you later OK. Yeah, I will, love you too, bye." He placed the phone back into its cradle firmly before shaking his head. "Emily, you have got to be fucking kidding me." He laughed sarcastically before making his way round his desk towards me. I stook rooted to the spot as he came and grabbed me firmly by the shoulders, his smouldering eyes piercing my gaze as he looked down at me. "How the fuck am I supposed to keep you, and Ivy safe, if I don't know the full story?" He was angry, but I could tell the annoyance was more at himself for not knowing all the information than at me for not giving it up. I dodged his question, having questions of my own that I needed answering first. I shrugged out of his grip and twisted away before plonking myself down onto his office sofa, my elbows on my knees, chin resting on top before firing away. "What did you mean when you said that was me when I mentioned about the anonymous tip off? How could you possibly know about that?" I directed my gaze towards, him as he slowly made his way back to his office chair, before sitting down gently, his face in thought. "Emily, I had already done some digging with the police before that meeting, they told me that they had received an anonymous tip off, I just was a bit shocked to learn that the anonymous tip off was you, that's all." He shrugged his shoulders, making it seem casual when his reaction has been anything but.

"Is that so hard to believe, that I would tip of the police at the knowledge of someone hurting a child?" My tone was a little bit more sarcastic than I meant, and I winced slightly.

"No, no it's not, Emily, it's just, this whole thing is madness, too many coincidences, too much that I don't understand, I just don't like it and I'm trying to figure it all out." His voice was soft, the anger dissipating as he went on. "Why didn't you tell me about the address?" I could tell he was hurt, hurt that I had kept that from him. Guilt nibbled away at me as I saw the sadness on his face.

"Alex, I'm sorry I didn't tell you. I'm a bit like you, confused, trying to figure it all out as well, we weren't in a good place then, it felt easier to deal with it on my own." I looked down at my feet, tinged with sadness at the memory of the night I left him.

Alex sighed deeply before shaking his head. "You really are a pain in the ass."

I shot my gaze up to meet his, smirking at his comment, grateful that this discussion seemed to be coming to an end. He smiled back at me genuinely, "I just think that if we are going to figure all of this out, we need to be more open and tell each other everything, there's no point in trying to build a picture if we both have one half each, OK?"

I nodded, genuinely in approval, he clearly knew things I didn't. "What else do you know?" I quizzed Alex, desperately wanting to know all I could.

Alex sighed deeply, running his palms over his face, "Not much more than you I don't think." He leaned forward and pulled a file out of his desk draw before sliding it over the top towards me. "This is all I have on him."

I shuffled slightly in my chair; my interest peaked at the thought of what would be inside. As though reading my thoughts, Alex gestured towards the file, "You can read it."

My insides buzzed as I stood up to grab the file, I opened it slowly before making my way back to the sofa. The first page was all about him, name, age date of birth, all the boring stuff. "Is this your corporate check?" I glanced up at Alex who was watching my intently.

"No, this is more advanced, the one I get on my employees is more of a character reference, credit check that kind of thing."

I nodded before turning the page, a photo of me and Jason from way back, was pinned to the top corner of the page. I threw my hand over my mouth in shock. "So, you already knew?" I spun the page around to face Alex, the photo in full-view.

He shook his head. "Not until the day of your argument with him, you know where you lied and told me you tripped on your desk and broke your globe?" I writhed at his admission; he knew back then.

"Wait, why didn't you say anything?" I shot back defensively, my mind raging at the thought.

"I literally only got the file that morning, I was trying to make sense of it myself, I wasn't sure what I was going to do with that information, wasn't sure if it needed addressing, and then I saw the look on your face that day I walked in on you both and realised there was way more to your relationship than what this file said." My eyes watered at the memory, his hands skirting up my bare thigh as I sat rooted to the spot, too scared to move.

"He touched me," I blurted out. "Right before you came in," his eyes widened as the words echoed around the room.

"He what…?" Alex's face was rigid, hard, pale staring across the room at me making sense of my words. "I swear to god, I will put this man behind bars if it's the last thing I do." He spat out the words with so much venom and hate, he even scared me. He made his way over to the sofa and pulled me in tightly, much the same as we had done this morning, yet this time, I felt his pain against my skin as he protected my body with his. "I'm so sorry, I wish I had of known at the time, it took all my might not to put my hands on him that day, never mind the fact that he abused you."

"It's ok," I whispered quietly, "we will get our revenge." I shook the file in my hand pulling his gaze down to the paperwork, his grip releasing slightly as I pointed to a line of text that sent physical chills down my spine – ex partner, Chloe Lopez – deceased, unknown cause of death.

Chapter 19

"Holy shit." Ali was repeating the same two words over and over. "Holy actual shit, do you really think he did it?" The last few days had passed in a strange blur, Alex had completely lost it, fully immersed in the mystery that was the death of Chloe Lopez. He read the line I had pointed to only once, before practically throwing me out of the way to get to the phone. The phone conversations, followed by numerous people in and out, asking a million questions had exhausted me. I didn't know how many times I could tell the same story over and over with the same confused face looking back at me. Why hadn't I called the cops back then, didn't I find it strange how he moved us both to a different state the next day, had I known that they were in a relationship, how could I possibly live in a house with someone I was so scared of, the whole time making me feel like I could have done more, like I should have done something more.

"Oh, Emily, you couldn't have possibly known, you were drugged, abused, you didn't really know what was going on." Molly had me pulled close on the sofa, desperately trying to ease my torment that surrounded the death of Chloe.

"I just feel terrible, every ounce of my being was telling me he did something that night, but I just didn't believe it, it honestly felt like a dream, I felt so out of it that I couldn't tell what was real and what wasn't, I barely remember anything, only really the morning."

"What an actual psychopath!" Ali was still adding her ten pence to the conversation while scrolling through her phone, Tom lazily chilling next to her with his feet across her lap. As soon as I found out, the girls and Tom were my first port of call, I couldn't really speak to Alex as he was so wrapped up and furious with the whole situation that I didn't want to burden him with more anguish and negativity in the form of my crazy mind and thoughts. They suggested we meet up straight away, for the usual gossip and catch up but now with a potential murder to add to the mix. It didn't seem real. It had taken a couple of days of madness to all find the time to get together and hiding out at Toms place for the night with people I really trusted was what I needed right now.

"So where is Jason now?" Molly tucked a strand of hair behind my ear tenderly. "We don't know," I whispered.

"No one has seen him since our fight at OSAR, Alex fired him on the spot and he presumed he had just gone home, found another job or something."

"So, what he's just disappeared of the face of the earth?" Ali chimed in sarcastically, "I mean, it looks like that, once we realised Chloe was dead, Alex called the cops straight away, when they got to his apartment, he hadn't been there in days, he had packed some stuff, his passport, clothes and was seen on the lobby cameras exiting out the front literally an hour after leaving OSAR that day."

"Wow, so he must have panicked and done a runner, thought you were on to him or something." Tom's voice was low and demure, a far throw away from his usual chirpy loud self.

"Mm hmm, I found some prescriptions in his work draw just before he was fired, in my name, Chloe's and another girl, he knew I had seen them and confronted him, I guess in that moment he knew I was onto him."

"I just still can't take it all in, as if you stayed with him a year after that night, you were in so much danger Emily!" Molly had switched over into Mom mode, going over the if, buts and maybes of our final year together.

"I had to wait for the right time to leave him, I had to make sure I had enough money together and some where to go, I guess Miami wasn't far enough," I scoffed loudly, still in disbelieve at how this whole situation had played out. How he had followed me unknowingly all the way to Miami. Manipulated his position at work to have me work there too, all completely unbeknown to me or Alex. He was smart, I'll give him that.

"Ahh, I found something!" Ali shoved Toms legs off her lap unapologetically as she sat upright on the edge of the sofa squinting closely at the screen on her phone.

"Local dentist dies in house fire," Ali spoke the words slowly, like the beginning of a horror story as we all looked at each other in horrified silence. Ali sighed loudly before making way of the article.

"Local dentist Chloe Lopez has been announced dead following a fire at her home in Wisconsin. Police were alerted to a house fire in the early hours on

February 10 by a member of the public where the woman, 25, was sadly pronounced dead at the scene. Police are not currently treating the fire as suspicious with no arrests being made at present." We all glanced around the room at each other in complete disbelief, why hadn't the police mentioned any of this in the interviews? Not suspicious, how can something like that be not suspicious? How hadn't I figured this out already, the smell of the fuel when I woke up that morning, the bloody clothes on the floor, of course he did it, of course it was him.

I stood up quickly and began pacing the room obsessively, running my hands erratically through my hair and over my face. "You stupid, stupid girl." I was chastising myself out loud, angry, and furious at myself for being so stupid. The pieces were finally slotting together and making sense in my head. I don't know exactly what happened that night, but I now knew the reason for the hasty move to another state that very morning. I hadn't heard nothing of the fire, nothing of the death of Chloe after we moved. We had no friends or family that lived there, no connections to the small town we had briefly called home, we pretty much just left out the back door unnoticed. I had my suspicions that he was having an affair with her, but he had always put my mind at ease, making me believe that I was being crazy, still not quite right so soon after the adoption, my emotions and mind all over the place, yet that mother fucker was doing exactly what I suspected him of. I wasn't crazy.

"Oh my god, Em," Ali's tone scared me, scared me enough to break me from my pacing and glare at her, knowing I wasn't going to like what she said. Ali looked around the room at the others, almost seeking permission to speak. Her words came out reluctantly, so softly, with pure emotion in her voice, as single tear fell from the corner of her eye. "She was pregnant."

"How long has she been like this?" I could hear Alex whispering gently, feel his warm palm against my skin as he stroked my head, yet I felt like I was watching from across the room.

"A couple of hours, she went crazy, smashed everything she could get her hands on, we had to hold her down, took ages for her to calm down, for the sobbing to stop, then she just went silent, she's been laid here ever since." Tom's voice was wavering, I could hear the tears he was choking back as he spoke to Alex.

"Tom, I'm so sorry about your things, I'll have you reimbursed for the lot, I just can't thank you enough for calling me, I can't stand to see her like this but

I'm so grateful she had you all with her, that she wasn't alone." He was speaking genuinely, but with a slight small talk vibe, like he didn't really feel comfortable discussing my breakdown with Tom.

"Of course, is there anything more we can do? Ali and molly are still here, they just didn't want to impede too much while you were in here, they are feeling as upset and shocked as Em is, we all are."

"Thank you, Tom, if it's not too much trouble I will stay the night here with her, I don't really want to move her while she's not quite with it, I don't want to unsettle her anymore."

"Yes, absolutely, of course, I'll leave you to it, if you need anything I'll be sleeping on the sofa, don't hesitate." Tom's voice was relived, like he was clocking out of crazy duty shift, Alex now taking over.

"I'll just have a driver drop off some bits for us both, it will be very soon, after that I won't bother you for the night, thanks, Tom."

I heard the soft patter of Toms feet leave the room, the slight click of the door let me know that we were alone. I felt the mattress move as Alex scooted in gently beside me, his warm arm snaking around my waist as he pulled me close. I heard him inhale deeply as he nuzzled my hair, "My Em," he murmured under his breath. A hint of a smile formed at the corner of my mouth, his presence slowly sobering me to the real world, my body becoming my own again. I stretched against his body gently before rolling over to face him, his eyes were wide as I met his gaze, his hands in the air, palm facing me in a submissive state, like he was assessing me.

"I'm OK, I'm not crazy," I murmured under my breath before nuzzling into his chest. I felt him let out the breath he was holding in as he pulled me close, kissing me gently on the forehead.

"I know baby, your just in shock, we all are." His voice soothed me, his words easing my mind to know I had him on board, that this crazy world I was living in right now wasn't just for me to figure out, he got me, he got everything that was going on in my life, and yet he was still here, early hours of the morning, in a stranger's apartment, someone else's bed, telling me that everything was going to be OK. I had so many questions I needed to ask, so many things in my mind that needed answering, yet I was exhausted, tired, and defeated from the last few days, yet my body still refused to give in. There was too much adrenaline in my system for me to sleep, the blow that Chloe had been carrying Jason's child, an innocent child who wasn't able to live because of him made me feel physically sick. An unthinkable evil who snatched away not only one but two lives. I felt bile rise in my throat as I wretched loudly.

Alex jumped out of the bed quicker than I had even seen him move. "No. No, Em, hang on." I could hear him clambering about the room desperately trying to find something for me to be sick into but to no avail, as I began heaving onto the bed in front of me. A tiny bit of embarrassment edged to the front of my conscience as he held my hair back, allowing me to heave until nothing more came out.

"Sorry," I managed through whispered breaths, genuinely feeling bad for the mess I had made of the bed, at now 5 am.

Alex laughed gently. "It's nothing I'm not used to, don't worry, come on, let's get you cleaned up." Alex folded the duvet over gently before pulling me up from the bed tentatively, leading me into the bathroom. I stood by the door as he spun the big silver taps round and round, the water cascading into the huge bathtub, the smell of jasmine now filling the air as the water swirled around, steam billowing up to the ceiling from the scorching temperature. "Arms up," Alex skirted his fingers around the hem of my jumper nervously. I stared into his eyes as he looked down at me, seeking my permission to touch me, like he was undressing me for the first time. I raised my arms above my head as he slowly pulled the jumper up, my hair cascading over my shoulders, barely covering my now naked breasts. Usually I would feel embarrassment, coy, shyness, but I felt nothing, no shame, no hesitation, I just did what I knew needed to be done, at pure ease and secure around him. I saw the tenderness in his face as he dipped slightly, lowering my jogging bottoms to my waist, before taking my hand and gently pulling me over to the tub. He spun the taps back around, stopping the flow before swirling the water gently, checking the temperature. "Yep, we are good." He pulled my hand up high, allowing me to step into the water with ease as I sunk down below the bubbles. The heat eased me immediately as I let out a loud sigh.

"Nice?" Alex asked seeking my reassurance.

"Yes, thank you," I replied quietly, still not feeling a hundred percent after my melt down earlier in the night and the subsequent vomit party I had just thrown for myself.

"We will figure this all out you know." Alex's voice was gentle, like he was treading carefully, assessing my mood, gaging my reaction.

"I know, it was just such a shock, after everything we had been through, to learn they were going to have a baby," I shivered, the water swishing up the side of the bathtub.

Alex sighed loudly. "I know, I still can't believe it either."

My mind swirled back over the last few days. "How do the police know nothing of this, nothing about Chloe's death was mentioned in the interviews, her name wasn't even brought up, every time I tried to speak about it, they glossed over the topic, wanted to know more about my relationship with him?"

Alex paused for a second taking in what I had just said, thinking his response carefully. "Emily, there's nothing linking him to her death. It was nonsuspicious, a house fire."

"Bullshit, I know what I saw that night, blood-stained clothes, the smell of fuel, what so it's just purely coincidental that the night she died, is the exact night all of this happened too?" I scoffed as I folded my arms across my chest and scooted back down into the water.

"I know he had something to do with this, we just have to prove it." Alex ran his hands through his hair, clearly tired. "I totally agree, and I'm sure the police are doing all of their enquiries behind the scenes, they just have to be diplomatic, they can't sit there and agree with our theory, nor can they start telling us details of someone else's death, I knew nothing of how she died either until I got the phone call from Molly, she was frantic." I logicalized his words in my head, annoyingly making sense before feeling bad for my friends. They had been so good to me, there for me through thick and thin, offering me a shoulder to cry on, an ear to vent.

"Are they still here?" I sat up slightly, looking towards the door, remembering we were still at Toms place.

"No, Molly had to go for the kids, she took Ali with her, she was in quite a state when I got here, Tom was passed out sleeping on the sofa when I grabbed the bags from my driver.

"Oh no, poor Tom," I remembered the mess I had made of his apartment, smashing up anything I could get my hands on as the rage and anger took over my body, never mind the state I had just left his bed in. "How bad is the place out there?" I winced slightly as I asked the question. He smiled, as he perched down on the edge of the bath,

"Let's say you did a good job." He laughed lightly.

"Oh my god, I feel so bad, I'm going to have to pay—"

"It's sorted," Alex cut me off abruptly, don't even think about it, he will be able to replace the apartment twice over with the cheque I wrote him.

"Oh, Alex, no," I sat up right in the bath, grasping his hands, water sloshing over the edge, soaking his trousers.

I pursed my lips trying to stifle my smile, "Ummm sorry?" I questioned cocking my head to the side innocently.

"You really are a pain in the ass." He laughed gently.

"You said that the other day to me, yet you're still here."

He smiled at me coyly, "Yet I'm still here."

I felt tired, as I sat at the kitchen island silently, Tom was still asleep on the sofa and I had left Alex snoozing quietly in the bedroom, fresh Gucci bedding adorning the bed, the sicky covers whirring around in the washer as I had rummaged through someone else's kitchen cupboards trying desperately to find some detergent to fix the mess I had made. I blew the steam off the top of my cup of tea as I shamelessly glanced around Tom's apartment. This place wasn't even his, he was a renting a room from the posh lady who was abroad, her name alluding me at this precise moment, and I had completely trashed it. Vases and photo frames lay broken in a pile, clearly swept to the corner of the room for now, the blinds torn down from the frame and the tv lay awkwardly over the coffee table, a huge crack slicing corner to corner. I was ashamed and embarrassed yet had no energy to make it right, I felt like shit. A cool hand on my waist made me jump, "It's just me," Alex charmed apologetically, whispering so as not to wake Tom as he wrapped his bare torso around my body pulling me in tightly.

"I was miles away there," I whispered back, feeling slightly coy at the state of the place, even though I knew he had seen it last night.

"Just as well really." He smirked pointing his chin towards the room.

"Really, Alex?" I smirked and shook my head taking a sip of my tea.

"I told you, don't worry, it's sorted, some contactors will be here at noon, the place will be back to its former glory before sundown." He mocked a salute in my direction playfully, clearly trying to take the edge off. I wanted to protest, to tell him he didn't need to and that I would pay for the damages, exactly how, I don't know but I knew that was the right thing to do, yet I sat in silence, allowing him to fix my problems as I knew I didn't have the means to make it right.

"Thank you," I whispered, offering a sweet smile by way of appreciation. A small squeak diverted both of our attention over to the sofa where Tom was now partaking in an over-the-top stretch and a theatrical yawn.

"Howdy campers," Toms high pitched voice bellowed around the apartment as he jumped up far to vigorously from the sofa, still fully dressed in lasts night attire, reaching to the ceiling in yet another dramatic stretch.

"Morning dude," Alex stepped over towards the coffee machine as he pulled down two cups, pouring fresh steaming coffee into both. I watched Tom's eyes dance with delight as he followed Alex's toned body across the room, I raised my eyebrow at him questioningly for eying up my man to be met with an abrupt shoulder shrug and nod of approval, I smirked as I took a sip of my tea.

"Glad to see your still with us," Tom joked as he wrapped his arms firmly around me, rocking me from side to side,

"Scared the living shit out of us all mind with you whole 'I've been possessed' thing going on."

He laughed as he leaned back, giving me the once over, "In all seriousness, are you OK?"

"Yes, I'm fine, Tom. I'm so, so sorry about all of, well this." I gestured towards the room apologetically.

"Ahh its only stuff," he waved his hand in the air casually like I hadn't just caused thousands of pounds worth of damage to his land lady's home. "Besides, my boss wrote me a check that will absolutely leave enough left for a shopping spree." He laughed loudly before taking the coffee out of Alex's hand, his face in bemusement at Tom's matter of fact attitude. "Oh, and while we're at it, you might want to let the boss know I won't be in work today."

Tom winked at me as he made his way down the corridor. "What shall I tell him?"

I yelled playfully over my shoulder, a moment's silence passing before he replied, "Headache!" He shouted giggling.

Chapter 20

"Do I, or don't I?" Tom was twisting back and forward in the mirror admiring his behind in a pair of dark brown jeans, the sixth pair of the same style, just a different colour.

"I just don't really know if I like them all that much." He screwed his face up sulkily as I gave him the death stare.

"Could you not have decided that before trying on six different pairs, Tom?" My tone was playful, but I must admit, shopping wasn't really my forte, and after pretty much three full days of hanging out with Tom, I'd had my yearly fix of retail therapy. We had spent the first two days spending Alex's much needed pay cheque to fix up the apartment, fortunately Tom's landlady was away for business for at least another eight weeks which meant fix up didn't have to be done right away, yet we had still nailed it, nonetheless. We had completely re fitted the entire apartment, from the television, right down to the sofa cushions, which were now firmly in place, a gleaming show home again with no trace of my meltdown to be seen. Fortunately, Tom had enjoyed the entire debacle, far too much in fact, whereas I had just tagged along, for the moral support and selfishly, to eb the guilt I was still harbouring after destroying his home and we were now on day three, spending the hazard pay, as he so graciously called it, left over from the refit. We had spent the morning trailing all the designer shops as he tried on mountains of clothes, shoes, and accessories that I guarantee he didn't need, yet the glee in is face as we went along was soothing. Tom had been so supportive since I found out about Chloe, everybody had, but I still couldn't help but wonder how I ended up with these amazing people around me supporting me when all I seemed to bring to the table was drama and hurt. It was something I don't think I would ever fully understand, nor would I fully accept it.

I slurped rudely on my iced latte and sighed deeply. "You OK?" Tom's voice was soft, like he had processed my thoughts and read my mind before even I had myself, as my eyes darted up to meet his. I opened my mouth to speak before hesitating and reminding myself that I didn't have to put on the superwoman bravado, not fully anyway.

"Actually, Tom, I'm really exhausted, I might call it a day you know." I forced a sympathetic smile with a small shoulder shrug, an attempt to soften the blow at potentially bursting his bubble. Tom exhaled loudly before shrugging brown jeans down to his ankles,

"Yeah, sure, I mean, it has been a mad few days, you must be tired, come on, lets head home."

"Umm actually, Tom, I think I'm going to stay at my place tonight. I don't want to overstay my welcome and I've got no more clean things with me." Tom stayed silent as he straightened the jeans and hung them neatly on the hanger, smoothing the material with his palm.

"But Alex specifically asked me to stay with you, that he wanted you to stay at mine, it's closer to him."

I sighed deeply; the annoyance obvious. "Look, Tom, it's been amazing spending the last few days with you, and I couldn't be more grateful for everything you have done for me, but I really could do with my own space tonight." He avoided eye contact as he pulled his linen shorts up, buttoning them slowly, like his thoughts were hindering his ability.

"Are you going to let him know?" Tom's tone was cautious, like he knew he was poking the tiger.

"Tom, I'm an adult, I'm perfectly capable of looking after myself, he doesn't own me, and you don't need to babysit me, I don't have to ask permission to stay at my own home." My voice was loud, curter than I had perhaps intended, yet my frustrations and anger spilled out onto the surface anyway.

Tom forced a smile, a hurt yet sincere smile. "OK, I'll walk you home," he offered the words gently, after spending a silent moment finding the words to say. His reaction should have triggered some form of guilt, yet it was too easy to numb, too easy to switch off my emotions, a talent I had perfected after spending an entire day speaking to the police as well as what felt like everyone else and their mother about Jason and Chloe. A protective method, that I thought had worked, yet all I felt now was like exploding, screaming from the top of my lungs.

"No, need, I've got it." I grabbed my bag and headed for the door hastily, the sound of Tom shouting wait, as I heard him busily trying to gather his belongings, potentially hot on my tail. I dashed out onto the sidewalk, desperately seeking some space as I took a deep breath of the warm evening air into my lungs, feeling lighter and freer in that very breath.

I swirled the now cool bath water with my hand, using my fingers to curl the bubbles into wintery peaks that looked like soft whipped meringues. I wasn't sure how long I had been here, yet the silence and alone time was something that I hadn't realised I needed so badly, a creature of habit that struggled to be around people for long periods of time, suffocating in the mask if I kept it on too long. I sighed deeply, the very delayed guilt now hitting me after my blow out at Tom, he didn't deserve it, yet being with him for such a long period of time had been exhausting, but that was no reflection of him, it was my strange and warped brain taking over.

I shook my head and ran my palm over my face, knowing I should probably text him, but not having the energy to explain myself right now. I shivered as I stood in the bath, the air cool against my already cold skin, pale and supple from my prolonged soak. I sighed loudly as I pulled my towel around me, still holding the warmth from the heated towel rail, a much-needed hug instantly lifting my spirits as I made my way into the bedroom. I grabbed my phone from my bag before making my way over to my bed, now likely in for the long haul as I plonked myself down onto my duvet with an air of ungracefulness, my permanent location for the foreseeable as I often spent far more time than I should sat on my bed in a towel, one of my less desirable traits. I touched the screen lighting up the display, my usual screen saver picture of the beach at sunset glowed back blankly at me, surprised not to see anything from Tom, or Alex for that matter. I glanced at the clock feeling sorry for myself, it was 11:20 pm, I wondered if Tom would still be awake, pondering over calling him to explain myself now that I was feeling a bit better, a little bit more human but decided against it, it was late and perhaps sleeping on it wouldn't be a bad idea considering. I swiped down to find Alex's number, slightly peeved that he hadn't tried to call me, but then checking myself when I realised his life didn't revolve around me and that I had actually told him to give me some space, hoping that it would relieve some of the pressure he no doubt felt under to look after me and work. He was hesitant but agreed that he would get as much work done during the day, and then we would check in every evening, just until he got everything underhand at the office and the station, a few days we hoped. He had been amazing the morning after my breakdown, making sure I had all the relevant people with me when I gave my statement to the police, taking my hand while holding me when the tears threatened to spill and my emotions got the better of me, a true gent. His suggestion that I stayed with Tom that evening hadn't come as too much of a surprise, I had a feeling that he wouldn't want me on my own, just in case, but was also slightly hurt that he hadn't asked me to stay with him, my mind making things up as I tried to sabotage myself into believing it was because he wasn't that serious about me and that he didn't want me around, ridiculous thoughts given the support and love he had showed my during the whole course of this crazy Jason, Chloe madness. He had, of course explained to me that he still had lots of work to do and that he didn't want me hanging around his place without any support if I needed it, slightly justifying his decision to have me stay with Tom, yet not stinging any less. We had been exchanging texts throughout the day, with him checking in on me during the evening with a phone call, his concern always genuine as he asked me about my day with Tom and if I needed anything. He sounded tired and exhausted when I had spoken to him last night, stressed and worn out from still running a business as well as dealing with all my problems as well. I sighed deeply, feeling guilty about not calling him earlier but still wondering why he hadn't called me, before tapping the green button. I was immediately met with an automated call message telling me my phone was out of service, I glanced at the screen to see my signal bar at zero, shit. That's why I hadn't heard from him, or hopefully Tom either. I clambered over my bed to grab my sweats and a hoody before pulling them quickly over my head, my damp hair clinging to my neck as I slipped on some sliders and made my way to the door. I clicked on the green ring button again as I paced the corridor, still no signal, still the same lady chiming into my ear, I huffed loudly, annoyed at not noticing my signal earlier, yet slightly grateful that it meant I wasn't getting the silent treatment from Alex and Tom. I was holding my phone in the air as I reached the lobby, still no signal bar in sight as I chuntered to myself, offering an expletive under my breath at regular intervals as I reached the door. I could feel Hernandez, one of the regular door men boring holes into the back of my head as I danced around the foyer, holding my phone in the air at different angles, hoping for some sort of miracle to occur as my phone still beeped out of service.

"Can I help you, Miss?" Hernandez's kind voice flowed across the foyer, attempting to save the day but no doubt knowing there wasn't much he could do.

"No signal, this damn phone." I smacked my palm to the screen, completely in vain as we both knew it wasn't going to help.

"Ahh, makes sense, the desk tried to call you earlier, but couldn't get through, you must have been off the grid all day." My senses peaked as I whipped round to face him. "Why were you trying to call me?" I hurried my words out, hungry for an explanation.

"Oh Mr Hutchinson, he came here to see you, but we couldn't get hold of you to let him in so we had to send him away." I felt relief first, then anger as I realised, he had been trying to get hold of me, and also that he now definitely knew that I wasn't with Tom any longer when I had wanted to explain myself.

"Urgh!" I threw my arms into the air in frustration as I headed to the exit,

"Sorry, Miss, should we not have sent him away?" Hernandez's kind face was peering over at me, full of concern.

"No, I mean, don't worry, I was just expecting a call from him you see," I waved my phone in the air.

"Ah, and you don't have signal so he came here to see you, and now he's probably worried." Hernandez eyes pinged as he realised my predicament.

"Mmm hmm," I offered back with an eye roll as I made my way out onto the pavement. The street was quiet, almost midnight with only a few cars passing quietly, the sparce streetlights barely glowing on the pavement in small underwhelming circles of light spread out close to the road. I held my phone out in front of me again as one bar pinged onto the screen before taking a few more steps to the left, alongside some old trash cans that were lined up to the entrance of the alley way leading down the side of my apartment block. Suddenly, two, then three bars pinged up as my signal reached full strength, I exhaled loudly, relieved as I saw six voicemails and ten text messages ping up on my screen, one each from Tom, the rest from Alex. My heart raced as I desperately scrolled down to his name, tapping the screen furiously to connect our call, as a rough hand suddenly clasped tightly over my mouth from behind. I felt pure fear flood though my veins like cold ice as my phone dropped onto the floor loudly, sliding off across the concrete onto the sidewalk as I was dragged violently from behind. My eyes desperately scanned the street for someone, anyone who may have seen me, but the street lay quiet, deserted, I was alone kicking and screaming as I disappeared into the dark alley way out of view. All my senses buzzed as survival mode kicked in, desperate to escape with my life as I fought with all my might, completely enthralled with adrenaline as my attacker slammed me furiously against the alley wall, slamming my head off the brick as my vison swirled blurrily. I felt the warmth run down the back of my neck as hot blood soaked my jumper and clung to my hair, familiar hands on my body as one grasped tightly around my neck, suffocating me of oxygen, the other covering my mouth preventing me from screaming. The dark clothed figure swayed in and out of my vision as my consciousness betrayed me, still tingling from the back of my head, as he held me against the wall, squashing my body with his as he pushed himself up against me, his erection obvious against my stomach as he pinned me tightly. He leaned in closely, the dark hood covering most of his face as he kissed my cheek gently before whispering my name into my ear.

"Emily." Suddenly, my body froze, refusing to move as my limbs disobeyed my brain, sinking to nothingness on the spot as I felt every ounce of oxygen leave my body. I gasped as the hand around my throat released slightly, allowing me a lifesaving gulp of oxygen which I drank in greedily, coughing as my conscience came back to me, the figure in front of me becoming clearer. He held me steady, still pinned against the wall as I found my feet, my breathing heavy and heart beating fast as I come to the realisation of what was happening to me, who was attacking me.

"You really think you can ruin me, really think that you are any better than me?" Jason's face was inches from mine as he spat the words murderously at me. "I'm going to take my hand off your mouth, if you scream, I'll kill you, do you understand?" I nodded furiously, tears now spilling down my cheeks as I gave in, admitting defeat and accepting the realisation that I would probably die here, he had almost succeeded before, when he supposedly loved me, what motivation did he have to keep me alive now. He locked eyes with mine before slowly taking his hand away from my mouth, his finger in a shushed position as he took as step back gently, watching my every move with fierce eyes and laboured breathing, He was enjoying this. I felt my subconscious skulk down the lowest point possible as I fully submitted to him, completely handing myself over to him as the old me came barrelling back full force, allowing him to dominate me entirely as everything I thought I had become, stronger, independent, a winner, fizzled out in its entirely.

"I'm sorry," I choked through the tears that were now turning into sobs, "I didn't mean."

"Shush!" Jason forced me back against the wall as I darted my eyes to my feet, desperately not wanting to have to look, to look into his eyes and have him know I was his again. "Now you've been a naughty girl, haven't you?" Jason tutted sarcastically as his hands wandered down my body before reaching my hips, he gripped me tightly before sliding my joggers slowly down an inch, my bare skin now touching his as he trailed a finger round the front of my waist band before slamming my hips violently into the wall behind him. He rested his chin on my shoulder as his warm breath spilled down my neck as he spoke, his hands still wandering over my body, completely and utterly frozen in fear as I realised, he wasn't going to kill me, just not yet, and in that moment, I prayed to God for him to end my life instead. "You know, you and I aren't so different, we could have been amazing together." I felt his hand palm against my stomach, his callouses rough and scratchy against my skin as he wandered up the front of my jumper, finding my breast and squeezing it hard. I tensed letting out a tiny yelp, as he thumbed my nipple and ground his erection into my stomach harder, more urgent as his breathing picked up pace, and his words got heavier. "You won't win you know, you will always be mine, always be my Emily, no matter who you are fucking," he spat the last word out like it was venom. "You think you know it all, think I'm the bad guy for following you here, I came here to protect you." He lowered his trousers down, releasing his erection as he took it in his hand, guiding my joggers down lower before they fell to my ankles, leaving me exposed and at his mercy. I felt the cold wall against my behind as I forced myself as hard as I could into it, desperate for every inch of distance I could scrape between us, the shiver and fear that cascaded down my spine as I froze solid having no effect on my outer appearance as I stood rooted to the spot, my breathing racing as my heart thumped dangerously. "You see I know things about you, things that you don't even know." He began kissing my neck softly as his hand moved slowly down my body, leaving my breast aching and sore from his grip. He slid his fingers down slowly over my belly button before tracing a line gently from one hip to the other, as he used his free hand to massage slowly up and down his length. I felt the bile rise in my throat as the tears stung my eyes, my body slowly trembling as the chill nipped at me and the adrenaline wavered.

"Please, don't," I offered as a quiet pathetic whisper, one final effort to not succumb to him, to not have him violate and own me again.

"Oh, you're getting it," he hissed in to my ear before sliding the head of his erection up and down my opening, stopping slightly as he gasped greedily into my ear. "And you'll enjoy it too," he spat his words painfully before grabbing my thigh and ragging it up to rest on his waist. I felt his heartbeat pounding against my chest as he kissed his way around my jaw, before sticking his tongue violently into my mouth, the crude taste of cigarettes tainting my mouth as he positioned himself at my opening, pushing slightly inside me as deepened his mouth on mine. I willed him, willed him to just kill me as uncontrollable sobs began to take over my body, I was his again, he had taken me, by force, and I had given in, weak scared, pathetic. I pushed my hips towards Jason, showing my submission, allowing him to enter me when out of nowhere, a familiar voice broke me from my onslaught as Jason froze suddenly against me.

"Emily." Hernandez's voice was like an angel calling me, saving me from this hell. I glanced urgently towards the sound of his voice, he was stood still on the sidewalk, holding my phone, looking up and down the street confused. I felt the panic as Jason dragged his trousers up furiously, his panicked eyes piercing into mine as he broke his touch from me, freeing my as he made off running down the alley, before disappearing out onto the next street. I breathed out deeply, relieved before dropping down the wall, my back grazing painfully as I did, but grateful for the pain, the pain that I deserved, the pain that was now being awarded to me for my weakness. I curled up into a ball as the emotions took over me, the uncontrollable wails that left my body, unrecognisable as my own as Hernandez came flying down the alleyway towards me.

Chapter 21

The air was cool, cooler than I'd like as the breeze whipped around my neck, tendrils of my hair flying upwards towards the black ink sky as I squeezed the wooden rail harder into my palms painfully. My heartbeat softly in my ears, my breathing matching each thrum gently as the eery dark water crashed loudly under the promenade, an unknown abyss under my feet, the long wooden planks, splintered at its joints keeping me from its depths. I breathed in deeply as I glanced out across the ocean, its current rough enough to carry me out, far out from my problems, away from the land and everything that confused me, everything that I didn't understand, a world that betrayed me and destined me to be alone. I released my grip slightly as I leant forward, a funnel of salty air pirouetting up against my chest, knocking the air completely from my lungs as I gasped for fresh air, my eyes wide in shock. My body felt free, my mind empty and at peace as I loosened my grip further, the darkness inviting me in, my favourite place so different at this time of night, yet still enamouring in its own special way, a way I felt only I understood. I took a deep breath and closed my eyes tightly as a cold rush flooded my body, my brain already anticipating the fall before I had even let go as a warm hand slid gently on top of mine, my senses springing back into life as my eyes opened suddenly, the bright sun stinging as I squinted away from its heat and glare. Confusion washed over me as the night seemingly turned into day in a moment, its chill and silence replaced with warm blue waves and people going about their day, sadness flipped onto this head, love, and life prevailing. I glanced down slowly to the gentle hand that was now gripping mine tightly as I subconsciously gripped it back, feeling the urgency behind the grasp as a tiny voice broke the air. "Mommy, please don't leave me, I need you." I locked eyes with the little girl, the dark-haired girl with eyes that mirrored mine, scared, shocked as the promenade swayed and creaked. I dropped down to my knees as I took her face in my palms, tears spilling out on to my cheeks as I breathed her name softly, my daughter's name.

"Ivy." I pulled her close, held her tightly against my chest as our bodies became one once again, the same as we were the last day I had seen her, the day I had lost her, lost myself as I took in every ounce of her presence. I breathed in her scent, her soft hair flowing down her back as I smoothed it with my palm, like a mother would as I beamed proudly, her grip tightening on me in return. We stayed, entwined in each other's arms for what felt like a mere moment, yet the world had moved on around us, the sun had moved on in its Luna cycle, setting again, plunging us into darkness, the cool breeze retuning as her grip on me tightened harder, forcing the air violently from my lungs as she squeezed.

"Ivy," I gasped as I used my palm to gently pry her away from me, a much-needed gulp of oxygen flooding my lungs as I leant back to look at her, wondering how such a small delicate girl had such a grasp on me. The eyes that met mine were not my girls, they were not kind, or loving like a mother and daughter should share, they were dark and angry, on the face of a monster, as the realisation that my daughter was gone, and I was now face to face with Jason hit me.

The sound of my own voice screaming her name scared me, like a feral animal in pain as I bolted upright, the room spinning as my head felt too heavy for my body. "Shhh, I'm here, I'm here," I watched in confusion as Alex bolted up like lightening from the foot of my hospital bed to my side in an instant. Dark circles blanketed his beautiful eyes, his shirt scruffy and untucked, clearly in need of some sleep. My eyes followed him as his warm hands framed my face, his forehead pressing gently too mine, a soft kiss soothing me as he whispered my name quietly against my skin. "Emily, oh my god I'm so glad you're OK."

His voice was desperate now, like he was trying to convince himself, and me. My brain swirled at what I was doing here, why I was laid up in a hospital bed feeling like I had fallen off of a building, the look on Alex's face scaring me more than my own thoughts as my achy limbs slowly began reminding me. He lowered me slowly back down, my head laying gently on the soft pillow as I winced in pain at the contact, my hand flying up to my head to protect it, my fingers bushing against rough stubbly hair on the side on my scalp. I watched Alex's scared eyes dart from mine to my head and back again as he opened his mouth to speak. "Emily, you, you had to have surgery." He sat aside me on the bed as he pulled me in gently under his arm, my brain not comprehending what he was saying.

"What do you mean surgery?" my words came out horse, scared as I shrugged my way out from under his arm to face him, my head still pounding as I moved too fast. Alex took a deep breath in and scrunched his eyes shut tightly as he began to speak.

"And a blood transfusion. You had a bleed, on the brain, you've been out for three weeks." I felt my heart race as I took in his words, his eyes glistening as they opened, tears brimming on the edges. Three weeks, I'd been out of it for three whole weeks. I felt the blood sink to my feet as my memories began slowly ebbing back, Jason's hands violating me as he helped himself to my body, the pain as he slammed my head against the wall, the fear as he took my innocence all over again. I stared blankly at Alex, as we shared a silent moment, the tears spilling onto my cheeks as I pulled the covers up to my neck in an instant, ashamed, embarrassed as Alex rushed to my side yet again, squeezing me tightly.

"No, don't you dare," Alex's words wavered, his emotions no longer hiding as I felt his warm tears fall onto my hand, "Don't you dare blame yourself." His voice was stern, angry, like these words had laid in his mind unspoken for some time and out loud, they stung. "This was not your fault; you have done nothing wrong." He squeezed me tighter as I began to sob. My skin crawled at the memory of that night, the fear I felt as he roamed my body, taking it for his gratification, dirty and tainted. How could Alex ever want to be near me again knowing what he had done, another man all over me. Alex's body was rigid and hard against mine, his breathing racing as he still held me tightly, a deep breath in as he held it before returning to its former state told me he was struggling to find the words to say.

"It's OK," I whispered gently, angling my head up painfully to look at his face, desperate to offer some form of calm. He closed his eyes and took a deep breath as he pulled me in tight again. "The doctors examined you," I felt him swallow before he carried on, "they couldn't be certain, but they didn't think that he'd…" His fists clenched undermine and his jaw hardened as he spat out the words like poison, "…raped you." I saw the pain and anger fizzle under his skin as he jumped up from the bed and paced towards the window, slamming his palms against the brick as he hung his head low between his shoulder blades.

"I'll kill him," he muttered through gritted teeth, his breathing loud enough to be heard across the room. I closed my eyes as I swatted though the memories, Hernandez's voice shrill though the dark alleyway as Jason prepared to violate me fully, the look on his face as he made off running still etched into my brain.

"He didn't," I spoke softly, gently as I remembered everything else, he had done to me, everything except for that, which was bad enough in itself, yet hopefully enough to sooth Alex to know he hadn't completely taken me.

I heard Alex's breathing stop as he stood upright, processing the information I had just given him, "He didn't?" Alex spun round to meet my eyes, his eyes still full of anger, but brimming with sorrow and relief at the same time. I felt my stomach clench at the realisation that this was hurting him just as much as it was hurting me, that this man felt everything I felt, and he still wanted revenge. I shuffled myself slightly upwards, Alex watching me intently as he cruised back over to the bed, helping me gently as I sat upright on the bed, his protectiveness flooding me as he eyed me intently.

"No," I gasped, grateful that he hadn't, grateful for Hernandez finding me right at that moment, yet still broken inside.

"He," I mimicked my hands over my body, the tears threatening to come again as the thought of his dirty calloused hands roaming my skin sickened me.

"OK, OK, you don't have to go through this all right now, you've just woken up." Alex propped himself on the bed next to me and pulled my head gently to his chest. He huffed loudly, clear relief on the surface, yet pure anger fizzled directly behind it. "I'll make this right I promise."

A solid knock on the door jolted us both from our sleep, I reached up to run my hands through Alex's hair, his head firmly snuggled into my chest as I sleepily came to, our legs entwined on the hospital bed as we shared a well needed nap. Before my hand reached his head, Alex was up and out of the bed, his foot blocking the door as he pressed his shoulder to it firmly. "Who's there?" he called out sternly, his hand grasping the handle firmly.

"Just me, tally ho!" Tom's shrill voice made me smile and I watched as Alex's body visibly relaxed, the air leaving his lungs as he pulled the door gently open.

"Hey, girl." He patted Alex gently on the cheek as he offered a cheeky wink, a small smirk in the corner of Alex's mouth followed by a subtle eye roll as he pressed the door closed quietly told me that he had clearly warmed to Tom as of late. Tom's lip pouted as he looked me up and down, "I mean, you've definitely looked better," he cocked his head playfully to the side as he placed the huge vase of flowers down onto the console table at the foot of my bed, the giant orange lilies a welcome pop of colour against the neutral white room. I beamed as Tom took a seat next to me before pulling me in tightly, "But I could not be happier to see you awake." The warmth of his skin and familiar smell soothed me from the inside as he rocked me gently. "How are you feeling?" Tom pulled me back gently before giving me the quick up and down with his eyes. "Besides the obvious," he planted a kiss on the top of my head as he snuggled me back in again.

"Overwhelmed, confused, scared." I saw Alex's face harden as I spoke the last word, wounded at my admission.

"But Alex's has been taking good care of me, I don't know what I would do without him." I desperately sought his gaze from across the room, he was sat in the white leather chair by the window, giving me and Tom some space as I spoke. He turned his head to face me before offering me a meek smile, his face anguished and sad.

"Ahem," Tom was eyeing me intently, "And the rest of us?", he faked an eye roll as he gestured over to the table. "And who exactly do you think had been bringing fresh flowers and keeping this one company as he pretty much refused to leave your side for more than thirty minutes." He glanced over at Alex who offered back a thankful smile. The door clicked open loudly as Ali and Molly came bounding through, disposable coffee cups bundled into their hands as the struggled to manage.

"And now tea!" Tom threw his hand up dramatically at the doorway as both girls beamed.

"Em!" Molly was beelining for me, as I grinned ear to ear, she pulled me into the tightest hug she had ever given me as I winced.

"Ow, Mol's," I giggled gently, "oh my god sorry, I just…"

She held me by the shoulders as she leant back wards to look at me, "I'm so glad you're OK." She smiled as she pulled me in again for a firm, but gentler hug.

Ali gleamed at me over her sister's shoulder, patiently waiting for her turn as Molly held on too long. "Come on, come on," she jibed at Molly before rolling her eyes at me, I smiled, the feeling of sense and belonging around these people hitting me like a truck as I realised, I was surrounded by family. Ali placed the cups down gently before moving in swiftly, offering up a huge hug as she rocked me back and forth.

"So good to see you, Em, you look well." Her eyes were sincere as she handed me the warm cup she had just placed down, smiling as she knew just how much I probably wanted it.

"You're the best." I closed my eyes as I took a huge sip of what must have been the best cup of tea I had ever tried in my life. I hummed loudly as I greedily gulped down more, "It's not tequila, honey." Tom laughed as I practically downed the lot, Alex shook his head smirking as he came over to retake his position at my side, snuggling me in firmly. Ali and Molly took a seat on one side of my bed whilst Tom helped himself and sat cross legged at my feet, his chin resting in his palms as he eyed me up the bed, silence filling the room. I watched as questionable glances crossed the bed, mainly directed at Alex, as he glared back.

"Umm what's going on guys?" I scrunched my nose up as I plonked my cup on the side table, wiping my mouth with the back of my hand as I read the room easily. I glanced around waiting for someone to speak.

"Well," Tom's voice broke the silence followed by an unapologetic interruption from Alex, "they still haven't found him." I felt his body go limp beside me as a disappointed sigh left his lungs. Tom glared his annoyance at Alex's interruption as I processed what he was saying to me.

"What, how haven't they found him?" I met confused eyes around the room as no one spoke. "For three weeks?" I shook my head as the realisation that Jason was still out there hit me. I swung my legs aggressively out from under the covers as my balance wavered, my upright position now threatening to floor me as I pushed myself up from the bed. Firm hands grasped my shoulders as Ali and Molly jumped up to stop me falling forward, Alex's hands guiding me backwards as I attempted to shrug out of his reach.

"We can't stay here, what if he comes for me again?" My voice sounded panicked, desperate as I glanced around the room for some support, for someone to agree with me.

"Em, this place is like a fortress," Tom waved his hand in the air gesturing around the room. I relaxed slightly as I turned to face him. "You literally need a passport to get floor to floor," he began absent-mindedly picking the skin on his finger, feigning a casual aura. "He isn't' getting in here," Tom swished his finger back and forward mid-air solidifying his point. I glanced towards Alex questioningly before he offered his point up.

"Emily, this is a private hospital, with world class security, I can assure you, you are safe here." He forced a smile as he waited for my response.

"So why the little display earlier before Tom came in, if it's that secure, why did you freak out so much when he knocked on the door?" I folded my arms across my chest in a win like demeanour, Tom was now wide mouthed with his hand dramatically palmed on his chest in a defensive stance, ready to begin his onslaught of how this was nothing to do with him.

"Relax," I gestured to Tom, eyes still locked on Alex. The silence between us fizzled as I waited for my reply, the tension in the room electric as I felt Ali and Molly look between each other.

"You had just woken up, I was on edge, emotional, I didn't know how you were going to be," Alex waved his hand around the room as he rolled his eyes, now looking around the room for support himself as everyone stayed silent.

"And, Ivy, my daughter, can you guarantee her safety?" I felt his skin burn as he whipped round glaring at me, his eyes boring into me as I cocked my head, still waiting for my answer.

"Right, that's it, I'm out, there is too much sexual tension or whatever this is for me guys." Tom jumped off the bed causally and held his hands up in defeat, Ali scoffed as she tried to hold her giggles in, Molly shook her head as she placed her hands over her face.

"She's fine," Alex's words pierced the air like a dagger as the whole room spun to face him.

"She's fine?" I repeated his words as a question, Alex just simply nodded.

"Your certain?" My hearth raced at the admission, the look on his face.

"A million percent." Alex shot back his words confidently as his chest puffed out, clearly trying to dominate the room. Molly and Ali shifted uncomfortably in their seat as they shared awkward glances, Tom was now at the door holding its handle, wanting to leave but not fully committed.

"So, you know where she is then?" My inquisitiveness was raring as I propped myself up onto my knees on the bed, practically pleading with Alex to spill all the information he had. "Where is she?" I was desperate now unashamedly grilling him as I grabbed him by the shoulders.

"Em, come on sit back down," Molly gently placed her hand on my shoulder from behind, desperate to alleviate the tension in the room.

"No, Molly I need her, I need to know that she's OK." I glanced over at Ali, her eyes brimming with tears as I glanced around the room, desperately wanting someone to speak.

"Tom?" I saw him exhale deeply before looking over to Alex, his eyes dark with anger, or fear, I wasn't sure which before he glanced back to me.

"Em, I love you, but this isn't a conversation you need to be having with me." He offered a sympathetic smile before leaving and closing the door softly behind him.

"Molly, Ali?" I crossed my attention to them, barely controlling my breathing as my heart raced. Molly smiled gently as she placed a soft hand on my face,

"Your daughter is fine, I promise you." She kissed me gently on my cheek as she tilted her head to the side, beckoning Ali to her side. Ali rubbed my back and just stared at me, her tears now running down her cheek as her and Molly excused herself leaving just me and Alex in the room. I grasped my hair in my hands on top of my head as I sank down onto the bed, staring into nothingness, my heart pounding through to my feet as a million questions thrummed in my mind. I felt Alex drop to the bed heavily next to me, his loud sigh admitting defeat.

"Em," I raised my head to look at him, to look him straight in the eyes as we spoke, not knowing what he was going to say next as my breath caught in my throat. Alex grasped my hand tightly as his words spun my world upside down.

"Emily, Ivy is my daughter."

Chapter 22

I stared at Alex, his face unreadable as I repeated the words he had just spoken in my head desperately trying to process them over and over as not one grain of it made sense.

"Ivy is your daughter?" I shook my head and huffed as I looked away from him, "What on earth are you on about, that's not even funny, Alex," I folded my arms across my chest as he angled his body to face me.

"Emily, please just listen to what I am saying to you." He grabbed both of my hands tightly in my lap, a slight tremble and clamminess obvious as he fidgeted around nervously. I looked up to meet his gaze, his eyes serious, full of emotion as the seriousness of what he was saying cut the surface slightly.

"I adopted her, she's my daughter." His voice wavered slightly as the words came out, his eyes begging me to believe him.

"I...I just don't understand, how, it's not possible." Alex sighed loudly, a small kind smile edging through as he stared deeply at me, with more affection, love, and endearment than I'd ever seen from him, it was flooding the room, his excitement and desperation obvious.

"I have no idea what the chances were of us ever crossing paths in our lifetime, but Emily, the day I found out that you were her mother, I just knew you were sent here for her, for the both of us." A small delicate tear fell from the corner of his eye as he gleamed at me, my brain absolutely not making sense of his words even though they were simple to understand. I had no words, nothing came out as I stared wide eyed at Alex, my heart beating too fast as my mind flitted from back then, to now, desperately trying to piece together the puzzle that had just been strewn so aggressively in front of me.

"I had no one, I didn't want to settle down, I just knew that I wanted to be a father." His voice was soft and gentle as he hung his head low, speaking through shaky words as I began to believe what he as saying. I reached across subconsciously, smoothing his back with my hand as he spoke, his body easing slightly at my touch, as I listened intently. He closed his eyes tightly as he squeezed my hand tighter, "Emily, I knew who you were way before the day I met you in the card shop, way before you began working with me."

My breathing froze as my brain registered his words, "What?" The words shot out of my mouth accusingly, trying to make way of the strange and impossible statement he had just made.

"Around a week before we met, Jason had mentioned that someone he knew from back home had moved to the area." My skin shuddered at the mention of his name.

"He happened to mention your name in passing and I immediately recognised it from the adoption." Everything in my body closed down, my heart in complete disbelief at what was being said as I nodded urgently, hungry for more information as my eyes filled with tears.

"I wasn't a hundred percent sure if it was you until I did the research, until I looked more into your history, came to see you at the card shop." I stared at Alex, taking in his every word as it slowly began to process. "Emily, the moment I saw you I knew it was you, you look just like her." He tilted his head to the side as he brushed a tender finger down my cheek, smiling proudly as he continued.

"I can't explain it, can't make sense of how we were brought together but there is no denying that it was meant to be, meant to meet, meant to be a family, I loved you from that very first moment." Hearing him say the words out loud, to my face floored me as the emotions I was holding in spilled over, tears flowing furiously as I brought his hands up to my face, nuzzling them lovingly.

"I love you too," I hushed back through my sobs.

"Please, don't cry, I know this is a lot to take in and I'm so sorry I kept it from you, I just could never find the right time, the hurt and sorrow I saw you go through was just too much when I had all the answers, I just didn't know if you were strong enough to understand," he perched a finger under my chin as he tilted it up to meet his gaze.

"Emily, you are worthy of being a parent, worthy of being in her life and I hope you will accept me too, as her father."

I shook my head in utter disbelief, complete turmoil fizzing through my mind as he spoke the words, my body desperately trying to absorb the words before they floated away.

"That sounds so strange," I giggled under my breath, "her father," I mimicked the words out loud, testing them again to see how they sounded on my lips.

Alex giggled with me. "Don't, she's going through a crazy stage at the moment, the whole father thing is difficult when you're playing good cop and bad cop." His eyes gleamed at the mention of his daughter, my daughter. I smiled genuinely as I began to compile the million questions I had in my head.

"So, tell me about the adoption," my soul painful as I remembered the saddest day of my life, his face proud as he remembered the best day of his. He sighed deeply before giving me the story.

"So, as I said, I wasn't ready to settle down, wanted to be a dad, and knew there were children that needed adopting." He pulled me back to lay on the bed, my head resting on his chest as continued, "Erica, my adoption councillor was in charge of finding me suitable matches—" I interrupted him rudely as I shot my head up to look at him, forgetting I had recently had surgery as I winced slightly.

"Erica, Erica?" I huffed loudly as a large piece of the puzzle slotted perfectly in place.

"Of course, she had mentioned the day I went to see her that her adoptive family were super protective, that an anonymous tip off would be enough for security to be ramped up," I giggled as I laid my head back down, a small mmm hmmm was all Alex offered with a beaming smile.

"And we did ramp up security, for Ivy, I just wish we had done the same for you," a slight hint of guilt stained his tone as he squeezed my shoulder reassuringly.

"If it wasn't for my meddling mother, you would never have found the place," his mind was clearly wandering now as the admission caught me of guard.

"Wait, what, your mother?" My head was back up, giving him the questioning look I had thrown at him more than once in the last few ten minutes.

He huffed loudly, "Yes, my mother," before giggling. "The day she met you, you know the day when you were having a huge go at me in my office and didn't realise, she was sitting there?" he cocked his head sarcastically to the side as he eyed me naughtily, the memory making me cringe slightly as I nodded, smirking as I laid my head back down. "Well, I had the grilling of my life after you left, she knew instantly as well who you were." I smiled at the thought. "Imagine me

156

trying to explain it all to her, the coincidence of us meeting when you were Ivy's mother, she hardly believed it herself if it wasn't for the same fiery attitude and bossy demeanour that she saw with her own eyes that day, exactly the same as her granddaughters." I smirked against his top as the memory hit me. "So, yes, I matched with Ivy, and adopted her and she came to live with me here." I felt his shoulders shrug underneath me as he told the story in a matter-of-fact way. "Of course, I had guilt, I had heard through the grapevine that the birth mother," I felt him shift uncomfortably beside me, "I mean, well you, had taken it pretty badly, that you were having second thoughts, but the paperwork had been done." I winced painfully at the memory, the day I placed my daughter with another family. "I sympathised, of course I did, all I knew was your name and that your reasoning for the adoption was because you had no family to help and didn't feel you could provide for her." I thought back to the conversations we had already had about this, my confessions to Alex and how he already knew, yet still listened every time, with tenderness and sympathy. "That's why I got you the snow globe, to remember her by," his words came out quietly, like he knew a nerve was about to be hit as he and I both remembered the day Jason smashed it. "You probably didn't realise it at the time, but that day completely broke my heart too, knowing the significance behind it but having to act like it was nothing." I felt my heart flutter at his tenderness, that my most prized possession was also meaningful to him as well, in a way I hadn't even realised.

"It took me a while to figure out Jason was bad news, but once I did, and once you told me you felt Ivy was in danger, that's when I acted, he was out, I just wish we had more evidence to hold him, but it was all based on the information you were drip feeding me."

I kicked myself mentally for my stupidity, "I'm sorry, if I had of known, I'd have told you the whole lot from the start."

Alex forced a laugh. "No, you wouldn't have, your stubborn and mysterious, just like your daughter," the reference made my heart beam, that we had similarities. "Although in a way I'm glad you didn't, you were cautious and clever, I admire that you wanted to keep her safe that your motherly instincts were there to protect her." Goose bumps spread across my body at his comment, like giving candy to a child, I craved more. I crushed my eyes closed tightly as I gripped Alex harder, I should have felt anger, confusion, and bitterness, yet everything was slotting so seemingly into place, making sense totally in my head, the turmoil and stress I had been secretly enduring over the last few months ebbing away quietly.

"So did Jason know that you are her father?" the thought suddenly haunted me at just how close he had been to my daughter.

Alex hesitated for a moment. "No, at least we don't think so." I felt him fidget awkwardly as he cleared his throat. "I kept my private life private, nothing about my home life gets brought into work, and ummm," he hesitated before falling silent.

"Oh, what now, I can't take much more." I sighed loudly, almost in a joke like way, thinking there can't be anything more that shocked me.

"Umm, well, her name is now Scarlett, her middle name is Ivy."

I held my breath subconsciously as I took in what he was saying, "Scarlet Ivy Hutchinson," I spoke the words robotically as I smiled. "That's got a ring to it," I giggled as I felt Alex relax.

"You're not mad?"

"No, I mean, it wasn't something that I had considered that her name could be different, but either way it was a good thing, Jason wasn't able to make the connection," I shivered again at the thought of just how close he has been.

"Exactly, we figured he hadn't made the connection and our digging seemed to just find that his threats to you were empty, he hadn't attempted or tried to find her or researched about her, it was you he followed here, not her." My stomach churned at just how ludicrous this entire situation had turned out, how out of all of the billions of people in the world, the three of us had found each other, through stormy waters, but here we were.

"It's just unbelievable," I hushed my words as they still didn't process fully.

"What about Jason, what else do we know?" my mind clicked into business mode, remembering my motive, his assault still visible, physically, and mentally.

"That prick, is going down, you mark my words," Alex answered immediately, his tone aggressive as he spoke his name. "I just don't understand his obsession with you," Alex quickly kissed the top of my head and offered a sympathetic hand squeeze. "Not that you are not absolutely perfect of course," he quickly offered up, trying to back track his words that I hadn't taken offence to anyway. "I mean, to follow you all the way here, then dupe me into getting you a job here just so he could be around you more." This time it was Alex who shivered, his body stiffening as the anger coursed, "I bet he had no idea of his stupidity, that he was actually leading you straight to me and Ivy, umm Scarlet."

I giggled at his error, "We are going to have to get used to that, aren't we?"

"I guess so," he offered back smiling. "So, my guessing is that the reason he lost the plot, and did what he did to you," he looked me up and down, his jaw rigid, "was because he didn't like the fact that we are together, it's the only thing I can think of," Alex shrugged his shoulders, "unless there is anything else." I could see the look in his eyes like he couldn't take much more, yet he knew that this was the time it would all come out if there was.

"No, honestly, you are the only person on the planet who knows absolutely everything about me, the whole lot." I watched his shoulders drop as he breathed a sigh of relive, as did I that for once and for all, every single secret was completely out.

"What about Chloe?" I moved myself into a sitting position on the bed, grabbing the glass of water at the side of the bed and took as sip as I waited for Alex to offer up any new information.

"Nothing," he shrugged his shoulders as he shook his head.

"Nothing?" I questioned confused, confused as to how there could be no more information on the death of the women Jason was having an affair with, followed by our swift departure out of state the very next day.

I saw Alex wince as he tried to find the right words to say, "So, umm, there wasn't much left of the house, or err, Chloe," his eyes stayed locked on mine as he gauged my reaction, I nodded urging him to continue. "The fire department weren't able to pinpoint a definitive point of ignition for the fire, just that they suspect accelerant was used."

"Fuel?" I remembered the smell distinctively on the night, its odour still lingering the next day. "Possibly, although she had a smell lean to building on the side of her house where she stored all of garden tools, fuel etc, so it can't be said if it wasn't just from that." He shook his head as he pondered over the information.

"OK, and I saw that her cause of death was unknown?" I pouted my lip in wonder as Alex explained.

"Yes, so Detective Green tells me that the remains that were left, was enough to blood test to identify and pick up on her pregnancy, but not enough for them to determine the cause of death." I shook my head in utter disbelief. "So as far as the paperwork goes, no cause of fire, no cause of death and it was all logged as accidental, case closed, nothing more ever came of it."

"And the police didn't think to pursue the father, Jason and ask some questions?" I was getting frustrated now, at the negligence of the entire situation and at how it wasn't glaringly obvious to the police.

"They didn't know who the dad was, it seems they were super secretive about their affair, no phone records, nothing linking her to anyone, a lot of their, um antics are suspected to be in person." I huffed loudly at the memory of Jason picking up his fitness regime, jogging at all hours for long periods of time and the proximity of her house to ours.

"Yeah, that sounds about right," I offered up sarcastically, a hint of annoyance.

"What about us moving, out of state the very next day, did that not look suspicious?" I felt confident of a valid point as he squashed my theory down yet again.

"Not really, people move all the time, with the fire and death not being looked into as suspicious, there was no one to look for, and from what I can gather, you and he didn't really have any friends or family who would have noticed your up and leaving." His words stung slightly as I realised just how much this man knew about me, my past and my present, as well as the memory of having no one, feeling suddenly grateful for my life here now.

"I guess so," I mumbled my words not convinced.

"You disagree?" Alex questioned me lightly, wanting my side of the story.

"No, no, well I mean it all makes sense what you are saying, but I just know, know in my heart that the fire and her death was not an accident, that Jason was involved somehow, I just can't work out how to prove it." I felt irked at the realisation that Jason was going to be harder to nail that I first thought.

"I promise you; he will go down; he doesn't have a leg to stand on now with the state he put you in."

I watched the fog mist over his eyes as he planned his revenge, "And as much as I would love to get my hands on him, we have to do this the right way," He nodded forcibly, like he was trying to convince no only me, but himself too.

"Which is?" I queried; hands palm up waiting for his solution.

"Leave Detective Green to do the digging, trust me, I'm paying him enough to find something, anything to pin him to Chloe's death, and once we find him, which they will, my solicitors will make sure he goes down for a long, long time for what he did to you as well," a glint in his eye and a smirk told me this was the sweetest form of revenge.

"OK," I shot back firmly, the look on his face was as confused as I had been at the start of our conversation, yet I couldn't understand why.

"Did you just agree to something and not argue?" Alex gasped sarcastically as he placed his palm to his chest, pretending to be shocked.

"Oh, stop it," I giggled as I jabbed him in the ribs lightly relieved that our heavy conversation was coming to an end, even though I still had lots to ponder over, and I would probably still come up with a million more questions.

"Well just as well you are in an agreeable mood, because you are moving in with me." Alex swiped the cup of water from my hand before downing it playfully and plonking it on the side table, the look of shock obvious on my face as he raised a finger to my lips. "Hush, it's happening." He nodded at me repeatedly, slowly encouraging me to nod along with him, I shook my head once as his eyes widened and my head subconsciously turned into a nod, agreeing with him involuntarily.

"I can't keep an eye on you while you are at your place, plus you need like, you know help with things." He gestured up and down like I was some sort of child incapable of taking care of myself, the offence clear on my face as a light knock on the door broke our pretend glares from each other. "Miss Moore, sorry to disturb you, the doctors will be in shortly to check you over, and all being well they will issue your discharge paper work so you can go home in the morning if you want to start popping your things together." She smiled sweetly as I nodded and smiled back, the door clicking closed softly behind her.

Alex threw himself back on my bed, resting his arms behind his head, his smile a mile wide. "Plus, I'm pretty sure there is someone there who wants to meet you."

Chapter 23

"So yes, umm if you want to put your things in here," Alex gestured towards the huge walk-in wardrobe, his face awash with nerves as he fumbled with his hair. He had been so sweet in the last 24 hours, refusing to leave my side in the hospital even though he had been the one to assure me that the place was more than secure. We had laid together on the bed until the early hours, absolutely exhausted but with far too much to talk about, too many questions that needed answering as we discussed everything new that we had learned. I was still in complete disbelief that this whole time, my daughter had been right under my nose, bewildered that Alex was able to keep it a secret, and that of all the people and all the places in the world, we should wind up together, we both believed that someone, somewhere was looking out for us and we were meant to be together, there was no other explanation for it. I was hesitant to move in with Alex, not only had I only known him a few months but our relationship had gone from zero to a hundred at the speed of light, with nothing but turmoil, secrets, and drama the entire way. I desperately tried to tell myself that this was going to be a new beginning, a fresh start, everything laid out on the table with nothing to hide, but a sickly feeling in my stomach told me otherwise and I just couldn't put my finger on it. I shoved my thoughts aside and gasped as I glanced through the doorway, the entire left-hand side was rammed full of high-end clothes and shoes, rows upon rows of crisp suit and shirts, more clothes than anyone could ever need in a lifetime. The right-hand side of the room was cold and empty, far too much space for my mere suitcase that I had brought with me, enough clothes and toiletries for maybe a week. I smiled meekly as I placed my case onto the floor and began unzipping it, before I knew it, Alex was at my side, gripping my elbow lightly as he guided my hand into his. "No, you don't need to do that, I'll have it sorted later for you, you need to rest." I stood slowly as I looked at Alex questioningly. "But you just said," I gestured towards the room, referencing the fact that he had just told me to put my things in here.

"I know, I um, didn't think, just leave your bag there, it's not urgent." He forced a smile as I could read his nerves all over, his apprehension and uncomfortableness obvious as my spirits sunk.

"Are you sure this is the right thing to do, me moving in here?" I folded my arms across my chest, popping my wall up slightly at the expectation of being rejected.

"Yes," Alex shot his words back before I could even finish my sentence, "I want you here" – he paused as he gathered his thoughts – "we both do." I felt my stomach flip at the realisation of meeting Ivy soon, something we had spent most of our time going over last night, discussing the best way to approach the situation. Alex had told me that Ivy already knew all about me, that she had known from the moment she could understand words that she had a mommy out there, that Alex was her father, but she also had another one, and that Mommy's name was Emily. My heart had swelled at the fact she had actually known about me all this time and I prayed she didn't hate me for placing her for adoption, something I was sure I would have to explain to her in time. I was shocked to find out that she had also known that I was around, that Alex had explained to her that he had met me, and that she had been begging every day since to meet me. He had been fending off her demands ever since, but was waiting for the right time to tell me. My mind was completely blown at all the things that had been going on that I had absolutely no idea of, not a clue that my daughter even knew I existed, never mind the fact that she actually wanted to see me and knew who I was. My emotions caught in my throat as the nerves I was holding deep inside bubbled to the surface, I had waited so long for this, yet I still wasn't sure if it was the right thing to do.

"Are you OK?" Alex read my face like a book, I smiled meekly as I sighed.

"Yes, it's just, a lot, you know," I was being truthful, yet I couldn't help but feel my statement was completely played down as opposed to what I was actually feeling right now.

"She's going to love you, don't panic," Alex placed a soft kiss against the top of my head as he pulled me in close, "Don't overthink it, OK?" he rocked me gently as I desperately tried to shake the feeling of uncertainty away.

"Why don't you go and have a nice hot bath, and I'll get us some lunch ready, then we can relax for an hour before she gets home from school?" he spoke the words so casually, like it was an everyday thing for him, which in fact it was, yet for me it was completely foreign, new and didn't seem real hearing it out loud. I nodded against his chest, a bath and freshen up would no doubt make me feel better, plus some time on my own, where I could gather my thoughts is just what I needed right now.

I smoothed my hair back in the mirror, the stubbly roots poking my hand, the scar ran from my ear, all the way to the back of my head. I traced my finger over the rough scar, now healed over, but still angry and red. Fortunately you couldn't tell when I had my hair down, but the emotional scars were hurting way more than the physical. I shook my freshly blow-dried hair into place and tucked it neatly behind my ear. I had lost weight in the time I had been in hospital, and I could still see the slight shadow under my eyes, my jaw line more obvious than it had been before as I had spent longer than I would on my makeup, trying to make myself look more human, more me. I heard the door open softy behind me as Alex stepped quietly into the bathroom, his face full of sorrow as he looked at my reflection. I stood silent as I followed his gaze before he pulled me in gently, hugging me from behind as we looked at ourselves in the mirror.

"You really are beautiful you know," Alex kissed the top of my head tenderly as he spoke, him towering over me with his large frame. He slid his hands slowly down my arms and over the tops of my hands, entwining his fingers with mine as he placed his hands into gentle fists, encasing my small hands with his entirely.

"I'm nervous," I whispered gently as he moved our hands to under my bust, squeezing me gently as he leant down to prop his chin on my shoulder.

"I know, you will be, but I just know she will love you," Alex's words were genuine, yet I still couldn't take them in, A bitter trait that had cursed me all my life, never being able to take a compliment, always seeing myself in a negative light.

"I hope so," I muttered nervously, "I'm just worried she will think I abandoned her, that I didn't love her," I felt my eyes swell with tears at the thought of my little girl, troubled with negative thoughts, not feeling enough.

Alex sighed deeply beside me, "Emily, she has never had those thoughts, adoption is something that is taken seriously, and my family has always made sure that your name was only ever mentioned in a positive light, that the whole situation was explained delicately to her, she's five years old, she only knows love." He smiled at me as he nuzzled me gently, easing my thoughts instantly.

"Please just put on a brave face for her, the rest will come naturally." I nodded gently, placing my warrior mask firmly in place as I prepared myself mentally.

"Alex!" I jumped lightly as I heard a woman's voice call his name from the hallway, a voice I recognised but couldn't quite place.

"She's here." Alex's face beamed as he took my hand and gently pulled me towards the living area. My nerves bounced violently in my tummy as we moved towards the hallway, the faint sound of a child giggling tugging at my heart strings as I realised, I was about to meet her. Alex held my hand tightly as we rounded the corner, the beautiful dark-haired girl pirouetting around Alex's mom as she giggled loudly coming into to full view as my breath caught suddenly in my throat and everything, I thought I knew about love smashed to pieces as I saw my daughter for the first time in five years. My skin prickled as took in every fibre of her, her aura, her beauty, her chiming giggle, my baby girl. My mind exploded as I desperately tried to absorb every second, in utter shock at the fact my daughter was standing so close to me after what felt like a lifetime.

"Daddy!" her shrill wail reverberated off of every surface as she spotted Alex.

Her little words like music to my ears as she made a beeline straight for him, "Hello, my munchkin, how was school?" he caught her mid-air as she flew into him, scooping her up with ease as she wrapped her arms around him, Alex planting sloppy kisses noisily on her cheek as she laughed uncontrollably. My insides twisted as I felt a new love for Alex right in that very moment, a feeling I had never felt before but that was overpowering and dominant as I watched him become a father, a role I had never seen him in before, with his daughter, my daughter, our daughter. Suddenly I felt the rooms atmosphere drop as silence sliced through it, the giggling quietening as I noticed her gaze on me, eyeing me intently over her father's shoulder as my heart raced.

"Hi," my voice came out as a whisper I wasn't sure she heard as she skulked down into Alex's chest, leaving only her big brown eyes peeking over his shoulder as she continued to stare. I glanced over to Alex's Mom nervously as she shot me a reassuring smile and a nod, enough to encourage me to breathe again, her admiration and love clear for all to see as she watched on. I looked back at Ivy as she wriggled gently in Alex's arms, her signalling him to get down as he placed her steady on her feet, her eyes never leaving mine. I smiled sweetly at her, offering anything that might ease her, make her realise that I was OK. She wrapped her arm around Alex's leg as she peeked around them nervously, I wondered what was going through her mind, what she was thinking, how she was feeling as I kneeled gently, our eye line now level as she took a tentative step out from his legs towards me. I could feel the buzz in the room, Alex and his mom both witnessing our first interaction, desperately watching her reaction as she laid eyes on me for the first time since the day she was born.

"I'm Emily," I whispered gently as she looked up to Alex for reassurance, he met her gaze with a nod before a light hand on her back eased her forwards towards me. My heart was beating so fast I was sure the entire room could hear it as she took a little step towards me, her hand outstretched. I flinched slightly as she placed it lightly on my cheek, her skin cool, soft as I closed my eyes and turned into her touch, my eyes brimming with tears. I stared into her dark brown eyes, exactly the same as I remembered, just as beautiful, as she moved her hand gently to my jaw. I didn't dare breathe or move as she eyed my face intently, taking in every detail as a small smile formed on the corner of her mouth. She turned slowly to look at Alex before her tiny little voice chimed sweetly in the air like music to my ears as she pointed at my face then back to hers, "Same," she gestured between us both at her dad, seeing the similarities between us with her own eyes as a single tear dropped on my cheek.

A small sob escaped my throat as she looked back at me slowly. "Mommy?" Her words floored me, like no emotion I had ever felt before, like everything I had felt up until this moment was in black and white as she flung her arms around my neck and squeezed tightly.

"My baby girl," was all I could manage as uncontrollable sobs took over my body as I held her back, my damaged and broken heart repaired as I held her close to me, becoming one again in that very moment.

"But, Daddy, I want Mommy to read my bedtime story," the sound of my name on her lips was still enlightening for me and I wasn't sure if it was something I could ever get used to. I saw Alex's face light up at the picture before him, Ivy, or Scarlett as I was trying to get used to, hanging off my legs, her needy eyes glaring up at me as she protested.

"Scarlett," Alex cleared his throat as he carried on, "Mommy," he eyed me slightly, the glee on his face obvious as he emphasised the word, "has got to rest, she's very tired."

I saw the pouty lip as the wail come immediately after, "No, no, no," her feet stomped cheekily on the floor to no avail, her fluffy slippers against the hard marble floors were no match for her.

"I don't mind honestly, I'm fine," I chimed sweetly as I looked down at Scarlett, her glinting eyes beaming up at me as her clever little brain worked her magic.

Alex looked at me, his face cocked to the side as I realised my error, "Oh, I mean, what did your daddy say first?" I kicked myself mentally, not intentionally undermining Alex but struggling to learn the word no when I had missed out on so many yeses. Alex glanced from Scarlett who was now hiding behind my legs and glaring up at her dad, I smiled at the change of roles in just a couple of days, how she had taken to me like I had always been here, me very much the same, that motherly instinct booming straight to the forefront the moment I saw her, it was completely natural.

"Why don't we both read it to you?" Alex offered up, much to Scarlett's delight as she shrieked loudly before running to her room, bouncing with every step. Alex grabbed my hand and giggled as he pulled me down the hallway after her.

"Told you she was a handful," he joked lightly as he giggled.

"She's perfect, Alex," I choked on my words as I thanked my lucky stars that it was him, she was placed with, that he was able to give her a life I never could, the happiness and love obvious in everything she did.

"Like her mommy." Alex swung my arm playfully as he winked at me, I shook my head sarcastically.

"No seriously, I don't think I can ever thank you enough for what you have done, you've given her a life I couldn't, and that's all I wanted for her," Alex hushed me gently as we reached her room, playing down the whole situation like he hadn't done one of the most amazing things in the world. Scarlett was tucked up in bed by the time we reached her room, her little lamp glowing cosily next to her bed, her book firmly in hand ready to get going. He little eyes lit up as she saw us both together, her gaze flitting from Alex to me and then back again like she was seeing something comical for the first time.

She patted the bed lightly with her palm as she looked at me needily, "Mommy," I closed my eyes and sighed peacefully, thankful for every time she said my name. I eased my way beside her gently as she pulled the blankets up and covered me gently with them, her head laid softly on my chest as she grabbed my hand and placed it on top of her head.

Confusion washed over me as she wiggled her head under my palm. "Tickles." She bossed me cheekily as I realised what she wanted, my fingers tracing through her silky dark hair as I tickled her scalp. Alex smiled as he got himself comfy at the bottom of the bed, his head resting on his elbow as he watched us both together, his eyes full to the brim with love as he took us in. It seemed unbelievable to be sharing this moment now, after everything we had been through, I just couldn't believe things could be so perfect.

"So, what do we have here?"

Scarlett handed me a book she had chosen, a big yellow duck plastered in the middle of the page, "Duckling goes for a swim," I began as I read the title, I felt her bounce with glee as I spoke, only warming my heart further. Alex reached up and placed his hand on my calf, his tender fingers tracing up and down affectionately as I continued with the book, not speaking a word yet his face telling me everything I needed to know, he loved me. Scarlett's breathing got deeper, and her bouncing at my every word subsided as I reached the end of the book, her sleepy soft snores blowing gently on my chest as I closed the book and placed it quietly on the side. I kissed her gently on the head as I gave her a light squeeze, feeling like I could stay there forever.

"You've done amazing you know," Alex was whispering gently so as to not wake Scarlett, I smiled back proudly, feeling completely overwhelmed with the weekend we had all spent together. We had spent every minute at Alex's place together, we had baked cakes, watched movies, and danced silly to loud music, everything a normal family would do on a weekend. I was gutted that it was Monday tomorrow, Scarlett would be back to school and Alex would be back to work and I felt sure the place would feel empty without them.

"I wish we could stay like this forever," I pulled Scarlet gently in my side, her eyelashes fluttering gently as she slept.

"I know, and I'm sure she wishes that too, but unfortunately, this little lady," he stroked her back lightly, his face full of love as he watched her, "has got a spelling test this week, so needs to go to school and learn lots of amazing things," his voice was flooded with so much pride as he spoke, as was my heart.

"Anyway, I totally forgot to mention." My attention turned to him fully as his tone changed, his voice still low and hushed. "My parent's wedding anniversary is this weekend." I giggled as I remembered him buying the anniversary card on the first day we met.

My mind cast back to the day we first met, "The card, you bought it that day?"

He smiled cheekily. "Yep, I needed an excuse to come in and speak to you, and technically I did need the card, just not until a few months later."

I giggled back at him and rolled my eyes.

"Anyway, my parents want you to come to the party." Alex smiled cheekily as he awaited my reaction.

My shock must have been obvious on my face as quickly continued, "What?" he looked at me confused as I screwed my face up. "Why would they want me to go?" genuinely confused.

Alex giggled lightly, "Emily, you are family, Scarlett's mother, of course they want you there, plus you've got a huge family to meet, and where better to start than there?" I breathed in deeply at the realisation that a family I never had growing up, the aunts and uncles, grandparents and cousins had now been given to me all in one go.

"Oh my god I never even thought of that," I gushed a bit too loudly as Scarlett fidgeted in her sleep. Alex smiled at my reaction, the excitement on his face clear at the thought of me meeting everyone.

"You won't be able to keep up, I've got a huge family, two sisters, a brother, plus you've not met my dad yet," a slight eb of guilt hit me as I realised, I never knew he had siblings.

"Sisters, a brother…I…I didn't know that."

Alex eyed me intently. "Hey, you wouldn't have known, we weren't exactly honest and upfront from the word go, were we?" the words were true, things seemed so different back then, a far cry from us laying here now, our daughter asleep between us as we casually spoke about attending a family event.

My heart soared, excitement cursing though me, "I can't wait," I beamed back genuinely, looking forward to meeting everyone, to spend another day with Scarlett. "Plus, I mentioned it to Tom when we were at the hospital last week, and he made me promise him an invite, well a plus three actually as he insisted on Ali and Molly coming too," he rolled his eyes as he spoke, yet the smile he was donning told me he didn't actually mind.

"Oh really!" I radiated happiness at the thought of my best friends being there, they had been amazing to me over the last few weeks and spending time with them was just what I needed right now.

"Yeah, there will be so many people there, what's a couple more?" I smiled sweetly as I just stared, no words to say as he reached over and stroked the side of my face tenderly.

"I love you, Emily," Alex looked at me with so much love and adoration that I couldn't deny it, no matter how much I tried to put myself down, or convince myself I wasn't worthy, I felt his words deep in my heart as I learned to anchor them in, to hold on to them tightly, a worthy owner.

"I love you too, Alex," I chimed back, feeling on top of the world.

Chapter 24

"Hello, my darling, Eric, nice to finally meet you," the friendly gentleman who I now knew to be Alex's father, shook my hand before slipping an extremely chivalrous kiss upon my knuckles.

"Isla and I are so grateful you could be here." I smiled sweetly, his salt and pepper hair blowing slightly in the breeze as he sat in his black expensive looking wheelchair. I could tell he was once a very handsome man, similar features to Alex's peeking through his porcelain skin and fine lines, only age diminishing his looks slightly.

"Thank you for having me, well us," I gestured back awkwardly towards Ali, Molly and Tom who stood silently behind me, Ali rudely trying to look over my head at the party desperate to get the formalities over and done with.

"Of course." He smiled charmingly, "I'll let you get on, enjoy yourselves."

I thanked him again before making my way over to the huge marquee that dominated their garden. It was a beautiful warm day and the blue sky cascaded over the entire area as guests enjoyed their drinks. A huge patio area that ran the full length of their giant swimming pool connected the house to the marquee with benches and flowered ornaments lining the entire area as guests mingled, the light sound of classical music thrumming through the warm air.

"You ready," I buzzed excitedly at my three best friends, not a penny spared when it came to our outfits as Tom had insisted on treating us all to new dresses.

"Let's go get 'em," Ali beamed as she made her entrance, gliding down the patio steps, the iron railing guiding her as she sashayed elegantly to the level of the guests, all eyes on her as she lapped up every second. The rest of us rolled our eyes in unison as we watched her performance, Tom offering up a wolf whistle followed by a howl as she flipped her hair.

I jabbed Tom lightly in the ribs, "Ouch," he quipped, "what was that for," he giggled loudly.

"I'm trying to make a good impression, this is my new family, I want them to like me, I don't want them to think we are calling a heard of animals." I smiled sarcastically as he pursed his lips tightly.

"Oops, sorry," he offered up laughing as we joined Ali at the bottom of the stairs. "Molly!" I heard her voice clear as day as Scarlett's head came bobbing through the crowd, her dark silky curls flowing behind her as she ran, her pink dress swirling around her legs.

"Hey there, you, well don't you just look beautiful," Molly scooped Scarlett up with ease as she clapped eyes on me.

"Mommy," she cooed gently, protesting against Molly as she held her arms out to me instead.

"Alright, alright fuss pot." Molly laughed as she handed her over to me.

"Mommy, they have donuts," she rushed her words quickly, out of breath as she excitedly gleamed.

"Hmm, I can tell," I giggled as I brushed a dot of icing from the end of her nose, "and how many have you had exactly?" I planted a kiss on her cheek as she squeezed my neck tightly.

"Far too many," a sweet voice chimed from behind me as Isla waltzed up looking absolutely stunning in her teal gown.

"Wow, Isla, you look absolutely beautiful," she hugged me lightly before tickling Scarlett lightly on the ribs, her squirming in my arms.

"And what did I tell you about running off young lady." She smiled cheekily at Scarlett before she stretched her arms out for her.

"Sorry, Grandma," she cooed, melting Isla's scolding in an instant. Isla scooped her over, her dangly earrings now the focus of Scarlett's attention as she tapped them playfully making them swing.

I cleared my throat as I remembered my manners, "Isla, umm sorry, these are my friends, Molly, Ali and Tom," I gestured towards them all before returning the welcome, "this is Isla, Alex's mother."

"Oh, darling, no need for the formalities, it is however lovely to meet you all, now please, make the most of the open bar and anything you need, don't hesitate to ask," I giggled as all three said thank you at exactly the same time, making the moment even more comical and awkward as it felt. Isla nodded her head politely before heading off across the patio.

"Wow this is amazing," Tom swished his hand in the air for dramatic effect. I laughed as I reprimanded him yet again.

"As if you talked Alex in to a free invite." I shook my head as looked at him.

"Listen." Tom had a single finger up as he turned to face me, I cocked my head to the side as I awaited his witty reply, "OK, OK, I have nothing, I just wanted to go to a party you know," he pouted his lip gently as we all laughed.

"Yeah, yeah, go on, enjoy yourself," I ushered him down away and he linked arms with Ali and headed off leaving me and Molly alone. I couldn't have been more grateful for my friends right now, we had spent pretty much the entire week together as Alex returned to work, them both taking emergency leave from their jobs to support me with Tom begging the boss for the same, with not much hesitation from Alex as he signed him off for the week. Them all meeting Scarlett for the first time had melted my heart as we all met in an ice cream parlour after school, Scarlett taking an instant shine to Molly as her natural motherliness oozed. I beamed with pride as I sat back and watch my friends play with Scarlett, loving her like their own and accepting her fully, knowing they would protect her fiercely if needed. The next day we had spent the afternoon at the beach, the school runs becoming a way of life for me as I proudly collected her from the school gates, swimming costume and towel ready in my bag as we met the others at the beach after. The emotions I felt as I sat there, watching Tom splash in the waves with her, giggling away together like they had known each other their whole life, something I never thought I would get to see as I watched on, a proud mother. Our evenings were spent at home, doing all the homely family things that we should be, Alex returning home after a busy day, the excitement of his arrival home never wearing thin as Scarlett squealed every time he walked through the door. Our relationship had become something different as the week went on, more natural, relaxed as the pressures of having secrets had evaporated, with nothing left to hide, it was like breath of fresh air and as our friendship blossomed, our romance boomed, our lust for each other feral. I was grateful when he took the day off work Thursday, allowing us to all go shopping and buy our outfits for the weekend, a feat which took all day, mainly because of Tom's indecisiveness, but also as Ali felt the need to visit every shop twice. We were stunned when Tom offered to pay for the day, all of us protesting, but eventually accepting when we realised that this was, in fact, still left-over money from Alex's generous cheque. We had teased him fervently when we pointed it out, him acting all coy and pleading his generosity would have been the same had he have not been rolling in the cash now. The laughter and time together was exactly what we needed after the last few weeks and we made sure to keep the topic of conversation away from all the drama and pain and instead chose to focus on the future, moving forward and this weekend which we were all super excited for. Spa day was Friday, with us all getting pampered and preened to perfection, massages all around as we spent the day relaxing and gossiping, the pain of my surgery and everything that had happened slowly ebbing away into nothingness as I kept my mind busy. Spa day ended up in a sleep over at Tom's as we, yet again, ordered far too much Chinese and watched all the movies you could imagine, face book stalked all the boys Tom currently fancied with mass disproval from everyone as we realised his tastes were very niche, and then laughed about it until our stomachs hurt. I hadn't seen Alex now for two days, and after spending far too much of the afternoon getting ready, I was eager to see him, my body craving his touch as my eyes scanned the crowd for him. I had put a bit of weight back on in the last week, my hips fuller and my bust rounder as my curvy figure snapped back with a vengeance. My burnt orange gown popped against my dark hair and eyes, the spray tan working wonders as my skin glowed healthily. The cut of the dress skimmed my curves and nipped me in at all the right places as I for once, approved of the image staring back at me, ready to take on the world and in particular, catch the eye of a certain gentleman. "Oh, my goodness!" Molly's shriek snapped me from my moment rudely as I whipped round to see her arms wide, as a red headed girl embraced her warmly.

"I haven't seen you in for ever, how are you, the kids and Mike well?" Molly was holding her at arm's length as she spoke, clearly old friends.

"Yes, they are great thank you, how have you been?" The red head beamed back at Molly fondly.

"Amazing yes, thank you, I'm actually here with my friend, Emily," she gestured over to me before introducing her friend to me.

"Emily, this is Layla, we used to go to college together," Molly's smile was a mile wide, clearly holding fond memories.

"Nice to meet you, you look beautiful tonight." I hugged her lightly, getting really good vibes from her as I felt like she was a lovely person.

"Mol, I'm going to leave you guys to catch up, I'm going to see if I can find Alex."

Molly looked at me hesitantly as she grabbed my forearm. "Are you sure, you'll be OK on your own?" I giggled at her as I shook my head.

"Molly, I'm not exactly going to be far am I, once I find Alex." I surged my shoulders and winked at her cheekily, her face making it obvious that she was trying to make a decision.

"OK, but make sure you come back if you need me," she ordered as she pulled me in for a hug.

"Yes, Mom," I giggled as I left the two girls laughing.

My eyes scanned the patio, I couldn't see Alex anywhere, small clusters of people were scattered around, looking a million dollars against what I could only imagine, was a multimillion-dollar backdrop as I smiled, truly grateful to be here. I strode delicately over to the gazebo, my dress flowing elegantly behind me as counted each step in my head, desperate not to trip over my high heel stilettos as I still searched for him. As I reached the small fabric tunnel attached to the entrance of the huge white tent, I could hear the music coming from inside, it had more of a beat to the delicate music that flooded the outside area and a deep blue glow oozed from the fabric lined arch leading me through to the main space. I stepped onto the silver expensive looking carpet that flowed all the way into the gazebo, the music getting louder with each step, the light ebbing away as I got further into the tunnel. I gasped as I reached the entrance, a huge area, vaster than it looked from the outside lay before me, decorated with the most beautiful theme I had ever seen. Dark branches twisted up every corner and along every beam, starting from the floor, climbing higher and higher until you could no longer see it, each twig beautifully adorned with wildflowers and small twinkle lights that sparkled magically. Large round tables dominated the main area, ten seats at each with at least thirty tables dressed in deep navy-blue cloths, wooded tree slices placed in the middle, flooded with yet more wildflowers, a huge glass dome in the middle with a giant white candle flickering away making each table cosy and quaint. The dance floor spread across the entire left area beyond the tables, its sleek, oak wood glistening under the DJ's lights. I smiled at all the people bopping away, Tom and Ali included as he swirled her round in a circle elegantly. I looked up towards the ceiling of the tent, my heart stopping momentarily as I gasped loudly, thick swashes of deep blue material sashayed from its highest peak, pinned in all the right places as it flowed right down to the floor, tiny small led lights absolutely blanketing the entire space made you believe you were under the most beautiful night sky as they faded in and out, blanketing the guests in a magical glittery dream. I barely found my composure as I glanced over to the right, a huge top table set higher than the level of the guests, with matching décor stretched diagonally across the lefthand corner, enough seats for about ten people with the bar mirroring its position in the righthand corner. I scanned my eyes across the bar, it was rammed full of men in their tailored suits, sat on bar stools, sipping whiskey as they joked with their pals, enjoying the evening, and making the most of the open bar. The entire marquee was beautiful, and a flitting thought came briefly to my head as I imagined one day my wedding looking something like this. Before I could dream further, our eyes locked as Alex came into view from behind a tall gentleman who was moving away from the bar. My breathing hitched in my throat as he eyed me greedily up and down, a slight lick of his lips as he set his drink down on the bar, his gaze never leaving mine as he moved towards me. I felt my heart beat out of my chest and by pulse quicken as I watched this man, a man who I now called my boyfriend, the father to my child and by far the most attractive guy in the room closed in on me, his eyes darkening as he got closer. He was dressed in the most tailored, perfectly fitted suit I had ever seen him wear, its navy-blue colour, I had no doubt, was chosen to match the theme of the night, his burnt orange tie seemingly matching my dress coincidentally. I wondered for a moment if this was an actual coincidence or if he had received a tip of from Tom. His dark hair was slicked back roughly, his dark stubble framing his masculine face. I felt my insides clench and my stomach flutter as he reached me.

"Wow," he gasped as he took my hand gently, placing a soft kiss upon it before pulling me in tightly and kissing me softly on the lips. I felt every pair of eyes on us as our contact electrified the room, like it wasn't just us who were drawn in by our lust, the whole room could feel it too. I glanced around sheepishly as he set me back gently, holding me lightly by the tips of my fingers as he admired me from head to toe. My suspicions were right as I locked eyes with far too many people, blushing as I looked away, now embarrassed at the thought if everyone watching our display.

"May I have this dance?" Alex bowed his head courteously and I felt like I was in a movie as I accepted his offer with a meek nod, my cheeks still flushed, my heart still racing. I stayed close as we wound our way through the throngs of people, hushed chatter and heads following our direction told me we were still centre of attention. As we reached the dance floor, it was like the DJ knew, as at seemingly perfect timing, the track changed to something softer, flowy, as Alex pulled me in tightly, his palm splayed on the small of my back, our hands outstretched together pointing to the other end of the room as he began to move slowly.

"Alex, you do know I can't dance, don't you?" I whispered gently, well aware the entire room was watching, he laughed gruffly.

"Do you trust me?" I hesitated a moment before nodding confidently.

"With my life," I confessed, I watched as his eyes glazed over at my admission, like igniting a flame inside of him as he swirled me round elegantly. My feet seemed to move involuntarily, like he was manipulating my body to move with his, and my legs had no choice but to follow suit as we moved seductively and elegantly to the music. I could see people covering their mouths, chatting in hushed tones as fingers pointed, wide smiles and jealous eyes on us when something came over me, a feeling of confidence, a feeling of no longer hiding away in the background, a confidence injected directly into me when Alex and I were one as I swayed my head backwards, my leg forcing its way up his thigh as he gripped it tightly, pulling me in closer as I felt every inch of him against my core. My vision blurred as my heartbeat faster, hot from the dancing, and hot for Alex as I thanked my lucky stars for sending this man to me as we continued our dancing, moving and existing as one.

I leaned back into my chair with not an ounce of lady likeness, I had been summoned to the top table by Alex's family, and although I felt embarrassed at first, they all made me feel completely at ease as we enjoyed a three-course meal, plenty of laughs and lots of alcohol and my dress was beginning to feel uncomfortable. Scarlett was sat next to Alex, yet she spent the entire time climbing over him to get to me, and my heart swelled as I sat around my newfound family. A sharp chime pulled me from my thoughts as I saw Isla holding a glass high, tapping a knife on it elegantly as she stood elegantly.

"To everybody here, Eric and myself cannot thank you enough for helping us share our thirty-year wedding anniversary, it means the world to us to be surrounded by our closest friends, old family, and new," she turned to face me directly as she said the last word before asking the room to raise a glass to me, her new daughter in law, I cringed awkwardly in my seat as the entire room cheered and clinked their glasses together, no doubt wondering how about the whole situation. Alex rubbed my leg reassuringly under the table and gave me an eye roll, making me smile at his mother's over-the-top gesture. I offered a genuine smile at Isla as I mouthed the words thank you at her.

"Now, I'm hoping that you will join us for the opening of our gifts, which we are more than grateful for and are excited to get to, what do you say?" The whole room cheered as a table full of gifts and cards was wheeled to the side of Isla and Eric by a suited gentleman I could only guess was a worker as they settled down to begin opening their gifts. Around ten gifts later, with speeches thanking each person individually for their generosity, my palms were beginning to sting at the repeated rounds of clapping, and I wondered if it would be rude to sneak off to the bar to get another drink. I glanced over at Alex who was beaming, his full attention on his parents as he took in their every word. Scarlett was kneeled on the floor by his ankles, a small tender head snuggled up to his leg as her soft snores purred sweetly, it had been a long night for her, but she had been so well behaved, I smiled as Alex subconsciously stoked her hair, or tickles as she called it.

"Oh, I don't know who this gift is from, it doesn't have a name on it," Isla's confused voice drew my attention over to her as she held a small box wrapped in silver paper up high, twisting it for the room to see.

"Does anyone recognise this?"

She held it up higher, the room silent as no one claimed the gift. "No, oh well we'll see what it is then." She unwrapped the small gift, a tiny green velvet box that fit neatly in the palm of her hand as she opened the box gently.

"Oh, how beautiful," her voice was sincere as she pulled the silver chain up high, the silver locket dangling elegantly off the chain, a familiar teal stone emblazoned into the middle of it. As shiver of pure cold ran through me as I recognised the locket immediately, the same locket I had seen all of those years ago, on the night that Jason had come home in the middle of the night, the night I suspected he killed Chloe, I hadn't seen it since but there was no doubt that it was the same one.

"Does anyone recognise this gift?" Isla was holding the locket as high as she could, waiting for someone to claim it as I jumped back in my seat, my face white with fear as the glasses on the table fell over spilling the drinks all over the table. I heard Scarlett whine, the knock waking her up as I stood, Alex grabbed my hand tightly, confusion awash his face as we both heard his voice at the same time.

"That gift is from me, Ma'am," Jason's slurring words as he rounded from the corner of the bar struck fear into me like I'd never felt before as I realised all the people I cared about the most were in this very room with him. Alex and I stared at one other, unable to speak, both as shocked as each other as his mother waffled through her words.

"Thank you dear but, I do apologise, I'm not sure I recognise you," Isla's words were sincere as she thanked this stranger for his gift.

Jason sauntered up to the top table as he ran his fingers lightly on the fabric, "I'm a friend of the family, well pretty much family actually," he scoffed as his eyes reached mine, brimming with tears, frozen to the spot.

"I'll fucking kill you!" Alex's voice burst loudly from beside me as he threw his chair violently backwards, rage smeared all over his face as he spat his words through gritted teeth.

"Kill me, you're not a killer, this one on the other hand," he whistled sarcastically, "brutal," he spat his words as he gestured towards me, Alex glancing between us questioningly.

"Enough!" Eric's voice silenced the room in an instant as Alex sat back down on his chair softly, clearly succumbing to his father's request.

"Will somebody please tell me what the hell is going on?" Eric's voice was stern, the entire room locked on him as confused faces shared glances across the marquee, Isla tightly at his side clearly scared.

"I'll tell you," Jason raised his glass and downed the contents before slamming it on the table directly in front of me, scaring Scarlett as she began to cry. I pulled her into my lap, desperate to sooth her, shushing into her ear as I rocked her back and forth.

"I'm not listening to this shit," Alex scoffed as he folded his arms across his chest, a last-ditch attempt at disobeying his father when he and I knew fully who held the power right now.

"Let the boy god damn speak will you, Alex!" Eric spat his word across the table as he gestured to Jason to continue.

"I am Jason, Emily's ex-boyfriend," he pointed at me accusingly as gasps from around the room began to form. "I followed her here from our home all the way back in Michigan," he strolled casually to the end of the table before plonking himself roughly onto it, the remainder of the upright glassed tumbling over. "Now you're probably wondering why I would do that, but I'm going to tell you that too." He giggled as he swung his legs playfully under the table. I willed someone to stop him, pleaded with Alex internally to drag him outside, but he stayed still next to me, rooted to the spot and silenced by his father as he too listened intently. I wished I had the courage to speak up, to finish his show that I knew he was enjoying so much, yet nothing came out. Fear and submission holding me. "Now I came here originally to protect dear Emily, to keep her safe from her past, her secrets, things she doesn't want others to know." I screwed my face up as he spoke, forcing a giggle at his ridiculous show. "And this" – he swiped the locket aggressively off the table before holding up high – "belonged to the mother of my child, the mother and child that she" – he pointed at me aggressively before throwing the locket at me, it hitting me in the chest and coming to rest in Scarlett's lap – "murdered."

I felt my blood run cold as gasps from around the room evolved into nervous chatter, my face awash with confusion as Alex snapped his head round to face me, equally as confused but with a flare of accusation at the same time.

I huffed loudly as I stood, placing Scarlett into Alex's arms, "What on earth are you talking about, are you crazy? You killed her; I saw you when you came back that night!" I was shouting now as tears spilled over my cheeks, my finger pointed sharply at him.

"No, no, no baby girl, what you saw was me returning from the murder, having covered it up for you, you were that drugged and out of it you don't even remember, do you?"

I shook my head violently. "No, I don't remember nothing, what are you even talking about?"

Jason closed his eyes before letting out a feral scream. "I'm talking about you driving a knife through the heart of the woman who was carrying my fucking child, the one woman who loved me, the woman who was going to make me a father but you ended both of their lives that night, Emily. You stole everything from me and I'm fucking done covering for you!" I didn't want to believe his words, didn't believe that what he was saying was true, but the foetal position he was now donning on the floor as he sobbed loudly was beginning to convince even me.

My heart stopped as I felt Alex drop his hand from mine. The tears brimming in my eyes as he refused to look at me, "I didn't do this." I pleaded with him as he looked further away, pulling Scarlett to the other side of his lap as pure fear and adrenaline buzzed through my veins, my voice barely a whisper as I scanned my eyes around the room at my loved ones, Molly, Ali, Tom, Scarlett, Alex, fear and confusion across each one of their faces as I felt them disown me. "Or at least I don't think I did it."

Chapter 25
Jason

I felt her move suddenly, bolt upright, jerking me awake from my sleep as our bed frame rocked. I squeezed my eyes tight and sighed deeply before rolling over to her side of the bed, trying to be the doting, supporting boyfriend I knew I had to be, the clock blinking 12:19 am. "Lay back down," I whispered, pulling her backwards as I had done a million times before. Emily had always had dreams like this for as long as I could remember, chatting away to herself, completely immersing herself, fully feeling every emotion, reacting to whatever it was that she was seeing in her sleep. I had always been there to calm her down, waking her up gently and stroking her hair as she fell back asleep, to then talk it through the next day, telling her what she had done or said. I deep down loved being the strong man she needed to make her feel safe, that her vulnerability meant she had to have me by her side. I felt like her saviour, and I would do anything and everything for her. Those were in the early days, during our first relationship when we were young and carefree, this time around things were different. Our life was volatile, dangerous, and confusing, her dreams more violent, offensive and real, fuelled by the masses of alcohol she drank to numb her pain.

I had always loved Emily, as high school sweethearts we had been inseparable for most of our school days, with us soon became completely besotted with each other spending every minute of every day with each other, lost causes with non-existent families, craving attention from one another as we desperately tried to fill the voids in our life. Our relationship was normal on the surface, but toxic at its roots, yet we were too young to notice. To anyone looking in, we had enjoyed a few years of innocent fun, cinema dates and strolls on the beach, kid stuff, but as life goes, things change, and after a couple of years, our intenseness fizzled out, no longer desperate for each other, no longer craving every fibre of one another. At least, those were the words we spoke, that the way we described it when we agreed to call it a day. To end our young carefree relationship and go out and experience the world. Inside I was completely gutted, totally and utterly destroyed at our separation, but knew it was for the best and what we both needed to grow, what she had insisted on, yet I couldn't help but think our toxic hearts belonged together. She never left my mind during the time I was gone; a few years had passed by quickly, I had left town after our split to travel, enjoying time exploring the mountains of Canada, hiking, countless road trips as the memories of my dark-haired girl, my Emily became only distant thoughts. Before I knew it, I found myself heading back to our hometown in Wisconsin a few years later. The money had run out, the pain of losing her almost completely gone, yet she was the first person I thought of as I arrived home. I had been back in town around a week before I saw her again, I just presumed she had left town, moved on, so I was shocked to see her sat alone in a bar, even more beautiful than I had remembered, her aura drawing me in stronger than before. To anyone else she looked like an ordinary girl, perhaps enjoying a drink after a hard day's work, but not to me, even after all this time, her eyes still gave her away, I saw the real her instantly, sad, and lost staring down into an empty glass swirling the ice around the bottom. Before I could talk myself out of it, I found myself crossing the room, my heart pounding in my chest as our bodies drew closer, the anticipation of being near her again humming through my veins. I paused as I reached the booth, expecting her to look up, yet she didn't, her lonely eyes and sad face remained emotionless. I scooted onto the seat beside her and without even saying a word, I pulled her into my arms.

"Emily." I breathed silently. It was at that moment that I knew I couldn't live without her, that everything I had experienced over the last few years was nothing compared to how I felt holding her in my arms. I shivered as her body began to heave, desperately trying to hold back the sobs as I whispered her to let it all out. What had happened to my beautiful confident girl? So broken and destroyed. It totally broke my heart as my guilt at leaving hit me full force. We talked for hours that night, and I fell completely in love with her all over again. I learned of her daughter she had fallen pregnant with after a one-night stand. My jealousy bubbled, yet I knew I had no place to be, that she was single, alone, and free to do as she pleased, yet the thought of another man's hands on her body sickened me. I fought back the tears as she told me she had placed her daughter for adoption, explaining her guilt and loss, a mother so completely besotted with her baby yet unable to give her what she needed, selflessly placing her with a new family who could. It was the early hours by the time I admitted my love for her, and how I had never stopped, her gleaming eyes and tender touch told me she felt the same and we vowed to give it another go. I promised to never leave her side, to give her the love and family she had craved so badly. We packed our bags that very day and moved across the country for a fresh start. Unfortunately, things didn't exactly work out how we planned. It took me a few months to figure out that Emily was drinking a bit too much to ease her pain, starting her day with a glass of wine, and ending it with a bottle. Her eyes would glaze, her speech would slur, and she would often go days without eating or showering. I desperately wanted to confront her, but also understood that she was grieving, letting her emotions fizzle in a glass of booze rather than face her demons, so pathetically, I let her be, let her grieve rather than the thought of rocking the boat, of losing her. I was there to hold her when she would sober up, screaming in pain, crying, I would be there to encourage her to wash, to call her old friends that I knew she had stopped bothering with. She knew I knew, but we never spoke of it, me instead becoming more of a carer than a boyfriend, not receiving the love and affection I needed in return as she numbed her emotions and switched them off to me entirely. That's when I met Chloe, a girl I had spotted around the town and who lived a few streets over, we would bump into each other when we went out for our morning run, sharing a conversation about the weather or what was on tv that night. I hadn't intended on it happening, but Chloe was giving me something I was vitally missing out on with Emily, that human interaction and normal everyday drama free life. I felt alive again, full of fire and drive. It wasn't long before our relationship had become physical, I felt guilty, deeply guilty but also justified it to myself and convinced also, that it wasn't my fault, I deserved to feel loved and wanted too and although the love I held for Emily was deep and sincere, the feelings Chloe ignited in me were something that Emily couldn't give me. Soon after our physical relationship began, even though she was on the pill, she fell pregnant. I didn't love Chloe yet knew from experience how important it was for me to be in my baby's life, that I had to own up to my responsibilities and do what I thought was right, and so I continued our affair for the sake of becoming a father. I knew how much it would destroy Emily, me not only having an affair but becoming a parent when she had given that opportunity away herself. I wasn't sure how I was going to tell her, but her drunk episodes that were becoming more frequent made it easy for me to get away with it, to continue having my secret family. Chloe was now around four months pregnant, we were having a baby boy, her attending her appointments alone, keeping our secret safe. She knew of Emily, and the predicament I was in, and had agreed to keep quiet, for now, as long as I played a part in the baby's life. It was stupid, and reckless and I felt bad every single day that I spent with Chloe, and then slept in a bed with Emily, but it had gone too far. I had seen her earlier in the day belly round and skin glowing yet back at home Emily had been drinking spirits since about 4 pm, not her ordinarily choice of booze, the glazed look and slurring words worsening as the evening went on, she was completely out of it, the worst I had ever seen her. I desperately tried to get her to call it a night as I slipped some pills into her drink to help her sleep, her still protesting, spitting out hurtful words, me letting it all slide because I loved her deeply, still besotted with her. She eventually gave up about 10 pm, I guided her to bed, swaying all over the place as her eyes stared through me. I pulled her into my arms and kissed her goodnight, our usual night-time ritual, thank full that the drink had been put down, for a few hours at least, yet here I was being woken up by her violent dreaming a few hours later, a normal event, yet feeling it was different as she mumbled next to me. I placed my hand around her waist as I tried to lay her back down, her rigid body still as she fought against me. I sighed deeply, annoyed, and tired as I flicked the lamp on next to the bed. She turned slowly to look at me, but I couldn't see Emily, just a vacant expression, cold, dark, emotionless. I shivered, scared as I whispered her name, just as she took a deep breath in and threw herself back, her hands at her throat, tightly twisting, I desperately fought with her, trying to pull her hands away, using all my strength to free her, but failing miserably. Had she taken something else? She was only slight, not strong enough to fight me off, yet here I was unable to simply pull her hands from her throat. I watched her face as she began to pass out, her hands finally releasing their grip as her lips tinged blue, "Emily!" I screamed desperately, shaking her, begging her to come back, tears now streaming down my face.

After what felt like minutes, but was only seconds passed, she gasped, the colour returning to her face, her gaze meeting mine. "What the fuck are you crying for?" She spat viscously. I glared at her questioningly, silently asking her what the hell just happened but unable to find the words.

"Don't pretend like you fucking care, Jason! You have your little readymade family found the corner, a perfect girl and a baby on the way, you don't give a shit if anything happened to me!"

184

Fuck. Every ounce of blood in my body ran cold. She knew, how long had she known for? Panic rose in my chest, still desperately not wanting her to leave me, not again, selfishly needing her in my life as well as living another secret one.

Before I could even explain, she jumped up from the bed, pointing at me violently, "You think you can have a family when I can't have mine, fuck you!" She laughed sarcastically before scaling the stairs and out the front door, slamming it hard as it smashed shut. I heard the car rev up and speed off down the street as I sat on the edge of the bed, completely bewildered, a million things going through my mind. *Fuck her,* I thought, I had put up with her drunk, absent-minded selfishness for too long now, I laid back down raging, gripping the covers tightly in a fist as I screamed into the pillow. Suddenly a sickening thought snapped into my mind, what did she mean when she said I can't have my family? She wasn't herself, her anger and viscous words cutting deeper than usual, had she gone around to Chloe's? Seeing her in that state would be a sure-fire way to scare Chloe off, taking my child with her, she was already completely in a trance, drugged up and more alcohol than I can remember down, she wasn't thinking straight. I jumped up out of the bed and ran down the stairs as fast as I could, my heart racing as I knew I desperately needed to find her. I ran my hands through my hair in frustration as I got out onto the street, remembering that she had taken the car. Chloe's house was only two streets over, so I ran, I ran as fast as my legs would carry me until I reached her house, breathless and wheezing as I snuck up the driveway quietly. I hoped that I was wrong, hoped that maybe Emily had just gone off somewhere in a rage and would come back once she had sobered up, but the split wooden door frame to the side of her house that was wide open, a garden spade strewn nearby told me otherwise. Still out of breath and full of adrenaline, I rushed into the house as a cold shiver trailed down my spine. Silence. No screaming Emily, no timid Chloe wondering what the hell was going on. I whispered Emily's name as I snuck quietly up the stairs to Chloe's bedroom, I closed my eyes as I pushed the door open gently, knowing that I wasn't going to like what I saw. I opened my eyes slowly as my breath caught in my lungs, forgetting how to breathe in that very moment as my stomach lurched. My whole life as I knew it had changed forever as Chloe lay on the bed, bathed in claret, laboured breathing, eyes panicked, as Emily stood over her, smiling, a knife in her hand.

"Emily, what the fuck!" I shouted, panicking as I ran over and grabbed Chloe by the shoulders, tears brimming in my eyes as the realisation of the situation began to hit me. She snatched her hands up trying to force me away, scratching at my throat drawing blood with her long nails, the pain not registering as the numbness set it. I looked down and saw a single hole in her night dress, exactly where her heart would be, blood saturating the fabric and now pooling around her on the mattress. My heart sank, my baby. I knew in that moment I wasn't going to become a father, that Emily had been true to her word. A pain I couldn't begin to describe to anyone, except maybe her, washed over me and I began to sob uncontrollably as I watched the life leave Chloe. Emily and I had now both lost a child. I looked over at her, and for the first time I fully understood her pain, understood how she felt, the vacant look on her face, the pain behind her eyes, I stood up and pulled her to me, she dropped the knife and began to sob with me.

"Emily," I whispered, "what have you done?" Even though she had done something unimaginable, I still completely and utterly loved her, I had to protect her, our promise to each other, our childhood obsession smashing to the forefront of my mind. My body cruised into auto pilot almost immediately. I ushered Emily to the shower, stripping her clothes off, and ordering her to wash, her expression still not her own, her eyes still glazed over. I left her there while I ran to the lean-to outhouse to find what I needed to clean this mess up. By the time I returned, Emily was sat on the bathroom floor, a robe wrapped around her, her own clothes bloodied on the floor. I desperately started pulling clothes out of the drawers, skinny jeans a hoody and a pair of black lacy knickers.

I threw them at her angrily. "Put these on and wait there!" Her face was still vacant, emotionless, drugged, drunk. I began pouring petrol around the house, I couldn't bear to look at Chloe, I had covered her with the bed sheets, knowing if I saw her face, I may risk giving it all up to the cops, giving up on Emily. I couldn't do that to her, I didn't love Chloe, not even close to how I felt about Emily. I ushered her down to the front door and onto the porch, it was pitch black outside, early hours of the morning, not a person in sight down the secluded street, the nearest neighbours completely out of view. I turned around, my lighter lit, before spotting a familiar silver necklace on the sideboard, a small teal stone cradled in the middle of the locket, signalling her birth month that I had bought for Chloe on her birthday, I picked it up and stuffed it into my pocket before throwing the lighter into the house, not looking back, too scared as we made off up the road into the darkness, Emily pulled tightly into my side as the house took up slowly in flames.

When we arrived home, Emily was still completely out of it, staggering around the house, bumping into things. I lead her to the bedroom slowly, taking Chloe's clothes off her, my emotions beginning to waver as the anger seeped though. I piled them in the corner of the room, dropping the locket on top as I pulled a night dress over her head, laying her down gently in the bed before pulling the covers to her chin, within seconds she was snoring softly, in a deep, deep sleep. Still semi on auto pilot, I headed to the shower, stripping off my clothes, it wasn't until I stood under the water, processing my thoughts, the adrenaline wavering that the realisation of what had just happened hit, my hands shaking violently as the shock hit me. That fucking bitch. She took away the one thing she knew would hurt me the most, all in revenge for me seeing Chloe behind her back. I hated her, hated what I had just done for her, me now equally implicated for covering up her crime, torching the house and all evidence to remain undetected. I stood there for a while, the hot water cascading over me, so hot that I hoped all traces of what I had just done would scald away before my attention was pulled back into the room, a loud clatter coming from the bedroom. I switched the water off, my heart beating out of my chest as I wrapped a towel quietly around my waist.

"You up?" I shouted. No response. I slowly creaked the bathroom door open, my blood boiling as I saw her sitting on the side of the bed, her eyes that were fixated on the pile of clothes on the floor snapped up to meet mine, clear, confused, back in the room. Anger surged through me, I lunged forward with gritted teeth and grabbed at her neck strangling her, pushing her back into the bed, she fought desperately, the drugs and alcohol now mostly worn off and unable to fight me, I saw the fear in her face as her body fell limp and she slowly passed out beneath me. I clambered back off the bed, my heart racing, a cold chill running down my spine, but feeling satisfied with my outburst, a small feat of victory after what she had just done to me. I glanced over at the bundle of clothes and slammed my fist down hard into the mattress, she had seen it. I rushed downstairs before throwing the clothes quickly into our fireplace, the flamed licking around edges as they quickly turned to ash. I wept as I placed the silver locket under a floor board in our spare room, desperately wanting to hold on to a small piece of my child's mother, but also fully understanding the danger of keeping it. I gathered my thoughts slowly, tired, and defeated as I wandered back to our room. I crept in quietly, creeping over to the bed to find Emily breathing softly, sleeping? passed out still? I was unsure, but one thing I knew, I had to keep up this loving pretence or she would know. I slid into the bed beside her and pulled her close to me kissing the back of her head softly, loving and hating her equally at the same time before drifting off into a deep calm sleep, the dim sound of sirens whirring gently in the distance.